River of Joy

JACK METZLER

The Storyteller's Collection

Destiny Image Publishers
P.O. Box 310
Shippensburg, PA 17257

ISBN 1-56043-658-1

Printed in the United States of America
For Worldwide Distribution

First copyright: 1987
First reprint: 1993 by Destiny Image

A note from the author:
I love to hear from my readers! You may correspond with me by writing:

> Jack Metzler
> 4650 S. Harrison Rd.
> Houghton Lake, MI 48629

When Nathan came back to the tepee after leading the horses out to graze, he found a venison loin lying on a piece of deerskin in front of the door.

"Where did this come from?" he asked as he entered.

"I don't know. One of our friends left it for us."

"*Our* friends? Do the people of this village really consider me a friend?"

"They would not have accepted your tobacco if they had not accepted you as a friend."

"Then Eagle Feather still regards me as an enemy." Nathan's countenance darkened, causing the silver in his hair and beard to appear more pronounced than ever.

"Eagle Feather and I were good friends. He wanted me to be his squaw. It is natural that he be angry. But his anger will soon melt like the spring snow, and all will be well between you."

"I hope you're right." He caught her to him fiercely. "But I know if someone tried to take you away from me, I'd fight. I love you far too much to lose you, and I imagine he feels the same."

"But we are married now," she soothed. "Nothing can change that."

To Brenda,
who makes my river of joy
run deeper…wider

Editor's Note:

Tachechana is pronounced *ta-chuh*-CHA-*na*

chapter

1

TACHECHANA USUALLY AWAKENED TO EACH NEW DAWN with an almost blinding flash of awareness, her Sioux blood singing in her veins. Not today. Slowly, almost dreamily, her dark lashes fluttered open to the pleasant light filtering through the walls of her father's tepee. How different . . . and yet, how much the same it was since the last time she had been in this place—the place she had learned to love, her home. Sensing that she was alone, she burrowed deeper into her bright red trading blanket, pulling it up around her ears . . . and thought of the last time she had slept here and all the events of the long intervening months.

Nothing about the tepee had changed. She could almost feel the strength of the structure as her eyes followed the twenty-eight poles supporting the buffalo skin covering to the smoke hole at the top. Twenty-eight poles, never more, never less, in a Sioux tepee. One for each day of the moon's cycle. One for each of the buffalo's ribs.

"If our brother the buffalo needs twenty-eight ribs to hold his skin over his heart in life, he should have twenty-eight ribs to hold his skin over the heart of his brother, the Sioux," her father would tell her each time they set up their camp in a new place. "And the ribs of our tepee must always be set in a perfect circle . . . the circle of life."

7

The circle of life, she thought. *How much it means to my people.*

In her memory Tachechana relived the night before she had set out in search of her own life's meaning, into the great unknown. It was then, for the first time, that her father related the sweet, sad story of the beautiful, green-eyed captive he had brought to this very tepee after a raid on a wagon train. Respecting the young woman's ladylike demeanor, the warriors had treated her with deference, and after a time. Great Bear had come to love her as a man loves a woman. They had danced the wedding dance together, and within twelve moons, Tachechana was born. Green Eyes, her mother, had died a few days afterward, but not before giving her child the name that meant "Skipping Fawn."

Sitting up on her pallet, Tachechana searched out a familiar patched hole in the buffalo skin just to the right of the doorway. What an uproar Plainsfeather had raised the day her small charge had made that hole with a bow and arrow Great Bear had fashioned for her. Although Tachechana was not allowed to treat the weapon like a toy, she had managed to bring it inside on one particular rainy day. As she was drawing back one of her father's hunting arrows, the arrow had slipped from her inexperienced fingers, whistled through the tepee wall, and thwacked into a cradle board Plainsfeather was making, missing her very ample bossom by less than an inch.

"Plainsfeather." A great flood of warm loving memories inundated Tachechana as she spoke the name. Plainsfeather— the only woman who had stood by her through all these years.

Tachechana's unorthodox exploits had long been the source of gossip among the females of the village, she knew. And while her Sioux sisters ridiculed her for her behavior,

Tachechana suspected they secretly viewed her with more than a trace of envy. All, that is, except Plainsfeather, who had been mother, sister, true and faithful friend. On this day of days, she would need her old friend more than ever.

My wedding day! she thought, springing from her sleeping place to apply a bristle brush to her long black hair. *Why am I lazing about like a sluggard?*

Most Sioux women wore their hair braided or pulled back and tied with colored rawhide, but Nathan liked her hair loose, flowing down over her shoulders or flying out behind her as she rode her horse Fox across the prairie.

Holding the mirror at arm's length, Tachechana studied her reflection. She had never thought of herself as pretty. Compared to the other women in her village, her nose was too small and her lips too full. All the Indian women she knew had dark eyes, but hers sparkled a translucent green, the gift of her white mother. Still, Nathan seemed pleased with the startling contrast of pale eyes and jet black hair. He had even called these strange features "beautiful," and his opinion was the only one that mattered, for today she was to become Mrs. Nathan Cooper!

That thought was enough to bring a surge of warm blood to her cheeks. Oh, how she loved him! What difference that his hair and beard were lightly frosted with the snows of many winters. He loved her as she loved him. Truly Nathan's God—and hers—had given each to the other just when they needed someone most.

Her mind raced back to the first time she had seen him. In exile from her village for her refusal to adopt the ways of the squaws, she was riding with a small band of warriors. When they spotted the tracks of a metal-shod horse, they pursued the white rider until they cornered him, and then she herself rode in to make the kill. She still could not comprehend why she had not instinctively taken his life that night on the prairie. Instead, she had been touched by his nobility, by an aura of goodness she had not been able to define. Later, he had taken her into his own cabin and taught her to read and write in English, to trust in the one true God, to be a lady like her mother before her. And when he had nearly died protecting her virtue from a band of outlaws, she learned the meaning of a love she had never known existed.

Great tears welled up within her and coursed down her dusky cheeks as she considered the long months of suffering and convalescence he endured after the gunfight that had preserved both her life and her purity.

At that moment she spied the long shadows of two men walking along the east side of the tepee. Quickly she swiped at the tears as Nathan and Great Bear entered.

"Chana! What is this?" Nathan asked as he brushed her wet cheek with a tentative finger. "Is anything wrong?"

"It is nothing. . . . It is only that the river of joy in my heart overflows."

Tenderly he took her in his arms. "Just so long as they are tears of joy." He kissed away her tears.

Blushing, Tachechana gently pushed Nathan away and smiled at Great Bear, who had discreetly presented his back to the couple. "My father, the chief, should have awakened me sooner so that I might have prepared his food," she said in her most formal Sioux.

"You are a sleeping bear," the chief replied with mock severity. "Nathan and I have eaten. Now Plainsfeather is waiting outside with a wedding gift for you."

"Plainsfeather!" she cried, and ran to the doorway. "Come in, come in!"

The ancient woman stood there shyly, looking not at Tachechana, but at her chief, entering only at his nod of approval.

10

Draped across her arms was a white buckskin dress, the bodice ornately embellished with fine colored beads and porcupine quills. How many hours of loving stitches had been required to produce such a magnificent garment, Tachechana could only imagine, not having acquired such skills herself.

"Perhaps the daughter of the chief would accept the handiwork of an old woman."

"Oh, Plainsfeather! It's beautiful ... is it not, Nathan, Father?" She clasped the ceremonial robe to her heart, then held it up to her body for their inspection. Then, without waiting for their reply, she threw her arms around her aged friend, who broke into a broad single-toothed smile as tears rained down coppery cheeks turned to leather from the heat of many summer suns.

Great Bear's voice interrupted their reunion. "We must leave the birds to preen for the wedding dance," he said to Nathan.

"But Chana has not yet instructed me in the steps."

"My father will tell you everything," she said, pushing him gently toward the flap of the entrance.

After the men left, Tachechana and Plainsfeather walked together to a secluded spot along the river where, despite the cold, Tachechana bathed in preparation for the ceremony.

Plainsfeather, carrying a long-bladed, heavy-handled knife, cut the center from an old Yucca plant and beat it with the handle of the knife. By adding water to the fibers of the plant, she soon had a handful of soapy lather. Little by little she rubbed it into the glossy hair until every strand was well covered.

Ducking beneath the crystal clear waters, Tachechana rinsed her hair free of the foam. Then, tilting her head toward the tall trees edging the river, she closed her eyes and slowly

11

stood. For a moment the water streamed over the sculpted contours of her face, the heavy, wet hair covering her supple body like a robe.

Then the women—the young bride and the old crone— walked back to the tepee where Tachechana shed her shirt and breeches and donned the wedding dress.

The drums began their wild, incessant beat, warning them that the time was near.

"You more pleasing to the eye than any maiden who has ever danced in village of Great Bear," said Plainsfeather, a suspicion of moisture forming in her faded brown eyes.

"Even more pleasing than my mother?"

"Even so."

"Tell me about her. In all the years of my growing up, you have told me so little."

"It was forbidden." Plainsfeather frowned. "Your father loved her well. He grieved much when she died."

The drums increased their cadence, issuing a command that all the villagers gather for the ceremonial dance.

"Please, Plainsfeather. I must know. Do I look very much like her? What was she like?"

"You are . . . just as she was," Plainsfeather grunted. "Now go to your husband." She busied herself with the discarded clothing.

A chill rippled through Tachechana's body at the mention of the word *husband*. But she resolutely stepped through the entryway of the tepee and walked beside Plainsfeather toward the council circle.

As a young girl, Tachechana had watched the elaborate ritual on a number of occasions but had stubbornly kept her distance, refusing to allow herself to be moved by the symbolic gestures of the wedding couple. She had resisted any stirrings within her ripening young body, knowing that these natural yearnings for love would lead inevitably to the submission of her will to that of some man who was undoubtedly her inferior in courage, in skill, in spirit. . . . Her fierce pride would never permit such capitulation.

And so she had looked on with disdain at the weak-willed woman who surrendered her freedom so easily. Soon that one would be like all the others—bearing babes, serving her mate as if he owned her very soul, resigning herself to a life of toil and drudgery. It was ever so with the Sioux, and Tachechana had vowed that no man would ever reduce her to such servitude. Until Nathan.

He had taught her about a love that longed to give rather than take, had pointed her to Jesus, the God-Man, who willingly yielded his heavenly throne to descend to earth, clothed in the flesh of a helpless babe, here to grow up to serve the creatures he had created and ultimately to die for them. Such love was scarcely to be comprehended, but it had broken her willful heart, and she had not been the same since that night.

Approaching the ceremonial grounds, it appeared to Tachechana that the entire population of the village had assembled in a huge circle around the council fire—the village elders and braves in the innermost circle, the women and young people behind them. The fire burned brightly at the northern end of the circumference.

Plainsfeather guided Tachechana to a place just inside the circle on the east side, and told her she must look only at the ground directly in front of her until the great drum began to sound.

Tachechana, her heart racing, stared at the spot with a might of will that surprised her. She yearned to look at Nathan on the opposite side—so near, and yet still so far away. Just when she thought she could bear it no longer, all the drums hushed. Her heart beat on so strongly she thought surely it could be heard by all.

At last the great drum thudded a slow deliberate beat. Slowly she raised her eyes to meet those of her beloved. Even in his wedding finery, Nathan bore the ravages of his ordeal, and she felt her throat clutch with her great love for him.

He was wearing a buckskin shirt that was too large for him, and although the garment was bleached almost as white as the dress Tachechana was wearing, the design was entirely different. *It was made by the hands of a white woman,* she surmised as Nathan rose to his feet and received a deerskin pouch from Great Bear.

At the chief's gesture, Nathan made an awkward attempt to toe-heel dance his way to the fire. There, he elevated the pouch above his head as if offering it to the Great Spirit. Tachechana recalled his words: "I will agree to your ceremony, believing in my heart that your Great Spirit is the same as our one God, but you must be willing to honor our customs as well and be married by a minister in a Christian wedding before we can live together as man and wife." The white man's customs seemed so strange to her, yet she had happily consented.

Her thoughts returned to focus on Nathan who was taking a pinch of the tobacco and willow bark mixture from the pouch and was sprinkling it into the fire. Afterward, he continued his slow shuffle back to the place where Great Bear was sitting, his arms crossed.

The chief held out a cupped hand into which Nathan dropped a portion of the mixture. Then, looking more like an intoxicated buffalo than a dancer, her bridegroom skipped to each of the elders of the village, distributing to each a sample of the bag's contents. Continuing around the circle, the procedure was repeated with every adult male. Each eagerly accepted the gift. All except one.

As Nathan clumsily made his way to Eagle Feather, the brave held out his hand as had all the others. Nathan dropped the mixture into the outstretched palm and was about to dance on when Eagle Feather bounded to his feet and flung the tobacco to the ground. Not realizing that his action was a challenge for the bride, Nathan moved on to the next brave.

"Why did Eagle Feather do that?" Tachechana whispered to Plainsfeather, noting that the brave had sulked off in the direction of his tepee.

Plainsfeather's face conjured up the image of a storm cloud. "Eagle Feather angry. He want you for his woman."

"But we were never more than good friends. We grew up together as children."

"No matter. He want you for *best* friend—forever. Your man best watch out for that brave. Sioux warrior no like to lose."

Tachechana recalled her own brash actions when she had vied with the men of her village, and realized the truth of the old woman's words. She felt a moment of remorse, then her attention was diverted to the man who had awakened in her the joy of her womanhood.

Nathan had distributed the last of his gifts and now held her gaze captive, willing her to come to him. The great drum quickened its tempo and she rose, her feet matching the lightness of her heart. Following the drum beat, they danced to the center of the circle, extending their open palms to each other and interlacing their fingers, her right hand in his left, his right hand in her left.

Locked thus, they lifted their hands above their heads, taking short quick steps until their bodies touched briefly before backing away until they stood at arm's length. Making a quarter turn so that Nathan faced the north, they raised their hands again, dancing in place, then coming together for

15

an instant. Three times more the ritual was repeated until they had saluted the four winds.

And now the time had come to pay homage to Great Bear and Plainsfeather who had nurtured the life of Tachechana, though today her eyes were for Nathan alone.

Making their final turn, they approached the fire once more, using the oft-repeated hand gesture, then danced toward the opposite edge of the circle. This time the ring of spectators parted, the villagers forming a corridor to the door of a new tepee where Great Bear and Plainsfeather waited, one on each side.

Tachechana scarcely saw the two beloved faces as she ducked into the tepee, heard the flap fastened shut behind them, and turned to regard her new husband, her eyes shining like twin stars.

"Nathan . . . ," she breathed, "now we belong to each other." Impulsively, she hurled herself into his arms, pressing her lithe young body against his.

The grimace on his face was one of pure pain. "Not quite, heart of my heart." He held her for a moment before gently disengaging her arms from about his neck and catching both her hands in his. "There is still the Christian ceremony at Fort Fetterman. Did you forget our agreement . . . that we should wait until then before . . . consummating our marriage?"

"But, Nathan, we have followed all the traditions of my people, even though it was not required. Do we not love each other as much now as we will after the white man's ceremony?"

"Tachechana, listen to me," he said with a groan, distancing himself from her in a single stride. "You know I love you more than my own life. I have proved that. No ceremony—neither Sioux nor white—can change that. But we are both Christians. We must guard well our example before the others—those who do not yet follow the Jesus way. Perhaps Plainsfeather or your own father will come to believe in him if they can see that believers are different . . . that they choose to honor God rather than the traditions of men."

"I never thought that any man could persuade me against my will," Tachechana said solemnly. Then her eyes flashed in merriment. "Strange. Today I find I have no will . . . except to please my husband . . . and my God."

Nathan smiled and pulled her to him for a warm and careful hug. They whispered to each other for some time. Then the drums began their frenetic pounding, and the shouts of the people summoned them to their wedding feast.

Pushing past Nathan, Tachechana led the way through the door and into the throng of well-wishers. Even the braves who at one time hunted Nathan, hoping to take his scalp, now smiled and danced around the couple, offering their congratulations and wishing them many strong and healthy children. All the braves except one.

At the far end of the village a pinto pony carried the solitary figure of Eagle Feather into the night.

chapter
2

THE EVENTS OF THE NEXT FEW HOURS passed in a blur of exhilaration and anticipation. Since the night was far spent before the feasting ended, the couple decided not to postpone their departure and made ready to leave for Fort Fetterman before the sun cracked the eastern horizon.

Dressed in buckskin breeches and sheepskin coats against the predawn chill, they saddled Nathan's horse, Rowdy, loaded the pack horse, and threw a buffalo skin across Tachechana's mare.

"It is time to be on our way," Nathan said in a low voice so as not to disturb any who might be sleeping after their night of revelry.

"But I must bid my father and Plainsfeather one last farewell," Tachechana insisted.

"We'll be back. Our cabin is not so far away that you won't be visiting. Besides, a part of your heart will always belong here."

"But my place will ever be with you, Nathan," she said softly and sprang lightly astride Fox and cantered out of the village without a backward glance.

Their route lay to the southwest where a Methodist preacher was said to be wintering at the fort, waiting for the spring thaw before making Oregon Territory. It was he who would perform the Christian ceremony Nathan insisted upon. With this happy prospect before them, they struck a brisk pace.

Nathan took the lead for the first few miles. Tachechana was content to follow at a reasonable distance, seeing his profile etched against the lightening sky. *How is it that this man has so captured my heart that I can forget I once was a Sioux warrior?* she pondered. *Is it because his love has changed me, or is it because the Jesus way is a way of peace?*

Feeling the heaving of the mare's sides beneath her, Tachechana reined in her horse to a slower pace and allowed her thoughts to roam free.

Soon she would truly be one with this man who had risked his life to protect her virtue. The gunfight with a band of outlaws had left him badly wounded, and it had taken all Tachechana's native skills—and the grace of God, Nathan often reminded her—to pull him through. In all of the time they were together, he had never pressed his advantage, even when he grew stronger under her ministrations. She had never met a more honorable man, nor a more honest one. Though she had come to expect honor among the Sioux, it was a rare thing in a white man, she mused.

Several times during the long day's journey, they were forced to detour around streams and rivers swollen from spring rains.

After an exceptionally wide detour and a stop for food and rest, Tachechana voiced her concern. "Will we make the fort by nightfall, Nathan?" she asked, a worried frown furrowing her smooth brow.

"If the horses don't go lame on us," he replied. "Our cabin is a day's journey from the fort, and your village is a good ten miles closer than that."

"Then we will have our Christian ceremony tonight?"

"You can count on it." There was a determined set to Nathan's strong jaw.

An hour before sunset, the couple rode through the gates of Fort Fetterman and within the half-hour had located the preacher.

"He's stayin' with the sutler, in the room over the store," said the blacksmith, pointing with a pair of horseshoe tongs toward the general mercantile store.

The clergyman, a bit surly at being disturbed during his supper, directed them to the chapel and told them to wait for him there.

When Nathan and Tachechana arrived at the small structure, they found it dark and cold, with no fire in the fireplace. Nathan lit one of the lamps and looked about for firewood. Holding the lamp high, he opened the door and looked out, hoping to find a woodpile. Instead, he found Captain Baker.

"I thought it might be you when the sergeant reported a man riding in with a pretty Indian woman," he said with a hearty clap on the back. "And what are you doing so far from your cabin?"

"Chana and I are here to get married."

"Married, you say? Here? That's good news indeed. And you'll be needing some wood for a fire, too. Let me see what I can do about that."

Stepping back into the little chapel, Nathan heard the captain barking out some orders. "Looks like we won't be having the quiet little wedding I planned," he told Tachechana, who was beginning to feel the fatigue of the long day setting in and more than a little confusion caused by all the commotion.

Almost immediately a tall, thin man garbed all in black, stomped into the room, his face a frozen mask.

21

"Why are you bothering to say your vows?" he demanded sharply, tilting his head back so as to peer at the two of them through the small spectacles perched on his elongated nose. "Most of you mountain men just take your squaws and start living with them. How do you expect God to bless the marriage of a white man to a savage?" He spat out the words.

Nathan stiffened, his jaw working furiously. "Now just you hold on, sir! This is the woman I love, and she's anything but a savage. She's a Christian."

The preacher cast a skeptical eye at Tachechana. "You speak English?"

"Yes," she replied evenly, holding her temper in check. "I speak your language, and I have learned to read and write."

"Humph! So you call yourself a Christian?"

"Yes."

"By what authority do you make such a bold claim?"

His gaze was withering, but she thrust her chin forward. "By the same authority as you."

"What impertinence! I am a minister of the gospel!"

"Then you, above all others, will understand. Did you not come to God as a lost sinner?"

"Ah . . . yes. . . ."

"And did you not ask him to forgive your sin because of what his Son, the God-Man Jesus, did for you?"

"Well . . . I suppose I did."

"Did you not become a child of God by believing the words of his Book?"

"Yes . . . but . . . but . . . " he sputtered impotently.

"Then we are both Christians by the same authority."

The preacher removed his glasses and wiped them with a handkerchief from his pocket. "Perhaps my judgment was hasty. My apologies, madam."

"Then you will marry us?" Nathan asked.

22

"Yes, yes," he agreed hurriedly, replacing his spectacles and bestowing a more respectful glance on them. "While I don't approve of mixed marriages, I must say your . . . uh . . . bride is quite convincing." The man moved to the front of the chapel, drawing a small black Bible from another pocket. "Just follow me, please," he called over his shoulder. Turning around to face them, he opened the Bible. "Do you have anyone to stand with you?"

"No," replied Nathan looking around. "We're alo—"

The door of the chapel opened before the words were out of Nathan's mouth.

"You'll never be alone when my troops are about," Captain Baker said.

The soldiers filed in, nearly filling the small chapel. Some of them set to work building a fire while others lit the still dark lamps.

"I've taken the liberty of sending for your wife and daughter to join the festivities, Preacher." Captain Baker was fully in charge, much to the man's discomfort. "Your wife can play that pump organ over there, and your daughter can stand with Miss Tachechana . . . if she'll have her."

Tachechana's green eyes widened, and she looked to Nathan for direction. He nodded his agreement. "Yes, please," she said simply.

"Captain Baker, I'd count it an honor to have you stand with me if you're so inclined," Nathan invited.

"I'd like nothing better. But don't you think it's about time you called me Tom?"

The two men were still smiling when the preacher's wife and daughter entered the chapel and took their appointed places. Soon the little organ was wheezing out an old hymn, and Tachechana found herself looking into the dark eyes of a feminine version of the preacher—except that in Rebecca's face, the thin features seemed more refined and delicate than waspish.

"Dearly beloved . . ." The preacher cleared his throat and began the timeless vows.

To Tachechana, the unfamiliar words held little meaning. But she was touched by the display of support on the part of the captain and his men, and by the aura of reverence in the room. She was making promises to Nathan and he to her *in the presence of their God*. Such vows could not be taken lightly. She would remember to ask Nathan more about them later.

Then the preacher's voice rang out loud and clear, and he was saying something about a token.

"This ring which was her mother's," Nathan replied to his question, and she felt the smoothness of the gold band as he slid it on her finger. When she looked, she found a small red stone mounted in the center.

The preacher droned on, ". . . by the power vested in me as a preacher of the gospel, I pronounce that you are husband and wife. You may kiss the bride."

Nathan took Tachechana's chin in his cupped hand and elevated it as he bowed his own head to meet her lips. At his touch she heard the sound of music, but it was sweeter far than that being produced by the strange instrument the preacher's wife was laboring over. She could have drifted off into the clouds at that very moment, except for the cheers and handshakes of what appeared to be the entire U.S. Cavalry.

"What are your plans now?" Captain Baker asked as the troop began filing out of the chapel into the cold April night.

"We kind of thought we'd take our time getting back to the cabin . . . maybe camp along the way," Nathan replied.

"Starting tonight?"

"Yep." Nathan's voice was deliberately brisk, belying the sag of his shoulders and the dull ache in his chest.

24

"You'll do no such thing, man. You're in no condition to ride. I insist that you and your wife take my quarters for the night. I'll bunk with my men."

"We wouldn't want to put you out. . . ."

Her husband's protests were growing weaker, Tachechana thought, her own head whirling with the exhaustion of the journey and the activities of the day before.

"Not another word. It's settled." Captain Baker turned to summon one of the men who was leaving the chapel. "Trooper O'Connel!"

"Yes, sir?"

"Fetch Mr. and Mrs. Cooper's saddlebags and deliver them to my quarters, then see to it that their horses are fed and watered."

"Yes, sir!" The trooper gave a smart salute and stood beside the door waiting for the newlyweds.

In the dizzying wave of emotion surrounding her wedding, Tachechana caught only a fleeting glance of a sturdy young man with the bluest of blue eyes set in a wide, pleasant face. The fringe of hair protruding from his kepi was the color of the carrots Nathan grew in his garden.

"I don't know how to thank you both," Nathan said.

"No thanks necessary, but you must promise me you'll be my guests for breakfast." He flashed a bright smile, then in an aside to Nathan that Tachechana could not fail to overhear, said, "It's imperative that we talk." Then, briskly, "Now, if you'll excuse me, I'll get what I need from my quarters. If there is anything else you require, Trooper O'Connel here will be at your service. Good night."

"Thank you again, Tom. Good night."

When the door to the captain's quarters closed and the newlyweds were alone at last, there was an air of restraint between them. Tachechana nervously fingered her new ring,

25

turning it over so that the red gemstone winked in the lamplight.

"Where did you get this ring?" she asked shyly.

"Your father gave it to me last night. It belonged to your mother. He has worn it in the medicine bag around his neck since the day she died."

Her eyes filled with tears. "I never knew."

"I doubt that anyone did." Nathan took the small hand in his, massaging the knuckles.

"He must have loved my mother very much." Tachechana's words were barely more than a whisper.

"Yes . . . and, though this will come as no surprise, he adores you." He pulled her to him and she rested her head on his chest, listening to his even breathing. "But not half as much as I do."

She lifted her lips for his kiss and wearily they sank onto the bed. Then Nathan leaned over and, cupping his hand about the lamp, blew out the flickering flame.

At breakfast the next morning, Captain Baker greeted the newlyweds, then got right to the point.

"You must be curious about my reasons for detaining you."

Nathan lifted a wiry brow, but his expression remained inscrutable. "A little," he admitted, "though . . . my wife and I . . ." he glanced at Tachechana's rose-tinted cheeks, "appreciate your hospitality."

"I was hoping to persuade you to stay here at the fort for a while longer." The tall man leveled a searching gaze at the couple.

"Why would you wish us to do that?" Tachechana's voice was a hoarse half-whisper, her senses instantly alerted.

"Now, now, Mrs. Cooper, you have no cause for alarm . . . personally, that is," the captain assured her, but he stroked his brown beard thoughtfully before continuing. "It is only fair, however, to warn you both that trouble is brewing in the northern plains. Big trouble."

"Again, Captain, we appreciate your concern, but you needn't fret about us. The word is out among all the tribes that Tachechana and I are man and wife, and they accept me as one of them."

"It's not the Indians that concern me—it's the army."

"What do these words mean?" Tachechana felt the uneasiness that accompanies the premonition of impending disaster.

"Many of the Indians have left the reservation," explained Baker. "The politicians back in Washington view such action as hostile, an insult to their generosity in sending food and clothing to the red man." There was a long pause. "They have ordered the army to drive all Indians back to the reservations . . . or wipe them out."

There was a moment in which both Nathan and Tachechana absorbed the full impact of his report.

Then her fighting spirit asserted itself. "But the agents at the reservation have not been giving the food to my people," she argued. "They sell it to the fort sutlers, who then sell to white soldiers, miners, and settlers. The Indians leave because they are hungry and must again follow the game trails."

"You and I know that," Baker interjected, "but Washington doesn't. At least they won't admit it."

"Then what is your judgment?" Nathan leaned forward.

"All-out war against any Indians found off the reservation." He paused. "It has already started. On the first of March, General Crook marched north to the Powder River, looking for renegades."

"The Powder is near my father's village!" Tachechana exclaimed.

"Exactly." Captain Baker nodded. "That's why I'm telling you now. Furthermore, Colonel J. J. Reynolds attacked a village recently, thinking it was the home of Crazy Horse. The Indians escaped unharmed, but there was much destruction. They lost everything—lodges, food, weapons.

"The refugees, Cheyennes, were received as brothers by Crazy Horse, and now he has taken them to Sitting Bull's village, where they're combining forces and planning a stand against the army. Mark my words"—and there was an underlying gravity in his voice that chilled Tachechana to the bone—"this summer of 1876, the plains will run red with blood, Indian as well as white."

Again there was a prolonged silence as the two so newly one contemplated Captain Baker's meaning. "I hear you, Tom," Nathan acknowledged, "but I'm still not convinced that either the Indians or the army will be a threat to us in our little cabin."

Baker sighed. "I can only hope you're right, my friend. But we know that Great Bear and his people cannot help but be discovered by the army . . . or by hostiles who will try to persuade him to support their cause. From all reports, he's a good man. But he's in for trouble unless he moves his people back to the reservation."

"What can we do?" Tachechana's thoughts raced like the pronghorn.

"Talk to Great Bear. Convince him to return to the reservation. Tell him that General Crook is already marching north and that, soon, Terry and Custer will be coming from Fort Lincoln and General Gibbon from the west. When they converge, there can only be slaughter and destruction."

"Captain, you underestimate my people." Tachechana's eyes glittered like green marble. "We have been pushed as far as we can go. There must be more *you* can do."

"I'm sorry, ma'am, truly I am. I give orders only to those immediately under my command, but when it comes to greater matters, I have to obey my superiors." For a moment the brave captain showed his vulnerability, Tachechana thought, and she pitied him.

"Then my husband and I will speak to my father. He is a proud man, and I don't know if he will listen to us, but we will try. . . . How long before your armies advance?"

"I only know the outcome will be determined this summer. You must tell your father to act quickly."

Pushing away his empty plate, Nathan stood, bringing the conversation to a close. "Tom, we're in your debt," he said. "We'll be heading back to our cabin today, but we'll deliver your message to Great Bear."

"Good. I knew I could count on you." The smile on Captain Baker's face was one of relief rather than satisfaction, Tachechana mused. "Trooper O'Connel, see that the Coopers' horses are saddled and brought around."

"Right away, sir!"

Tachechana kept her thoughts to herself as Nathan and Captain Baker talked on in subdued voices. *Strange,* she sighed, *that I could be so happy only a few hours ago . . . and so sad at this moment.*

chapter

3

NATHAN AND TACHECHANA RODE OUT INTO THE PALE GREEN mist of morning. Dewdrops, diamond-bright, glistened on a prairie awakening to new life and color, as if eager to shed the somber hues of winter.

Viewing the peaceful terrain stretching in all directions as far as the eye could see, Tachechana suppressed the nightmarish sensation that Captain Baker might have been speaking the truth when he said this land she loved would soon see much bloodshed. She shook her head to shrug away the dark clouds marring her happiness. Whatever the future, this week must be filled with love and joy.

Still, the feeling of foreboding persisted, and she nudged Fox into a canter, bringing her alongside Nathan mounted on Rowdy.

"What do you think of Captain Baker's words?" she asked, hoping for some reassurance from her new husband.

He squinted, as if gauging the distance between them and the first cry of battle. "The officials in Washington believe their cause is just; the Indians believe otherwise. I'm afraid a collision of wills is inevitable."

"That means war?"

"That means war."

They entered a small forested glade where the sun could not penetrate and where frost hung in hoary whiskers tight to the needles of the ponderosa pines. Tachechana felt a chill course through her body that seemed an ominous exclamation point to Nathan's terse statement.

"But it is not fair that the Sioux, who have lived on the prairie forever, should be confined to such a small part of it. Even our sacred Black Hills are being robbed of gold by the white man."

"Life is not always fair, Chana, but I'm afraid there is nothing the Indians can do. You have seen how your people suffer because the white hunters are killing all the buffalo. What will they do when the buffalo are gone?"

"Such a thing cannot be when the great beasts fill the prairie like pebbles in a stream bed!"

"Believe me, it is possible. If necessary, the white soldiers will not stop until they have starved the Sioux into submission."

Her small chin rose in defiance. "Then the Sioux will fight! We call the buffalo *Pte,* our uncle. We shall defend him!"

"Yes, I'm sure the Sioux will fight, and the Cheyenne beside them. Many good people will die."

"What will we do, Nathan?" Her voice dropped plaintively.

"First we'll talk with your father to see if we can persuade him to take his people to the reservation, at least until this mess is resolved. Then, I intend to write General Sherman and President Grant to see if anything can be done at the military and political level."

"Will the white fathers listen?"

"We can only try."

As they rode out of the glade the warmth of the sun drove the chill from her body, and Nathan's confidence helped to set her mind at ease.

The sight of a mule deer roe, heavy with fawn, bouncing away from them on stiff, coil-spring legs, caused them to rein in the horses for a better view. They watched her bound into the safety of a shallow draw, not speaking until she had disappeared.

"Let's not allow Captain Baker's news to spoil our trip home," Tachechana said, edging her horse up next to Rowdy.

Nathan leaned over and kissed her. "Let's not allow Captain Baker's news to spoil anything about our life together."

As they traveled on through the day they talked only small talk, saying those things which are common to lovers everywhere. They spoke of the life they would have together, their cabin, even the garden they would soon be planting.

"Lots of carrots," she said, "and no beans!"

Nathan chuckled. He remembered the face she had made at her first taste of beans. "It hardly seems possible that only nine months ago I thought of you as a barbaric little savage," he said.

"And I thought of you as an old Gray Beard!"

"Then how could two such unlikely people ever manage to fall in love?" he teased.

"We were both looking for something," she replied, "and we found each other."

"Such sage words!" Nathan leaned forward in his saddle and gave his bride an impulsive hug. "Now you *sound* like the Gray Beard!"

About mid-afternoon they came across a crystal stream flowing through a grove of cottonwood trees, and while it was yet early, they decided to make camp. Nearby, a tall outcropping of rock would act as a barrier to the cool night breezes.

Tachechana immediately busied herself collecting saplings

to build a frame over which they could throw their canvas tent material, while Nathan took a pail from the pack horse and went to the creek for water.

They were more than a little surprised when they unpacked the tent. There, carefully wrapped in tissue paper, they found a beautifully hand carved wooden plaque which read, "God Bless Our Home," with a note from Trooper O'Connel offering his best wishes for their happiness.

Tachechana's smooth brow creased in a frown of puzzlement. "I do not understand. This Trooper O'Connel, this white soldier of war, speaks of God and home. How can such people as this one and Captain Baker be murderers?"

"Chana, no one is all good or all evil. Each of us is the victim of circumstances, of these days in which we live. I'm sure many of the soldiers would rather leave the Indians alone, even as many of the Indians would like to live in peace. But as long as there are greedy people in this world, we will have conflict."

"There must be a way to end this ... this conflict ... without spilling blood," she insisted.

Nathan sat for a long time, the muscles of his jaws bunching and relaxing as he thought. "There *is* a way," he said. "Jesus showed us how to live in peace. When offended, turn the other cheek, go the second mile, give rather than take. It is the way of love. But there are too few who believe, too few who walk with him. Each person wants only what is best for himself."

When they had set up camp, they went together to collect enough wood to cook their meal and keep the fire burning through the night. There was plenty of broken wood among the cottonwood trees. The last armloads, however, took them out onto a spit of sand bordered on three sides by water. In the calmer water on the downstream side of the bar, they could see silvery trout quickly darting to take refuge at their approach.

"Too bad there are no grasshoppers around, or we could eat fresh fish tonight," Nathan said.

"Maybe you could swim after them and catch them," Tachechana said and gave him a little shove.

She hadn't intended to push him into the water. But, Nathan, not expecting her playful mood, found himself knee-deep in icy water. With a giggle of delight, Tachechana ran for the cottonwoods, Nathan close behind her. It was not a real race. She knew she could outdistance him whenever she pleased. In and out of the straggly trees she ran, dodging first one, then the other.

Tiring of the game, she allowed Nathan to gain on her and made the supposed error of turning into his waiting arms.

"Now I've got you, and you're the one who's going swimming!"

He caught her up in his arms and carried her back onto the sand bar. Swinging her back and forth as if ready to throw her in, he spun her around and deposited her on the sand to the cacophony of her squeals and giggles. They lay together on the sand, panting for breath, until Tachechana's giggles ceased under Nathan's lips.

The sun sank behind the rock that was their windbreak when they finally brought the last armload of wood back to their campsite and prepared their evening meal. Then, lounging under the canvas roof of the lean-to, they watched the stars appear and listened to a pack of coyotes sing into the ever darkening sky. Gazing into the dying embers of the fire, they fell asleep in each other's arms.

It was the chilly temperature rather than the sun that awakened them the next morning.

Nathan threw some kindling on the coals and scurried back to his blanket, waiting until the heat of the blaze warmed the tent. Later he had to break ice in the bucket to get enough water for the coffee. By the time breakfast was ready, they were feeling the warming effects of the fire and the rising sun, but the sky showed itself too red to suit Nathan.

"It looks as if we're in for some bad weather," he said, nodding to the overcast northern horizon.

"Does that mean we have to go back to the cabin today?" she asked.

"No, but we better keep our eyes open. I wouldn't want us to be caught in a spring blizzard."

Although she didn't speak, Tachechana did not understand his concern. The northern plains were home—in fair weather or foul—and she was used to the ways of Mother Earth. The thought of being snowbound with Nathan in their makeshift quarters caused the beat of her heart to quicken. But whether here or in their snug cabin, they would be alone together, growing closer each day, and savoring the delights of expressing their deepest feelings.

"And just what are you dreaming about?" Nathan asked, breaking into her thoughts, even as he cast a wary eye on the scudding clouds.

"Oh, nothing," she said with a sigh and set about her chores.

The stars were not visible that night, and the hunting coyotes were too far away to serenade them. The stars were still in Tachechana's eyes, however, and her heart provided all the music she needed.

Sleeping soundly, they failed to notice the fine mist of rain that began to fall, or when it turned to soggy flakes. The wind came up with the sun, sticking the white slush to the northwest sides of the trees and rocks. The flapping of the tent awakened them.

"I was afraid of this," Nathan said as he surveyed the flat whiteness outside.

"Shall we stay here until it ends?"

"We'd best cut and run," Nathan replied. "But I think we'll head for your father's village. It's closer by two hours than the cabin."

They struck the tent and were shortly on their way, sucking and chewing on pemican and jerky.

Tachechana resisted the urge to run the horses hard to cover more distance before the snow got too deep, but any Sioux warrior knew better than that. It was wiser to pace them carefully, lest they flounder later in heavy drifts.

About noon, however, the snow stopped altogether, and the sun came out.

"It's clearing, Nathan!" Tachechana cried. "We can easily reach the cabin by nightfall."

"We're only about an hour from your father's village, Chana. We might as well ride on in and pass Captain Baker's message on to him."

A chill gripped Tachechana. She had been forcing that issue from her thoughts since they left the fort, but now there was no way to avoid it. What would she do if her father decided to fight? She loved him dearly. And she hoped to count some of the white soldiers, like Trooper O'Connel and Captain Baker, as her friends as well.

And what would happen if her father went back to the reservation? Would there be food enough for them and grass for their horses? "Life was much simpler when I was a child," she mused.

Crossing a small fold in the land, they spotted the tepees of Great Bear's village piercing the horizon, and Tachechana knew it would be too long a time before she and her husband would be alone again. In spite of the cold and snow, a council would be called, if not for tonight, at least by tomorrow. The decision to move to the reservation, or to stay and fight the army would not be made by Great Bear alone. All the elders and braves would voice their opinions.

They rode into the village, but when there was no sign of recognition or welcome, Nathan was puzzled.

"It is the way of the Sioux to leave a newly married couple to themselves until the couple starts the conversation," Tachechana explained."

"But we must tell your father about Captain Baker. Each hour we delay puts the village in more danger."

"First we must go to our own tepee and unpack our horses or the people will think we do not like the lodge they built for us," she said.

"I never realized how complex the Sioux culture was," Nathan admitted.

"We are not savages as so many of your people seem to believe."

"At least I know one who is not!" Nathan grinned. "You are half white, which means that our children will be three-quarters white."

"Children!" The thought caused her to rein Fox to a standstill. "Oh, Nathan, will we have children?"

Nathan laughed so hard he nearly fell from his horse. Gaining control of himself, he wheezed, "Married people quite often do," and again succumbed to laughter.

"Can we have a whole tepee full?"

The idea of a tepee full of children quickly sobered him. "I guess we'll have to see what the Good Lord has to say about that, though I hope we have them one at a time."

"What other way is there of having them?" she asked and galloped her horse to the front of the new tepee.

Chuckling, Nathan followed her and began unloading their provisions.

"How long must we wait before it is proper to visit your father?" Nathan asked.

"We must first build a fire to signal through the smoke hole of our tepee that we are happy with our lodgings," she said, then added mischievously, "and spend the first night here before we speak to our neighbors." Her eyes twinkled with this addition to the Sioux custom.

When Nathan came back to the tepee after leading the horses out to graze, he found a venison loin lying on a piece of deerskin in front of the door.

"Where did this come from?" he asked as he entered.

"I don't know. One of our friends left it for us."

"*Our* friends? Do the people of this village really consider me a friend?"

"They would not have accepted your tobacco if they had not accepted you as a friend."

"Then Eagle Feather still regards me as an enemy." Nathan's countenance darkened, causing the silver in his hair and beard to appear more pronounced than ever.

"Eagle Feather and I were good friends. He wanted me to be his squaw. It is natural that he be angry. But his anger will soon melt like the spring snow, and all will be well between you."

"I hope you're right." He caught her to him fiercely. "But I know if someone tried to take you away from me, I'd fight. I love you far too much to lose you, and I imagine he feels the same."

"But we are married now," she soothed. "Nothing can change that."

By noon the next day the warm sun had thawed most of the snow, and Nathan had delivered Captain Baker's message to Great Bear. As expected, the chief called a council for that very evening, sending several young boys to the tepees with the news. Nathan accompanied the braves as they gathered the wood for the council fire, and watched with interest as each piece was carefully laid in place.

"Is everything ready, Gray Wolf?" a voice called from behind him.

He turned to find Great Bear and Tachechana standing there.

"Why do you call me Gray Wolf?"

"Now that you are one of us, you must have an Indian name. I have chosen 'Gray Wolf' because you are swift and cunning like the wolf," the chief explained, referring to the incidents in which Nathan had eluded both the Indians and whites who sought his life. "And because of the color of your hair . . ."

". . . and your face!" added Tachechana, barely suppressing a giggle.

Great Bear, irritated at this interruption, slanted his daughter a look of warning. "In the land of the Sioux, you shall be known as Hityoni, the Gray Wolf."

"The chief has greatly honored a white man," Nathan said.

"Tonight you will sit at my right hand at the council fire as my son, and your wife will sit at your right hand. You will each speak the message of the white chief, Captain Baker."

"But, Father," Tachechana injected, "a woman has never spoken to the council before."

"If only Gray Wolf tells the words of another, the people might not believe him. You must say that you, too, have heard the words of the white chief."

"But will they listen to a woman?" she asked.

"You are the daughter of Great Bear. It is enough."

40

Nathan, observing the ritual of lighting the council fire and the passing of the peace pipe, was not called upon to speak immediately. First, the chief must declare his reasons for calling the council and explain why a white man was sitting with them.

"Gray Wolf is my son! He speaks the truth. Skipping Fawn has also heard the words of the white chief. She will tell us that Gray Wolf's words are truly the words of the white chief, Baker."

Nervously at first, but gaining confidence as he proceeded, Nathan addressed the assembled elders. In firm tones, he explained that many people, red and white, would die if the Indians did not return to the reservation, at least temporarily.

"The Sioux are brave and strong," he said, clenching his fist and striking his chest. He paused. "But what will happen to your little ones if the soldiers should ride into your village while you are at the hunting grounds?" He stood, feet spread wide apart in the manner of the Sioux, and looked into each dusky face, letting his words sink deep before he took his seat.

Glancing around the outer ring of the circle, Tachechana noticed the mothers hugging their babies close. This touching gesture bore mute testimony to the truth that they were stirred by Nathan's speech, even though she could detect no visible sign of emotion in the faces of the men.

Eagle Feather was the first to spring to his feet. "Why should we listen to the words of this man or his white chief?"

"Gray Wolf, the husband of my daughter, is my own son! His words are my words!" Great Bear thundered.

"But the words of the white chief cannot be trusted," Eagle Feather returned. "Other white chiefs have said we would be fed on the reservation. They lied. They said we would forever have our sacred Black Hills. They lied. How do we know this white chief is not lying?"

41

Chief Great Bear got to his feet. "Among the Sioux there are coyotes who do not know how to speak the truth. Does that mean all Sioux are liars? So it is among the white men. Gray Wolf and Skipping Fawn know this chief. They trust him. Their judgment is good."

"But if we do not fight, the white soldiers will think we are cowards. They will never stop pushing us onto land we do not want, or giving us food we cannot eat. They will continue to take our maidens and force them to bear their children. I say . . . we fight!" Eagle Feather lifted a clenched fist.

Another young brave took up the refrain. "If we do not fight, our own women will hate us!"

"But there are many more soldiers than Indians," one of the elders reminded them. "If we kill and are killed, soon there will be no Indians left."

"Then we must strike first!" said Eagle Feather. "We have all heard how the white soldiers attacked the Cheyenne and destroyed their village and food."

Into the night the argument raged. At last Great Bear stood and stretched out both hands. A hush descended over the group and all was still, except for the snapping and popping of the fire.

"Let us hear the counsel of the wise ones," he said and sat back down.

The elders remained seated as they spoke. As a whole they favored peace, but only a "peace with honor." They must have some guarantee that the white soldiers would not murder them in their sleep.

At last Great Bear rose for the final time. "If my son Gray Wolf can bring us such assurance, we will again try to live in peace with the whites." The chief looked at Nathan. "Can you do this thing?"

"I will ride to the fort at first light," Nathan replied, looking grave. "If there is a way, Captain Baker will see to it. I will ask him to come to the village in peace and speak to you himself."

chapter
4

AT SUNRISE, NATHAN LEFT FOR Fort Fetterman with Great Bear's proposal for peace. He rode alone, despite Tachechana's pleas to remain at his side.

"Trust me, Chana," he said, leaning down from his saddle to pull her into his arms for a farewell kiss. "It's better this way. One rider can make better time than two."

"Then fly like the wind," she said, "and God speed your return!"

Throughout the long day, Tachechana found little to hold her attention for more than a few minutes at a time. Watching her flit from one activity to another, her father remarked that she had become more like the bumblebee than the skipping fawn.

When she was summoned to the tepee of a young woman in the last stages of childbirth, she was both relieved and apprehensive. Seeing Plainsfeather's coppery face wreathed in smiles, however, did much to ease her fears.

The woman was strong and healthy, and the delivery proceeded without incident. When at last Plainsfeather handed the crying infant to Tachechana, she wrapped the small one in soft deerskin and cuddled him for a moment before placing the bundle in the mother's outstretched arms.

Looking into that tiny face, she felt such a surge of tenderness that the breath was nearly drawn from her mouth.

"How long will it be before I have a baby of my own, Plainsfeather?" she asked as they walked back to the old woman's tepee.

"Ha!" she cackled. "That depends on your man—how much he gives himself to you."

Tachechana blushed, thinking to herself, *Then soon I should be with child.*

Eating her evening meal with Great Bear that night, she asked, "How long after you danced the wedding dance with my mother before I was born?"

The chief's face resembled a thundercloud before the sun breaks through. "Ten or eleven times the moon changed," he said, slanting a dark look in her direction.

"Oh."

The look of disappointment on her face brought a smile from the chief. "Why ask such a question? Do you think you carry a wolf cub?"

"No, I don't think so, but I would like a baby very much, a whole tepee full of babies."

Great Bear chuckled. "Ah . . . many children to call me Grandfather." His expression took on a faraway look. "Perhaps until the last war horse is dead, it would be better to have no new ones."

A shudder rocked Tachechana's body, and she silently offered up a prayer for Nathan. *What would I do if I should lose him now?*

"When will Nathan return?" she asked.

"Gray Wolf," he corrected, "will be home before the sun sleeps tomorrow."

She slept lonely and alone in their new tepee. No matter how high she banked the fire, she could not make the lodge as warm as when Nathan's body was next to hers. In the four nights they had been man and wife, she had grown accustomed to his nearness, and her heart ached with the dull pain of separation. *Tomorrow . . . tomorrow . . . I will see him again* . . . and she slipped into a dreamless sleep.

Nathan rode into the village on the afternoon of the following day. He stopped first at his own lodge to greet Tachechana, then, together, they walked to the tepee of Great Bear.

"Does my son bring good news?"

Tachechana was always amused when her father, only two years older than Nathan, called her husband by the affectionate term, but she made no comment.

"I bring news," he said, "but the chief will have to decide if it is good news or bad."

"Shall I call the Owls to a council fire?" the chief asked.

"It would be better if we talked first in private." Nathan nodded toward the door of the chief's lodge.

The chief held the flap open and the three of them went in, settling themselves cross-legged on mats.

"What are the words of the white chief?" Great Bear asked.

"They are not good words." Nathan sat in silence for a time. "Many of the whites would like to see the red man banished from the plains."

"Why do they hate us so?" asked Tachechana.

"The white man puts much value on the ownership of land," he replied. "Some will even kill to possess it."

"But how can anyone own Mother Earth which the Great Spirit has given for all men to walk upon?" Great Bear asked incredulously.

"It is sad that all men cannot see it that way, Chief Great Bear. Besides, there is much gold in the Black Hills. The

47

white man uses gold to trade for other possessions. It is enough to drive some white men crazy with greed."

The chief shook his head as if unable to comprehend what he was hearing.

"Then there is the matter of Indians killing whites and mutilating their bodies," Nathan went on. "I know the whites do the same to the Indians, but only the white man's story is told in the great cities of the East. Now, even the white fathers are saying, 'The only good Indian is a dead Indian!'"

"So ... we must fight." Great Bear's tone was one of resignation.

"No, there is still hope for a peaceful resolution," Nathan said. "Captain Baker and his soldiers left this morning on a three-day patrol. On the last day they will visit the village of Great Bear."

The chief frowned.

"Don't worry. Baker will come in peace." Nathan hastened to ease Great Bear's fears. "His word is as my word or the word of the chief. He has known of your location for some time, but would not come near, because I told him you were a man of honor and peace."

"But will the blood of his soldiers run too hot, or my young braves be too eager for the coup?"

"We must do all we can to promote a peaceful talk with him, but he has orders to send all Sioux back to the reservation."

"If these orders are to kill us, we will fight. Sioux are not dogs to lie down and be trampled underfoot."

"Baker doesn't come to kill the Sioux," Nathan contradicted. "He comes to reason with you. If you choose not to lead your people back to the reservation, perhaps you can bargain with him, call a truce. All he wants is a chance to talk with you. You alone will decide what is best for your people."

"I have the ears of a jack rabbit," said Great Bear. "My people will listen to the words of this white chief. If he truly comes in peace with good medicine for my people, we will listen and the wise ones, the elders, will decide what to do. But if he comes with his wolves, like the others, and if he wants to make war, he will find the warriors of Great Bear to be the fiercest bears of all the tribes of the Sioux. We will fight for the lives of our women and little ones, our lodges and our horses. No Sioux fears the long darkness."

"It is so." Nathan nodded. "But the chief will find that Captain Baker shares his hope that neither his men nor yours will taste the bitterness of war and death."

"When will he come?"

"The day after tomorrow when the sun is at the top of the sky."

"Then we will be ready for him before the sun rises."

A shadow of concern flickered across Nathan's even features. Tachechana suspected that he was thinking of the white general called Custer and his habit of attacking in the predawn grayness. After they left the tepee, she was not surprised by her husband's question.

"Will your father meet with the soldiers and talk of peace with them . . . or is he planning an ambush?"

"My father is a man of his word!" she retorted angrily. "If he says he will talk, he will talk, but neither is he a fool. He will be prepared if the soldiers try to deceive him."

The day before Captain Baker's scheduled visit, Tachechana noticed Nathan studying Great Bear's every mood and action. His eyes followed the chief as he walked among the lodges, speaking in subdued tones with his warriors. Grunting in acknowledgment, they would then disappear for a time, bringing back their weapons for the chief's approval.

Nathan grew increasingly tense until, at last, he took Tachechana aside. "Why does your father prepare the village for battle? Doesn't he believe me when I say Captain Baker will come in peace?"

"He believes you have given him the captain's word, but he does not yet trust the captain to do what he says he will do."

"Do you think I have misjudged Baker?"

"No." She spoke with confidence. "Captain Baker cared for me when you were wounded . . . when we didn't know if you would live or die. He is a good man."

Nathan sighed. "If we are wrong, many people, red and white, will die here tomorrow."

That night a dance was held, and while it appeared to Nathan and Tachechana that it had been staged to encourage the people to accept the overtures of peace when they were offered, the festive atmosphere soon gave way to an ominous stillness. One of the singers began a war chant, and soon an old squaw took up the death wail. As the evening wore on, the villagers wandered back to their lodges to await the morning.

Long before dawn Tachechana and Nathan awoke to the sound of horses plodding, single file, out of the village. Rising quickly to determine the source of the commotion, Nathan found all the warriors armed and mounted. They were heading west, but before the darkness hid them completely, Nathan saw them separate into three groups and split off toward the north and south.

When the couple reached Great Bear's tepee, they found him similarly armed. "Where are the warriors going?" Nathan demanded.

Great Bear scowled. "We will not be prairie dogs in the dawn as so many of our brothers. If the white chief Captain Baker plans treachery, he will be greeted by my own. If he is an honest man, he will see the sun set today."

With uneasy tread Nathan and Tachechana walked back to their lodge to await the sunrise.

She recoiled at the sight of Nathan opening the action of his rifle to be sure a cartridge was in the chamber. "Do you think there will be killing?" she asked.

"Only God knows what this day holds. . . ."

"If there is fighting, who will you fight against—your people or mine?"

He held her gaze with a solemn look. "We are all one, Chana. We must pray that there is no choice to make."

Shortly after sunrise the group of Indians who had ridden to the south came trotting into the village. Eagle Feather, who appeared to be the leader, galloped directly to Great Bear's tepee.

"From the look on his face," Tachechana observed, "he did not find the soldiers."

"And if I don't miss my guess, I'd say he's sorry he didn't," Nathan added with a wry look.

Shortly thereafter, another group arrived from the north with a similar report. All eyes turned toward the west. Only one group remained.

Ten minutes later two braves galloped in, their ponies white with lather. "The soldiers are far from the village. They ride in columns of fours."

"Then they come in peace." The chief nodded in approval.

Quickly he readied an area just west of the village to be used as a meeting place. Blankets for the elders were spread in a long row. Adjacent to these, three blankets were placed for the chief and for Tachechana and Nathan, who would act as interpreters, then three additional blankets for Captain Baker, his lieutenant, and sergeant. The braves would sit on the ground directly behind the elders, and the troopers would fall in behind the officers.

Just before high noon Baker's troopers were spotted, coming in at a slow trot. The braves riding out to meet the soldiers flanked the column on either side at about one hundred yards. When the Indians came within range of the village, they galloped ahead and took their places with the other warriors.

Standing at her father's right side, with Nathan on Great Bear's left, Tachechana felt a thrill course through her body. Perhaps God had permitted her to learn English for this very day—to help bring peace to her beloved prairie.

She glanced at her father's profile. How proud and strong he looked today. He was wearing his ceremonial war bonnet, the giant eagle feathers framing his noble features. She could not read the expression on his face, but she knew that he was unafraid.

Suddenly all eyes turned to the soldiers, who had advanced to within fifty yards of the chief. Captain Baker raised his hand and the column halted.

The one called Sarge shouted, "Dismount!" and the troopers obeyed as one body. "Fall in—in three ranks!" he bellowed.

One soldier from each column took the reins, while the others moved forward and formed three rows parallel to and opposite the elders. Captain Baker stepped out ahead, closely followed by two of his higher-ranking officers. The rest of the contingent fell in behind.

Captain Baker and his men approached the waiting assembly. There was no sound until Nathan's voice shattered the silence.

"Chief Great Bear," he said, "this is Captain Baker, an honored chief of the Great White Father in Washington. Captain Baker, Great Bear, a chief of the Lakota, mighty warrior and man of truth."

The captain removed his glove and offered his right hand to the chief. Tentatively, he accepted the captain's handshake of friendship.

"If the White Eagle, Captain Baker, comes in peace, he is welcome in the village of Great Bear," Nathan interpreted.

"May our peace be long and happy," returned Captain Baker.

At a signal from the chief, the guests of honor seated themselves, followed by the elders and the remainder of the captain's entourage. Eagle Feather, poised in stubborn defiance, was the last to be seated.

"What words of peace does the white chief bring to the village of Great Bear?" he asked.

"These are sad days," Baker began, "when the heart of both red man and white are filled with hatred and killing."

"If the white men did not kill the Indian, his women, and children, and steal his land and its gold, there would be no hatred in the heart of the Indian," Great Bear insisted.

"It is true that many bad things have been done by the white man, and many by the Indian." Baker paused. "But it is our job, yours and mine, to find a way to live in peace.

"I bring you news. The president, the Great White Chief, wants all his children, the Sioux, to return to the reservation where he will provide food and horses for . . ."

"Do not insult the chief with that nonsense!" Nathan fired a retort. "He has heard those promises before and received rancid meat and wormy bread for his faith. He will not willingly return his people to those conditions."

Baker narrowed his gaze, choosing his words with care. "Then tell him the Great White Chief has no recourse but to return all hostiles to the Agency."

"You call us 'hostiles'?" Great Bear was indignant. "We wish only to live in peace, but we wish to live *here*—on the breast of our Mother Earth."

Baker rose and began to pace. "If you insist on remaining here, all white men will believe you to be hostiles . . . and I cannot guarantee your safety."

The chief scowled. "You will find that the Sioux are turtles—slow to die."

"Chief Great Bear, I know the Sioux are great warriors, and I have no wish to fight them, but soon this prairie will be covered with blue-coated soldiers—as many in number as there are grasshoppers in summer. I do not want to see you and your people harmed.

"If you would go back to the Agency, at least for a time, perhaps this matter could be settled. Then, when there is peace over all the prairie, you might be able to return. If you don't go back soon, however, it will be too late, and you and your women and children will suffer."

"And what of my brothers the Oglala, the Sans Arcs, the Miniconjous, the Brules, the Cheyenne? Will you kill all of them?"

"Chief, it is not our desire that any should die. We wish that all would return to the reservation of their own free will. If they refuse . . . then we have no alternative but to use force." Allowing for a meaningful pause, Baker resumed his seat on the council blanket.

Great Bear got to his feet slowly. Tachechana, looking on, knew her father's heart was heavy, but no flicker of emotion betrayed his deep feelings. Passing before the elders, he looked into each face, then leaned forward to confer with them. The waiting was like the passing of an eternity.

At last, he straightened and addressed Captain Baker, pausing as Nathan translated. "The wise ones of my village say we should stay here until we learn whether our brothers will return," Great Bear said. "We will not fight, but neither will we be the first to give up our place on the land."

The tension crackled as Captain Baker considered Great Bear's proposition. Knitting his brows in concentration, he said, "If the chief will give his word that he will return to the reservation with the others . . . if he pledges that his braves will not attack the white man in battle, then Great Bear's village will be spared."

"But how do we know other soldiers will honor these words between us?"

Again the captain weighed his words carefully. "We will leave our red, white, and blue flag here to fly over your village. If other soldiers come, they will see the flag and know you are friendly."

"No! The white chief speaks false words!" shouted Eagle Feather who came running to Great Bear's side. "The Blue Coats gave a flag to Black Kettle, the Cheyenne, on the Wishita River. The soldier called Long Hair, Custer, came at dawn and killed Black Kettle and his wife and many woman and children. He even took Black Kettle's daughter, Me-o-tzi, and forced her to be his woman for three years. Do not trust the Blue Coats!"

The captain turned to his sergeant. "Weren't you with Custer at the Wishita?"

"Yes, sir."

"Tell him it's not true!"

"I'm afraid I can't do that, sir. He has it just about the way it happened."

"Do you mean to tell me . . ."

"Yes, sir."

Captain Baker's lips thinned into a white line, and red blotches appeared high on his cheekbones. "Chief Great Bear, this is the first I have heard of Black Kettle. I assure you this news comes as a great shock."

"The Blue Coat lies!" Eagle Feather screamed. "He lies!" Unsheathing his knife, he sprang at Captain Baker.

To her horror, Tachechana watched the drama unfold before her eyes as if in slow motion. Instinctively, Great Bear stepped in front of the captain, just as Nathan, glimpsing Sarge going for his gun, shouted, "No!" She saw her husband leap up to deflect Eagle Feather's charge, saw her father grapple the young brave to the ground. She heard the sharp report of the sergeant's gun, felt Nathan's body crumple against her as he took the bullet intended for Eagle Feather.

Without thought, she threw herself over Nathan's body in a gesture of protection. "Make . . . your father understand." He ground out the words. "Captain Baker . . . didn't know . . . about Black Kettle."

"Doc!" Baker called frantically. "Cooper's down!"

Tachechana did not need to hear the urgency in the captain's voice to know that Nathan was seriously wounded. It took every ounce of will power to resist issuing the keening wail of the Sioux death chant. Instead, she murmured a prayer of deliverance for the man she loved as her own life. Through a haze of grief, she was barely aware of Eagle Feather, still pinned to the ground by two of her father's most trusted braves.

Great Bear knelt beside Nathan, his head cradled in Tachechana's lap. "What is your counsel, my son?"

"Go back . . . or accept the flag," Nathan said with a long, low groan.

"Come! Take Gray Wolf to his lodge!" His gesture brought four braves to Nathan's aid. Then, rising to face Baker, Great Bear spoke in measured tones. "We will fly your flag over my village. Tonight, you camp across river. Tomorrow, we talk more. But I warn you"—he glared at the captain with eyes of black granite—"we will not believe what our eyes cannot see. Like the hawk circling in the sky, my warriors will be watching all white soldiers." Without another word, he strode away.

"Is there anything I can do?" Captain Baker asked helplessly as Tachechana followed her father and the litter bearing the inert form of her husband.

"No. Nothing," she called over her shoulder. "This day the white man has done too much already."

chapter
5

TERROR GRIPPED TACHECHANA'S HEART as she saw her husband carefully lowered to his sleeping mat and prayed that his strength and tenacity for life would not fail him now. Only four months ago he had been felled by the outlaw's bullet. *Can his body endure another wound so soon after the first?* she wondered.

She prayed while Doc administered a large dose of laudanum to ease the pain. She prayed while he probed for the bullet. She prayed even more fervently when she saw Doc give up, cleanse the wound as best he could, and cover it with a clean white cloth.

"There's not very much I can do, ma'am," the soldier said regretfully. "If I try to take that bullet out, your husband may bleed to death, or he might be paralyzed. Men have lived with bullets in 'em before. He might just be one of the lucky ones."

Tachechana grimly acknowledged Doc's words and wiped Nathan's brow as she had done so many times before. She looked into his expressionless face for some reassurance that he would survive, but the opiate was doing its work and he lay still, the slight rising and falling of his chest the only indication that he was alive.

Great Bear entered the tepee and scowled when he saw

Doc. "The soldiers crossed the river," he said. "What is this one doing here?"

"It is all right, Father," Tachechana said. "This is Doc. He is the one who helped Nathan get well when he was shot before. He is a friend."

"Sometimes I think you have too many white friends," he grunted. "Twice your husband has been shot by white ... friends."

"But this time it was Eagle Feather's fault. The sergeant was only trying to protect his chief just as your warriors would have protected you ... just as Nathan tried to protect both you and the captain." A sob caught in her throat.

Great Bear heard her words and stood without moving, watching Tachechana take the blanket from her own pallet to cover Nathan.

"We must keep him warm," she said, "but I don't want to leave him to get more firewood."

"I will send someone. Gray Wolf must not die." Abruptly, Great Bear turned and ducked out of the tepee.

A grunt at the flap of the tepee announced the arrival of a brave bearing an armload of firewood. It was Eagle Feather, and the look of shame on his face would have amused Tachechana at any other time.

"Your father, the chief, said you needed wood. I told him I would get it."

"It is the least you could do!" she snapped.

"For what I have done, your father, the chief, has made me a woman for today and tomorrow. Even if your father had not ordered it, I would do it. Though I count Gray Wolf my enemy, I had no wish to harm him. He ..."

"Enough!" Tachechana interrupted. "It is by your hand that my husband lies wounded, maybe dying. Still, it is not proper that a Sioux warrior should be doing squaw's work."

As Eagle Feather turned to leave, he paused at the doorway. "If you had danced the wedding dance with me, this would not have happened," he said.

"If I loved you, I might have danced with you, but I love Gray Wolf. What is done is done and cannot be changed."

Throughout the night Tachechana and Doc sat close by, watching Nathan's labored breathing. Just before dawn their tired bodies could take the strain no longer and they dozed off, only to be startled to wakefulness by Nathan's weak cough. Instantly alert, they sprang to his side. His eyes fluttered open and he smiled weakly.

"This isn't exactly ... what I had in mind ... for our honeymoon," he managed.

At the sound of his beloved voice, the river of joy in Tachechana's heart overflowed its banks once more. Nathan was alive!

"How long have I been lying here?" he asked.

"Just the hours since nightfall."

"What did Great Bear decide ... about Baker's proposal?"

"They will meet again in a few hours to talk more," she explained.

"I must be there." Nathan looked at Doc for some sign of approval.

"I don't know," Doc said. "Moving around might break open that wound. Wouldn't try it, if I was you."

"I must," Nathan insisted.

Tachechana's heart sank, but she spoke with stoic dignity. "Then it will be so."

Nathan was fully conscious at the time appointed for the confrontation between Captain Baker and Chief Great Bear. Tachechana saw that he was comfortably settled with a back rest before her father signaled that the meeting was to begin.

In her eyes, both groups seemed to be large snakes, coiled and ready to strike. The blue-gray haze hanging over the prairie reminded her of the smoke that had blossomed from Sarge's gun the day before.

Great Bear rose to speak, but first paced the ground between his people and the soldiers. Even Tachechana marveled at his display of power and strength. His skin-tight buckskins could not conceal the ripple of muscles beneath.

He glared into the faces of each of the soldiers, then, almost contemptuously, turned his back on them to gaze at his own warriors. Lastly, he looked into the cold black eyes of Eagle Feather.

At last, with Tachechana interpreting for him, the chief spoke. "He who commits any act of hostility will die by my own hand." He addressed Captain Baker. "Eagle Feather was wrong to threaten you. Your soldier was wrong to shoot Gray Wolf.

"Because he is the husband of my daughter and a proven friend of the Sioux, I will follow his counsel. Your totem will fly over my lodge from this day on. My people will no longer attack the white man, but"—and his eyes narrowed to slits— "if your soldiers, or any other white man attacks, we will fight as she bears with cubs. Even our women and children will become warriors before you.

"If the Great Father in Washington speaks the truth, we will go back to the reservation and live like obedient children. If he treats us like we are crazy women, he will see how crazy women can fight. I have spoken."

Captain Baker glanced over at Nathan, whose face had taken on an ashen cast. "What does the chief mean by 'crazy women'?"

"Unfaithful . . . wander from husband to husband."

Captain Baker half smiled. "Tell him I have no desire to

62

fight crazy women, that I will do my very best to keep all white men out of this area until Sitting Bull and the others return to the Agency. Then I will come in peace and personally escort Chief Great Bear and his people to the reservation."

Haltingly, Nathan relayed the message to Great Bear, who walked over to Captain Baker. Baker and his two aides rose, and the two leaders shook hands.

"Sergeant, where are the colors?"

A flag bearer sprang forward and presented the banner to the captain.

"This is the symbol of my country," the captain said, holding the flag reverently before extending it to the chief. "I will do all in my power to see that it protects you and your people."

"Now, you must go," Great Bear said brusquely. "My warriors are hungry for blood."

"I understand. Gray Wolf is our friend, too." Baker offered Nathan a brisk salute. "Sergeant! Prepare the men to move out!"

The dust rose in swirls under the hooves of the horses as Captain Baker's men galloped from the village.

Lapsing into unconsciousness, Nathan took no notice of their departure or of the litter-bearers who gently deposited him in his lodge. He did not know when night fell or that Tachechana kept her vigil beside his pallet throughout the long hours, leaning over him to catch any words he might speak in his delirium.

In the gray predawn, he called her name. "Chana, . . . Chana!"

"I'm here, Nathan. I'll always be here."

"But . . . my love . . . I'm afraid . . . I won't." She could barely make out the message, so soft were his words. "Before I go . . . you must know . . . how much I love you."

"You must not speak of death," she soothed. "You have suffered wounds before. You are strong."

But the flow of her tears belied her words, and with the little energy left to him, he touched the trail down her dusky cheeks.

"Whatever God wills," he murmured. "I'm . . . not afraid, Chana." He smoothed the dark hair that enveloped him like a cloud as she covered his hand with kisses. "Don't weep for me. . . . Someday . . . we'll be together again. . . ." The pained look left his eyes, and he was at rest.

The Sioux death chant rumbled up from Great Bear's chest when he realized the end had come. Members of the village waiting outside the tepee picked up the chant and passed the news. Gray Wolf, the husband of Tachechana, the son-in-law of Great Bear, was dead.

For hours the death chant moaned through the village to the beat of the Great Drum, the same drum that only a week before had thudded out their wedding dance.

"Is he to be covered, as a white man, or raised, as a Sioux?" Great Bear asked at last.

"He lived his life as a white man, so he should be put into the ground." She could not bring herself to think of her beloved's body hanging on a scaffold in the manner of the Sioux. Somehow, it seemed more fitting that Nathan should be cradled in the bosom of Mother Earth.

"Where shall we cover him?" Her father interrupted her reverie, then waited respectfully for her decision.

"He must be taken back to our cabin at the box canyon. There, he must be put into the ground in front of the large rock where he liked to pray . . . and he must be wearing the clothes of the white man."

Great Bear nodded and left to dispatch his braves to carry out Tachechana's requests.

With Plainsfeather's wails in her ears, she lay down opposite the body of her husband. Tomorrow Nathan would make his final journey to his cabin and to the prayer rock that was to become his headstone and memorial.

Why, Lord? she pondered. *Didn't Nathan teach me about you from your Book, and did we not try to obey all your commands? Why have you taken him from me?*

Through the smoke hole at the top of the tepee, she could see a few pale stars. They glittered no reply.

chapter
6

THE SUN, AN OMINOUS RED BALL, rose beneath a bank of pink-bellied gray clouds on the day of Nathan's funeral. It would rain before nightfall. The wind scarcely stirred and even the songbirds seemed hushed in the exercise of their morning vespers.

Outside the flap of her tepee, Tachechana could hear the voice of Plainsfeather as she took up the death chant once again. When she wasn't busy attending to the needs of the dead and Tachechana, she sat outside the lodge wailing that sad song in honor of the dead.

"Dear Plainsfeather," Tachechana thought, "always near when I need her."

A deep-throated cough announced the entrance of Great Bear. In his usual manner he backed into the tepee, a habit he had acquired when the changes in Tachechana's body told him she was no longer a child.

"Did my father sleep well?" she asked, knowing he grieved with her.

"How can I sleep when my daughter follows a horse with no rider?" He looked down into her normally radiant face and saw his own loss mirrored in the green eyes. "Come. There is meat and bread in my lodge. Let us eat together so we may have strength for what must be done today."

"But I must prepare Nathan for the burial."

"Plainsfeather will prepare the dead. The living must eat. Gray Wolf would tell you so if he could." Taking Tachechana by the arm, he coaxed her from her tepee.

Although she normally relished the small steaks cut from the loin of a deer, this morning she only picked at the meat.

"Are you a mouse that you only nibble at your food?"

"I feel no hunger, Father."

"Still, you must eat or you will become a rabbit, too weak to do what you must."

Dutifully she ate a little more. Getting to her feet, she said, "I must prepare a travois for Rowdy to pull."

"Plainsfeather has already seen to that."

It seemed to Tachechana that her father took longer than usual eating breakfast. Only after she left the tepee with him did she realize the purpose of his leisurely pace. A funeral procession had formed and was waiting for them as they emerged.

At the head of the procession stood Great Bear's favorite war horse, a beautiful pinto, closely followed by Rowdy, Nathan's horse, fitted with a travois. Upon the wooden frame lay the body of her beloved, looking especially handsome, his hair combed, his face shaven.

Her own horse, Fox, pawed the ground directly behind the bier, and to her great surprise, beside Fox, on a rather nondescript bay, sat the preacher from Fort Fetterman in a suit almost identical to Nathan's. Behind him, a single file of soldiers, and beside each soldier, a Sioux warrior. At the end of the procession, on another of Great Bear's mares, sat a very uncomfortable Plainsfeather.

"Begging your pardon, ma'am," said the preacher, removing his top hat, "but your father sent word of your great loss. We are here to pay our respects and to say some words at the burial, if you would have us."

Tachechana looked out over the crowd, picking out familiar faces, all of whom looked somber and downcast. There was Doc and Trooper O'Connel, his bright red head bared to the sun, the only cheery note in the dismal scene.

"Thank you for coming," she said, "and while you cannot bring back my husband, you can help me bury him like a Christian."

The chief mounted his pinto and took Rowdy's reins. Tachechana threw herself on Fox's back and they began the long journey, each hoofbeat driving her deeper into despair.

She followed close behind the bier, looking into Nathan's lifeless face as though she were riding in a dream, waiting for the moment when Nathan would tenderly stroke her cheek to awaken her and tell her all was well. But it was no dream. And, too soon, they arrived at their destination.

At the graveside, the preacher asked Tachechana, "Will you translate for me so that . . . your people . . . will understand?"

She nodded. "My mother was white, but in her heart she was a Sioux. I am Sioux, but part of my heart will always belong to Nathan."

Great Bear and Plainsfeather carefully wrapped the body in a blanket and lowered it into the grave. The soldiers stood at attention on one side of the grave; the warriors, on the other. The preacher led Tachechana to the foot of the dark hole that yawned up at her. How could she bear to have Nathan's body covered with dirt? Blessedly, her attention was drawn to the words the preacher was reading from a small black book.

"Let not your heart be troubled; ye believe in God, believe also in me." He waited while Tachechana translated.

"Do not worry or be troubled," she said. "You believe in the Great Spirit; believe also in his Son, Jesus. In the Great Spirit's dwelling place are many lodges. I tell you the truth. His Son went there to prepare a tepee, and if he prepares a tepee for you, he will come again to take you to that tepee."

Looking into the faces of her Sioux brothers, Tachechana wondered how they were receiving these words, if they thought them strange superstitions as she herself had at first.

At last, the reading was over, and the preacher sprinkled a handful of dirt over the grave. A huge knot formed in Tachechana's throat, and she could neither swallow nor speak. At that moment, she wished for nothing more than to throw herself into the grave and be covered over forever with her beloved.

Plainfeather's coarse old voice rattled the death chant once more. Great Bear soon picked it up and was joined by the warriors, but no words came from Tachechana's lips.

Two of the soldiers began covering the grave, and the preacher led Tachechana by the arm to the cabin, where she sat on the stool that had been her seat since the first day she arrived there many months before. The preacher took Nathan's chair.

She shook her head. "Please . . . that is where my husband sits . . . sat."

Quickly he moved over and perched on a box. "What are you going to do now?" he asked.

"I want to stay here, to be near Nathan's grave. I suppose I'll trap to get those things I can't make. Nathan taught me well."

"But it isn't good for you to be alone," he insisted.

"I must have time to think, to find out what I am to do . . . to find out why God allowed this thing to happen."

"Why can't you just trust God's Word?" he suggested. "He has promised to care for you in all your trouble."

"Have you ever lost a wife?"

"No."

"Then you don't know what I am feeling now. What good can come from the death of such a man, one who loved God as Nathan did?"

"I don't know, but I'm sure God does."

"That's why I must be alone . . . to learn those things. He must tell me."

A knock on the door brought the conversation to a close. "Enter," Tachechana called.

The door opened to reveal Trooper O'Connel, his arms full of firewood. "It's beginning to rain, so I thought I'd get some wood inside where it would stay dry," he said as he plunked it into the woodbox beside the stove and proceeded to build a fire. Turning to her, he regarded her sadly. "And, ma'am, if there's anything else a soldier can do to ease your grief, I'm hopin' 'tis me you'll choose."

Great Bear and Plainsfeather entered just as Trooper O'Connel left for another armload of wood.

"Why are you building a fire? We must be going. The Great Spirit gives water to the grass," the chief said.

"I will not be going with you. This is Nathan's home . . . my home. I must stay . . . to be with him . . . so I don't forget."

"Your home is now in our village, with me."

"Not yet, Father. I need time to be alone, to remember."

"Then Plainsfeather will stay with you to cook and care for you."

"I can cook for myself."

"Plainsfeather will stay tonight!"

"Yes, Father, but she will return to you tomorrow." The firmness of her tone matched his.

The two women watched the soldiers and Indians ride out. At the forest south of the canyon wall, the soldiers turned west while the warriors continued south.

The rain came down in torrents, its interminable beat drumming on the cabin roof. Normally Tachechana would have relished its comforting cadence, but tonight it only deepened the despair of her heart.

71

Tachechana watched as Plainsfeather, curious about cabin life, began poking into the various boxes, shelves, and drawers. Perhaps because she was hungry, she seemed most interested in those boxes and tins that contained food, and Tachechana began preparing a simple meal.

She set out only one dish for Plainsfeather, but the old woman took another out of the cupboard and insisted she join her. Rather than argue, Tachechana accepted the plate and even spooned some food onto it. But try as she might, she could only swallow a few small mouthfuls and a sip of the water carried in by Trooper O'Connel.

Having concluded the evening meal and chores, Tachechana showed Plainsfeather to the bed Nathan had built for her in the little trap room and indicated she was to sleep there. She herself would move into the big bed, the bed that should have been hers to share with Nathan.

How empty the bed looked now. How strange to crawl into it and know he would not be joining her. Again she wanted to cry, but tears would not come. Her body yearned for the warmth of Nathan's body to drive the chill of death from her. Still, the tears would not come. But the stress of the past few days did its work, and her grief-numbed senses surrendered to deep sleep.

Sometime during the night the rain stopped, and the earth smelled fresh with the day's dawning. Tachechana drew in a deep breath, then glanced at the lonely side of the bed, and once again she felt the crushing weight of her grief.

Hearing Plainsfeather's soft padding about the kitchen only annoyed her, and she hastened from the bed to send the old woman on her way.

At the door Tachechana paused, rubbing her arms for warmth. The coals in the stove had burned low, and

Plainsfeather had opened the door to add kindling, the open door fanning new life into the dying embers. Tachechana could not help smiling at the sight of her old friend struggling with the strange black beast.

Catching sight of the young widow, Plainsfeather gave her a one-toothed grin. "Be warm soon, I think."

Breakfast stretched into another ordeal for Tachechana. Her body was not yet ready for food, and she resisted Plainsfeather's urging.

"I cannot eat if I am not hungry," she complained after forcing down a few mouthfuls. "When I get hungry, I will eat. Now," she said briskly, changing the subject, "while it is not raining, you must prepare for the ride back to the village. Will you have trouble finding your way?"

"I look outside," Plainsfeather acknowledged. "Tracks of travois easy to see, and chief say he leave signs on rocks for me."

"Then you must go before the rains come again."

"I wish daughter of my chief worry more about herself than me."

In a burst of affection, Tachechana threw her arms around the old woman, and when she drew away, Plainsfeather's leathery cheeks were stained with tears.

"Please . . . I stay with you," she begged.

"Only God and time can comfort me now, Grandmother," Tachechana said, using the Sioux term of endearment for the first time.

With this, Plainsfeather broke out in loud and bitter crying. Tachechana envied her. She wished she could weep, pour out her grief, release the awful pain inside, but her body would not oblige. Her throat constricted, and the wrenching of her heart became nearly unbearable, but she could not shed a tear.

When Plainsfeather at last rode out of sight, Tachechana

drew a sigh of relief. At last she was alone to mourn as she pleased. No longer must she consider how her actions would affect others.

Walking slowly around the corner of the cabin, she realized she was moving toward Nathan's grave. She climbed onto the prayer rock and sat silently for a long time, staring at the mound of freshly shoveled dirt. She felt she should pray, but words would not come. Then, unbidden and from some-where deep within her soul came the mournful wail of the Sioux death chant.

How long she sat there, she could not guess. She knew only that the clouds had blown away and the sun was shining brightly when she left her resting place and walked back to the cabin. There, she noticed that the water buckets were empty.

The path to the river was pleasant, and a stroll would do her good, she thought, gathering up the buckets. On the way she turned the horses loose into the west pasture, behind the shed. They were skittish, sensing something amiss, but she could not communicate with them beyond stroking their soft muzzles and crooning soothingly.

As she passed the place where she had been caught in the snare set for her by Running Coyote, she recalled how tenderly Nathan had cared for her. "That was the day he began to love me," she said aloud, though there was no one to hear.

Filling the buckets, she got her feet wet and shed the deerskin moccasins. She glanced around and recalled the first time she had gone swimming here and how she had embarrassed Nathan.

She loved the river, swollen by melting snow, loved the way it swirled and rushed on its way to a sea she had never seen. On impulse, she poured one of the buckets of water over her head. The iciness sent a thrilling chill through her body, numbing her pain temporarily. Quickly she slipped out of her dress and began walking out into the frigid water.

How easy it would be to lie here until I died and went to be with Nathan in heaven, she thought.

She rolled onto her back and looked toward the shore. There she imagined she saw Nathan peeking through the bushes as he had that first time he saw her swimming. This time, instead of turning and skulking back to the cabin, he stepped out and called her. So plainly did she hear his voice that she called back, "Nathan! Nathan!"

She swam to the river's edge and pulled on her clothes, grabbing the buckets of water and running as best she could on legs numbed with cold. But she could not find him.

"Nathan!" she cried. "Where are you?" The only answer was her own mocking echo bouncing off the walls of the canyon.

So sure was she that she had seen him, she diligently searched the ground for his footprints. She found none. Taking up the buckets once more, she staggered toward the cabin where she threw several heavy pieces of wood on the fire and fell into the big bed. No matter how deeply she snuggled into the bed, however, warmth eluded her. Still shivering, she fell asleep.

chapter
7

TACHECHANA LOST ALL RECKONING OF TIME. Lying in bed, delirious and lethargic, her fever-clouded eyes saw only what she wanted to see. Nathan. She would call out to him, and he would come floating into her consciousness. She saw him caring for her, but she saw him from somewhere outside her own body, as if she were a third person watching him teach her to read, or catch a trout with a grasshopper. Sometimes she imagined him reading to her from his Bible, or telling her about God.

She often asked him why God took him from her, but each time she questioned, he would disappear from her dream and she would call his name over and over until he returned. Then she would lapse once again into a dream world in which the pain of losing Nathan vanished as the nebulous images appeared.

One day as she lay on the bed, dreaming that Nathan sat at her side, the vision was shattered by an urgent pounding on the cabin door. Hoping the intruder would go away, she lay still. But when the pounding persisted, she called out weakly, "Enter."

The door opened with a blinding glare. Shielding her eyes with an uplifted hand, Tachechana squinted into the daylight, recognizing the figures of Sarge and O'Connel as they burst into the room.

"What's happened to you?" Sarge asked, appalled at the apparition before him.

With thickened tongue and parched lips, she replied, "I've been sick, but Nathan takes care of me."

"O'Connel, wet a cloth to bathe her face."

"The poor woman, she's nothin' but skin an' bones," O'Connel said as he handed Sarge his own wetted neckerchief. "What can we be doin' for her?"

"Well, it's a sure bet we can't do her much good, us on patrol and all. She needs somebody around the place to keep an eye on 'er, fatten 'er up. What say, we take her to her old man's village?"

"No," Tachechana said, an urgency in her voice. "I must stay here. Nathan cares for me."

Sarge looked at O'Connel and shook his head.

"Can you ride, ma'am?" O'Connel asked.

"Of course I can ride. I am Sioux. But I will not leave Nathan."

"Well, he can come along, but we're takin' you in where you can be looked after proper," Sarge insisted. "And, O'Connel, round up the horses. They look half-starved, too."

It took both the men to get Tachechana on Fox's back. The horse, protective of its mistress, balked at their attempts to help her.

"Where is Nathan?" Tachechana asked over and over. "I don't want to leave him behind."

"He'll be along directly," Sarge lied.

"Why isn't he here with me?"

"It's resting that he is, ma'am. We'll be carin' for you for a while," O'Connel spoke reassuringly.

"Look, Nathan. That's where Running Coyote caught me. Remember? You saved me."

"What have you been eatin'?" Sarge asked.

"Nathan brings me trout from the stream. He catches them with grasshoppers. . . . Why are the trees all blurry? They look like they are standing in the fog. . . ."

She felt O'Connel's arm slip around her just as she would have toppled from the saddle. Fighting back the blackness, she peered at him closely. "When did you get the soldier suit, Nathan?"

"Beggin' your pardon, ma'am, but 'tis me, O'Connel."

"It's good to feel your arms around me again, Nathan."

About a mile out of the village, Tachechana heard Sarge tell O'Connel that he would be going ahead to give Great Bear the news. She clung tightly to O'Connel, who was holding her in the saddle and murmuring words of encouragement.

Upon reaching the village, both the chief and Plainsfeather met the little party, lines of worry etched deep in both faces.

By now Tachechana had lapsed into another siege of delirium, and she moaned and talked into the night, slipping from reality to fantasy. In those rare lucid moments, Plainsfeather dripped gruel into her mouth or squeezed in a few drops from a cloth soaked in spring water.

By mid-afternoon of the following day, Tachechana's fever broke and she heard the hoofbeats of an approaching horse. Judging from the sound of metal-shod hoofs striking the baked earth, she knew it was the horse of a white man.

"It is the one called Doc," Great Bear said as the soldier, medical bag in hand, burst into the tepee without ceremony.

Noting the bucket of water and cloths that Plainsfeather had used to bathe the girl's face, Doc nodded. "Good!" And though her command of the English language was limited, Plainsfeather understood and stood back, a slight smile playing about her lips.

Digging into his bag, Doc produced a bottle of laudanum which he administered promptly.

"She needs rest," he told the interested observers. "This should do it. She'll sleep now, though it will take time before she'll be her old self."

The next time Tachechana awoke to full awareness, she glanced about the tepee with interest. The effects of the opiate still clouding her mind, she looked to her father with a puzzled expression on her face.

"What am I doing here?" she asked. "Who brought me here?"

"You been sick," Plainsfeather explained. "Soldiers brought you here to get better."

"Who is caring for Fox and the other horses?" She raised up on one elbow, her Sioux spirit asserting itself.

"They are with my horses," replied Great Bear. "Have no fear."

Quirking an eyebrow at Doc, she asked in English, "What day is this?"

"The sixteenth of May. I reckon you've been right sick for almost a month now."

"May 16!" Her eyes flew wide. "I danced the wedding dance with Nathan on the second day of April."

The mention of Nathan's name sobered her, the pain in her expression bearing witness to the pain still lodged in her heart.

"I know, ma'am, but he'd want you to go on livin'," Doc said in a gentle voice. "And to get well, you've got to eat."

For the first time Tachechana accepted the broth from Plainsfeather's hand, but after four or five spoonfuls, she began retching.

"It's the laudanum. In a day or so that will go away, and she'll begin to eat like a bear."

Doc left for Fort Fetterman the next day, assured that Tachechana was well past the crisis. Though she still suffered bouts of nausea, she was able to retain most of her food, and daily she grew stronger.

The sadness and grief over the loss of her husband did not diminish as her strength returned. Each afternoon she walked to the river and sat alone, watching the water carry away sticks and debris. How like the floating sticks she felt—carried along by forces over which she had no control.

As she sat surveying the river, Great Bear came and sat beside her. "My daughter no longer smiles for her father. Is she angry?"

"Can I ever truly be angry with my father? No, it is only because I miss my husband that my lips refuse to curve. It's as though the river of joy in my heart has dried up. I cannot even cry for him. There are no tears left."

"What do you see before you?" he asked, pointing at the Little Powder River.

"The river?"

"Is it as deep now as when you danced with your husband?"

"No."

"What will it be like during the moon of the yellow aspen leaves?"

"Nearly dry."

"And next year when the grass turns green?"

"It will overflow its banks again."

"So it is with your river of joy. In time, it will flow once more. It is the way of things . . . the circle of life where all things come back to their beginning."

They walked back to the tepee. Tonight would be a special night, Tachechana decided. Tonight she would play the part of a squaw and prepare the evening meal for Plainsfeather and her father.

81

Two more days passed, and Tachechana still struggled with weakness and nausea. "Sometimes I don't think I will ever be well," she complained to Plainsfeather.

"But your food does not come back each time you swallow?"

"No . . . just when the day dawns."

Plainsfeather studied on the matter. "How long has it been since you were after the manner of women?"

"It was before I became Nathan's wife. . . ."

"I think . . . maybe you will have a small one!"

"A child! But Nathan and I were together only one week."

The woman cackled and threw her arms around the astonished Tachechana.

"A child . . . Nathan's child!" Tachechana repeated over and over trying to comprehend Plainsfeather's statement. "I must tell Father!"

She found Great Bear in the rope corral, examining Fox and another mare with a practiced eye. Though Tachechana pranced about him, he did not acknowledge her presence until she spoke.

"Father," she said shyly, "I have come to tell you some news of great importance. Soon there is to be a new life."

"Two of them," he replied absentmindedly, running his hands along Fox's flank.

"Two?"

"Nathan's horse, Rowdy, has gotten both your mares with foal. Soon you will have as many horses as I."

"Father!" she cried, putting her hands on her hips. "I have not come to speak of horses!"

Great Bear looked up at last. "What is this?" he demanded. "It has always pleased you to learn that a mare was to foal."

"I was speaking of myself! I am carrying Nathan's child!"

"I eeeeeeee!" The war cry erupted without warning. "I am

to be . . . grandfather!" he shouted, pounding his chest in triumph.

Then it happened. Somewhere deep within the hidden recesses of her heart, a small spring began to gurgle. It was not running bank full, but Tachechana knew that her river of joy had begun its long journey to the sea.

chapter

8

THE WARM SUMMER SUN had descended to meet the horizon when Tachechana took her customary walk to the bluff overlooking the river. There, she was startled to find Eagle Feather waiting for her.

"Is Eagle Feather well?" she asked, using the formal Sioux greeting.

"No." His reply was unexpectedly curt.

"What troubles you?"

"You have told me you no longer hold me responsible for the death of your husband, but it is not the same between us as before. You do not act as my friend. You have no words for me when we meet by chance in the village."

"I am married now. You would not want me to act as a crazy woman, running from one man to another."

"Your husband is dead. You are free to find another husband. No one would call you a crazy woman."

"But I still love Nathan. . . ."

"He is dead. You have no more husband, and I have no wife," he insisted stubbornly, the planes of his face golden-brown in the rays of the dying sun. "Since we were children, I hoped we would dance the wedding dance together. Now there is no reason for us to wait longer."

Stunned, Tachechana sank onto the grass at his feet. "Eagle Feather, you must understand. Nathan's death was an accident as much of his own making as of yours. But my love for him did not die with him. . . . And, before many moons pass, I shall have his child."

Eagle Feather sat down to consider her words. He shook his head. "How can you love someone who does not exist?"

"He is alive in my heart, and he will live on in his child."

"Your child will be my child." He waved aside her argument with a sweeping motion of his hand, and his heart could be read in the sheen of his dark eyes. "I would be a good father . . . and you would make me the happiest warrior of the Sioux nation!"

In the face of Eagle Feather's stirring declaration, Tachechana struggled for composure. "It is more than that, Eagle Feather," she replied. "I have promised God, the Great Spirit, I would be the wife of Nathan Cooper forever. I must not break my word. Even if I could, it would not be fair to you, for what I feel for Nathan is stronger than our friendship."

"And what of me?" He rose and paced the grassy slope. "Am I to walk alone forever, with no woman to warm my heart and my tepee, with no children to bring me comfort in my old age?"

Tachechana's eyes misted. "Someday you will find a woman to love you and give you many children. You must wait until you find the right woman. Then, and only then, will you be truly happy."

Hanging his head, Eagle Feather said, "I have already found her. No one else can bring me happiness."

"Forgive me, Eagle Feather, but I had to speak the truth." Tachechana's heart went out to him.

"Then I must leave the village, for seeing you gives me great pain here," he said, holding his hand over his heart.

"But where will you go?"

"West, to find the village of Crazy Horse. He has invited all Sioux and Cheyenne to join him."

"But he schemes against the white man—to kill him."

"Then the prairie and the Black Hills will belong to the Sioux again, and the white man will not steal our wives from us."

"There are too many white men for that, Eagle Feather. The Great Father in Washington will send ten more for every one that is killed."

"Then it is better to die than to live in the shame the Great Father sends. He would make us all his slaves."

"No. It will take time, but we can learn to live side by side. We must work for peace."

"Your husband worked for peace, and the white soldier shot him. It is more honorable to die fighting than to die talking."

"It is better still to live in peace than to kill or be killed because of impatience."

The warrior rose to his feet. Looking down into her face he said, "I will fight the soldiers. We will see who it is that gets killed."

She watched him walk away with a determined stride.

That night, Tachechana prayed for Eagle Feather, asking God to keep him from foolish counsel and to send him a wife to give him the love that was not hers to give.

The sun had approached its zenith the next day before Tachechana realized Eagle Feather was not in the village. Inquiring as to his whereabouts, she learned from Swimming Otter that the brave had ridden out during the night. When she searched the rope corral, she found both his horses gone, along with his war lance, and she felt a pang of fear for her childhood friend.

Tachechana ran all the way to her father's lodge. "Father, Eagle Feather has gone to join Crazy Horse to fight the soldiers."

"How do you know that?"

"He told me last night, but I didn't believe him. Swimming Otter heard him leave during the night."

Great Bear glowered. "The foolish young pup! I gave my word to the white chief that none of my warriors would fight them, and it was agreed."

"Perhaps I am to blame. Eagle Feather asked me to be his wife. When I refused, he said he would go to the village of Crazy Horse."

"Then I must bring him back."

She watched her father's spirited pinto disappear into one of the unseen folds of the prairie with a prayer for his safety . . . and for the headstrong warrior he was seeking.

Six days later the chief returned to the village, leading two tired ponies. Across the back of one lay the still form of Eagle Feather, a crusty red-brown bloodstain on the left shoulder of his deerskin shirt.

A crowd quickly gathered around the chief and Eagle Feather. At Tachechana's bidding, gentle hands lowered him from his horse and carried him into his lodge.

Looking at the wound, a warrior said, "A white soldier's bullet made that hole."

The braves had often seen the damage inflicted by army rifles. The large caliber bullets ripped through muscle and bone, leaving a formidable hole, surrounded by mutilated flesh. Yes, even to Tachechana's untrained eyes, this was the white man's work.

"Prepare a council fire," her father ordered. "The entire village will hear of this deed. We will not wait until the sun dies. Do it now!" He rode to his tepee to partake of the food Plainsfeather was already preparing. He would need all his strength.

Knowing it was useless to ask questions, Tachechana joined the other women and children gathering wood and making the fire ready for the chief and elders. Twice, however, she ran to Eagle Feather's lodge to tend his wound. The entrance and exit holes were well-packed with sagebrush leaves to control the bleeding, so all she could do was bathe his forehead and go back to her chores.

Finally all was in readiness. The chief, elders, and warriors sat in a tight circle around the fire, the young braves circled around them, and the women and children on the outer fringe. For the first time Tachechana was content to sit with the women.

Tobacco was thrown into the fire as an offering to the Great Spirit, and the peace pipe of the village was lighted and passed around the circle of elders. Tachechana thought her father drove the warlike side of it into the ground harder than usual, burying the hatchet.

Ever so slowly the chief rose to his feet. "Let all the Lakota hear the voice of Chief Great Bear. Seven nights ago our brother, Eagle Feather, left our village to join Crazy Horse in his fight against the soldiers. He knew, as all of you know, that I had told the white chief Captain Baker we would not fight. Eagle Feather made his chief's word a lie! That is why I went looking for him.

"Yesterday I came upon the camp of my brother, Little Bear, who has also joined Crazy Horse. Little Bear told me how Eagle Feather fell.

"The day before, the white chief General Crook sent his army down the Rosebud Creek, looking for the village of Crazy Horse. Sioux and Cheyenne scouts had watched the soldiers for several days, so Crazy Horse was ready for them and rode out to meet them.

"There was a great battle. The Sioux and their brothers, the Cheyenne, killed many soldiers and would not let them pass down the river. All day they fought, and at the falling of night, the warriors rode back to their lodges. When the next day broke on the horizon, the soldiers headed back to their fort in the south. Your brothers won a great victory.

"Little Bear found Eagle Feather and was bringing him back to our village when I came upon them. My brother is returning to the camps of Crazy Horse and Sitting Bull on the Little Big Horn River, where they will dance the Sun Dance and have a great feast.

"Some of you will want to join them. You may do as you wish. But"—his voice took on the sound of a hammer striking the anvil—"if you decide to leave, you must take your lodges, your wives, and your children. If you make the word of Great Bear a lie, you cannot come back. You will be my enemy, and I will kill you for making me a liar."

One of the braves jumped to his feet. "The white men have lied to us many times! Their word is as good as horse dung! Why should we not fight them?"

Great Bear raised his hands to quell the murmur brought on by the outburst. "Am I a white man? Are you? No! We are Lakota! We are Treton! Our word is true."

Another brave rose to his feet, but without the rashness of the first. "What will happen to Eagle Feather? Will you kill him for his deed of valor in fighting?"

"Eagle Feather is badly wounded. He will probably die. If he dies, it will be the punishment of the Great Spirit. If he lives, he will either show the tribe he has repented . . . or he will fight me to the death. But be warned. There is no repentance for you. If you disobey my command, you will die."

Tachechana heard her father's words in stunned silence. She had never seen him so angry.

At the close of the council, she followed him at a respectful distance. Inside the lodge, she waited for him to speak first, but he said nothing.

Unable to contain herself any longer, she burst out, "Would my father really kill Eagle Feather?"

"Your father will not have to. Eagle Feather will probably die from the hole in his shoulder."

"But if he doesn't, will you kill him?"

Great Bear's countenance was grim and his words slashed the air like the blade of a hunting knife. "He has already condemned himself to death."

"Everyone thought Nathan would die when he was shot the first time, but he lived," Tachechana dared to persist. "Eagle Feather's wound is higher, not in the lungs."

There was an ominous silence before Great Bear spoke again. "If he lives . . . he must admit his wrongdoing before the entire village."

"He will live, Father. I will pray for his life, and I will nurse him back to health." She turned and left the tepee without a backward glance.

From her place of vigil near the doorway of the tepee, Plainsfeather took note of Tachechana's departure and followed her across the village to Eagle Feather's lodge where they cared for him throughout the long night.

The sun burst on the new day with a blast of heat that was unusually strong even for the Great Plains.

Rising from her makeshift pallet in Eagle Feather's tepee, Tachechana roused Plainsfeather, and together they rolled the covering of the lodge from the bottom, allowing whatever breeze might blow to cool the interior.

91

Quickly assessing her friend's condition, she took the cloth from his brow and dipped it again into a bucket of water.

"I fear for Eagle Feather's life," she admitted to Plainsfeather. "He burns with fever, and he refuses both food and water."

"I fear for *your* life," scolded the old woman. "And the life of small one you carry. What of him? You eat nothing, drink nothing. Ptoo! If you child again, I use the back of my hand."

At that moment the flap of the tepee parted and Great Bear entered, bringing with him some bread and thin slices of roast buffalo tongue.

"Eat."

Reluctantly, she accepted the food and placed it on a small stand near Eagle Feather's head.

"Now!" insisted the chief.

At his sharp command, she reached for the food, tore off a bite of bread with strong white teeth, and began chewing slowly.

When Eagle Feather stirred, Tachechana abandoned her own meal and offered him water, dribbling it into his mouth. The water returned, flowing onto the pallet beneath his head.

"Humph!" snorted her father. "The fish swims on his back. He will die."

"No! He will not die! You speak as if you wish it so!"

"What will be, will be," he shrugged. "This brave has no desire to live."

Perplexed, Tachechana turned inquiring eyes on her father. "Why do you say that?"

"Little Bear told me of his actions in battle. Wherever the fight was the hottest, Eagle Feather was there. When Little Bear tried to help him after he was wounded, he asked Little Bear to let him die honorably on the field of battle. Now, he resists even your attempts to help him. He wishes to die."

"But why? Why would anyone wish to die?"

"Because he cannot have that which he wishes more than life."

A rush of heat stained her cheeks. "Father, he cannot die because of me. He is a good man and a brave warrior. I don't want him to die. . . . What can be done for him?"

The chief leveled a long look at her. "Only you can decide."

chapter

9

AGAIN THE NEXT DAY the earth-scorching sun blazed down
on the village with such vehemence that no one wished to
leave the shade of their tepee. The sides of each lodge were
rolled up to catch any whisper of breeze. The only sign of
activity was the splashing of the children in the cool waters of
the Little Powder River. Even the horses could do no more
than stand in pairs, each looking in opposite directions, idly
flicking away the flies with their tails.

At high noon, while all were resting in the shade, a dusty
column of soldiers rode into the village. Captain Baker and
Sarge were in the lead, followed by ten other men riding two
by two, their sweaty faces caked with dust and grime.

They nodded to Tachechana as they rode by Eagle Feather's
tepee, and she noticed Sarge calling Captain Baker's attention
to the wounded man in her care. The captain acknowledged
the information with a curt nod and continued on his way to
Great Bear's tepee.

But Trooper O'Connel took off his hat and smiled broadly
as he passed. Tachechana could not resist smiling back. The
muddy residue of perspiration and dust had matted his red
hair and ran down his face in stripes, like a Sioux warrior
painted for battle. Still, there was a warmth in his boyish

good looks that tugged at her heart. He had befriended Nathan, and that made him her friend, too.

The chief greeted the captain with the gesture of peace. "Why does the white chief honor us with a visit?" he asked as Tachechana joined them at the doorway of Great Bear's lodge.

Without reply, Captain Baker asked a question of his own. "May my men water their horses in your river?"

"The Great Spirit made water for all his children."

The captain and Sarge dismounted, signaled the men to lead the horses to the bank of the river, then followed Great Bear into his tepee.

"Your men pant for lack of air," the chief observed, "as if they ride hard and long."

"Yes. That's why we have come. General Crook and his forces met the hostiles at the Rosebud Creek where we fought them to a standstill, but they disappeared during the night."

"Why does the white chief call them 'hostiles'?"

"The army has been ordered to regard all Indians not on the reservation as hostile. I wanted you to have one final warning."

"But we have pledged not to fight."

"How good are your promises, Chief?"

Great Bear drew himself up proudly. "The word of the Sioux is the word of truth and honor."

"When we rode in just now, we noticed one of your braves being treated for a gunshot wound. Are you trying to say he was not involved in the battle we have just left?"

The chief made no reply, a scowl furrowing his brow.

"In fact," the captain continued, not waiting for a reply, "my sergeant thinks he personally shot that man off his horse. He says he can even identify the horse."

"It is so," Tachechana interrupted, "but it was not his fault.

He left the village because of me. Eagle Feather wished to die, so he placed himself in the thick of the fighting."

"That can't be helped, ma'am. He's in violation of the chief's own truce, and he's under arrest. Our orders are to take any hostiles back to Fort Fetterman for trial and execution."

"Captain Baker," said the chief in a tone that brooked no argument, "my brave lies near death. He will remain here. If you take him to your fort, he will die, and I will not be able to control my warriors. They are many, you are few right now. Would it not be better to have him die here, a hero, rather than lose more of your men and make Eagle Feather a martyr?"

"I see the wisdom in what you are saying," he nodded. "But the chief must realize that some of my men are hot-headed, too. They will feel I let them down if this village is permitted to ignore the order to return to the reservation. Things are getting worse on the prairie. Armies led by Custer, Gibbon, and Terry will join General Crook. They do not agree with Crook, who wants to urge the Indians back. Only if you go back to the reservation can you be protected."

"The last time we were so protected, we nearly starved to death," spat the chief.

"I regret to hear that. But we have been working to bring about many improvements on the reservation. I'm sure the conditions there are quite different now."

"But your government expects us to live in square houses and grow corn. We are Lakota of the Sioux. The Great Spirit made us to live in round lodges and to sleep on the ground, the bosom of Mother Earth. We are hunters, not farmers. We live by our wits and our horses. We need the open prairie."

The captain heard him out before responding. "Your way of life and the white man's way cannot both continue. The white man needs his railroads and gold mines for commerce. But there is still hope for compromise."

Great Bear snorted in disdain. "My people don't want change. It has always been so. The sky, the earth, and the buffalo are all we need. Why does the white man slaughter our uncle, the buffalo?"

"If the buffalo are not thinned out, they will hinder the building and operation of the railroad."

"I have heard it said that if the buffalo were exterminated, the Indian would soon die."

"Yes, there are those who wish all Indians dead," admitted Captain Baker, "just as Sitting Bull would like to drive all white men back across the Father of Rivers."

"How can we be sure the white men are not putting the Indians on the reservation so they might kill us all at once?"

"Many people realize Indians are good people. They would not permit such a thing."

"What you say, Captain Baker, is a hard thing. We are a small village. Alone, we could not fight off your armies, but if we joined with the other families of the Sioux . . ." Great Bear paused. "Perhaps Sitting Bull's vision is true. If my warriors fought with our brothers against your four generals, the Indians would win, and there would be no more white man to disturb the peace of the prairie."

"Chief, you are a man of wisdom. You know you cannot defeat four armies all at once, but even if you could, it wouldn't be wise. Many warriors would die. Who would care for their women and children? No, we want no more bloodshed. Consider our proposal carefully. It's your last chance."

Great Bear's jaw tensed. "I will talk with my people. Tomorrow, when the sun cracks the sky, I will give you our answer."

"Until tomorrow morning, then." Captain Baker rose. "Chief, my men and horses are tired. We ask permission to camp across the river."

"It is done, but you will not eat your hard bread. You will all come back to my lodge to eat your evening meal. I will send someone when it is time."

Baker bowed, then he and his men mounted up and splashed across the river to set up camp for the night.

When they were well out of range of hearing, Great Bear motioned to Tachechana. "Find three or four women to help you prepare a feast. Tell them I will give each of them a deerskin if they agree."

"But, Father, there is not enough meat in the village," she explained.

"A hunting party went out at dawn. One came back with news of a buffalo kill. They will be here soon. Tell them I must have the haunch to feed my guests."

Tachechana scurried back and forth as she and her helpers built cooking fires and dressed the meat for her father's feast. Between chores, she looked in on Eagle Feather. His wound was healing nicely, and the pallor of his skin was taking on a healthy glow beneath the burnished planes of his face.

Occasionally, Tachechana paused to rest a moment. It was then she found herself glancing across the river, only to find Trooper O'Connel gazing back.

Plainsfeather, who had lost both of her husbands to the white man's guns, could not fathom the kindness her chief was showing the soldiers. "They are only twelve, we are many," she muttered under her breath. "We should kill them all and feed their bones to our brothers, the coyotes. That is the feast I would like to see."

When everything was in readiness, Tachechana went to her father's lodge. "It is time to call the soldiers to the feast."

"Since you alone speak their language, you must ride to them with the news yourself," he instructed. "And you must sit with them at the feast to tell them my words."

Delivering her message quickly, Tachechana returned to the tepee where she stepped out of her fringed deerskin and pulled on the green dress Nathan had always admired. Then, unbraiding her hair, she brushed it to a glossy sheen, leaving it to flow about her shoulders.

Hurriedly, she filled a wooden plate with the buffalo stew and entered Eagle Feather's lodge.

"You must eat," she urged. "Our uncle, the buffalo, has given his life so you can grow strong again."

But there was no reply from the astonished brave who gaped at her from his pallet.

With eyes the color of the prairie grass in summer, with unbound hair falling like midnight around her face, she was a stranger to him. He noted the snug fit of her garment, revealing a trim waist, though she was carrying the white man's child. His eyes took it all in, but his heart would not believe what he was seeing. Then his gaze dropped to her slender feet, shod in soft deerskin, and his heart leaped within him. As long as she walked in moccasins, there was hope.

Still, he made his voice stern when at last he found his tongue. "Where is Tachechana, the Sioux princess? Or is she still trying to please her white brothers?"

She shook her head. "You forget. I am a married woman, no matter what you believe. I dress to please no living man— only the one whose memory I carry always in my heart. Now," she said briskly, handing him the stew, "my father needs me. Eat and soon you will join in the hunt rather than lie about like a helpless old man!"

When Tachechana returned to Great Bear's lodge, she

found the soldiers arriving to greet her father. Although they were not marching in stiff columns, nor was there a single rifle in evidence, each man carried his revolver in a holster at his belt.

They scarcely resembled the bedraggled men who had ridden into camp just hours before. Officers and enlisted men alike had washed the grime from their faces and beaten the dust from their clothing. One face was especially pink and shiny from hard scrubbing, the fringe of red curly hair revealing the identity of Trooper O'Connel.

Wearing his long trailing war bonnet of eagle feathers, Great Bear appeared in front of his tepee and motioned to the soldiers, indicating that they should sit in a circle—Captain Baker on one side of the chief, Tachechana on the other. She was not surprised when Trooper O'Connel appeared to ask the honor of sitting at her other side.

"You may sit wherever you wish," she said, smiling politely to ease his embarrassment.

Throughout the meal Tachechana's services were in demand by Great Bear and Captain Baker, but whenever there was a lull in their conversation, O'Connel's mouth was filled with compliments and questions. He commented on the weather: "This summer has been a real scorcher!" and the food: "Didn't know buffalo could be tastin' so fine!" He rattled on and on, and at times Tachechana had difficulty in suppressing her amusement. It had been a very long time since anyone had made her feel like smiling.

After everyone had eaten his fill, Captain Baker presented Great Bear with a pouch of real tobacco. The chief accepted it and shook the captain's hand in the manner of white men. One by one the soldiers passed by Great Bear, thanking him for the feast and shaking his hand. O'Connel was the last one in line.

"Thank you, Chief," he said through Tachechana. "'Twas a lovely meal ye were servin' and a lovely lass ye've got for a daughter, too!"

The tall redhead lingered behind as the other soldiers walked on to untether their horses. He was still talking with Tachechana when his comrades mounted and splashed across the river, making for camp.

"It's in your debt I am, for permittin' me to sit at your side, ma'am. I'll not be forgettin' it."

"Why is your speech so different from the others?" she asked.

"Ah, and it's because I'm from Ireland."

"Is Ireland a city in the East?"

"And now it's my leg you're pullin'."

"But I have not touched you!" she said, taking a step back.

"Oh, I'm sorry, ma'am, truly I am. I meant only that you're makin' sport of me."

"But I wouldn't do that."

"Ye mean ye've never heard of Ireland?"

"No. What is it?"

"Just the prettiest piece of sod on God's green earth. It's an island far across the sea, a nation where everyone speaks as I do."

"It almost sounds like a song when you talk."

"Your own mither must have come from the Green Isle, for ye have a touch of the old malarky yourself."

"I never knew my mother. She died when I was born."

"Oh . . . 'tis sorry that I am for bringin' it up, God rest her soul."

"He did."

"Who did, and what did he do?" O'Connel seemed perplexed.

"God did. You said 'God rest her soul.' My mother was a

Christian. When she died, God took her to live with him. She is resting with him now. Are you a Christian?"

"Aye. And all my family was brought up in the church," the soldier replied, once more on familiar ground.

"When did you let Jesus become your Savior?"

"Ah . . . I'm not sure that 'tis following ye I am." He shifted uncomfortably from one foot to the other.

"The Bible says that all men are sinners, that we must repent of our sins, that we must ask Jesus to be our Savior and forgive us before we can live with him in the next world."

"But 'tis the church that is savin' us."

"There is no church here, yet I am saved. Haven't you ever asked Jesus to come into your heart and forgive your sins?" She was growing a little confused.

"I guess not . . . at least not in the manner you're meanin'."

Thinking back to the times Nathan had discussed this very matter with her, Tachechana began to reason with O'Connel. "You must know that you are a sinner."

The soldier bowed his head contritely. "Ah, Miz Cooper, that I am. Some of the things I have done would make my poor ol' mither turn in her grave if she knew of it."

"If your mother would be displeased, think how God must feel."

"You're shamin' me to the core, ma'am."

"If you're really ashamed, all you have to do is ask God to forgive you and receive Jesus as your Savior. Then you would not do those things anymore. You would not even desire to do them."

"Many a time I've tried to turn over a new leaf, but I always fall back to my sinful ways." The young trooper now appeared truly penitent.

"Turn over a new leaf?"

"To start over. To be a better person, fresh and clean, like a new page of a writing tablet."

Tachechana smiled. "God doesn't give us new pages to smudge. He wants to erase the marks of sin forever. When you accept Jesus as your Savior, you become a child of God, and he takes all your sins from you—as far as the East is from the West."

"Ah, Miz Cooper, if I could be sure of somethin' like that, I'd—"

"O'Connel!" Sarge's voice came booming across the river, followed by a string of words that Tachechana had not heard before. Whatever they meant had a startling effect on the young soldier.

Springing to his horse, he called a hasty good night to Tachechana and galloped across the river at full speed.

chapter 10

TACHECHANA, WATCHING FROM EAGLE FEATHER'S TEPEE, saw Captain Baker and Sarge slowly cross the river and walk their horses to the entrance of Great Bear's lodge. The chief greeted them with the open hand, and sent a young boy to fetch Tachechana. When she arrived, they were breakfasting on venison jerky.

After a formal greeting, there was an awkward moment while each waited for the other to speak. Great Bear's eyes bored into Captain Baker's, and Tachechana was afraid her father had decided to join Sitting Bull and Crazy Horse.

Under the chief's intense scrutiny, Captain Baker could wait no longer. "Has the chief decided to return his people to the reservation?"

"My people are divided. Some want to fight. Others want peace, but are afraid you speak out of both sides of your mouth. If we go back to the reservation and our brothers defeat the soldiers, it may be that they will hate us for not helping them. Or you may kill us for spite if our brothers defeat your armies. Either way, the lives of my people are in the hands of the Great Spirit."

"If you go to the reservation, we can protect you from renegades, whether red or white," Captain Baker said.

Great Bear chose to ignore this bold assertion. "I have decided. My people will return to the reservation, but it will take time to prepare for the journey. We must choose our path carefully, for there are many white men who would slaughter us on the trail."

"I could arrange an army escort for you."

"No." Great Bear's answer was firm. "We will not be herded like the buffalo, and we are not your captives. We are free people, going to the reservation of our own will. Within two weeks, I will register at the Pine Ridge Agency."

A cold chill swept through Tachechana's body as she repeated her father's words. She remembered well the hardships her people faced the last time they stayed on the reservation.

"Chief, you have made a wise decision," Baker said, obviously relieved. "Give the system a chance to work. There are many white men who would like to be your friends. I am one of them."

"It is good," was the chief's reply.

They shook hands once more, and the two officers swung into their saddles. Sarge raised his hand, signaling to the soldiers on the opposite side of the river. When he lowered his hand toward the west, the mounted men crossed the river, two by two, falling in behind Baker and Sarge. Their faces appeared grim as they rode by Tachechana, except for the one rimmed with carrot-colored hair. O'Connel, riding rear guard, smiled broadly and lifted his kepi as he passed.

She watched until they disappeared from sight, then sighed, thinking of the long days stretching ahead. Then a strange thought took root in her mind. She wondered about the life of an army wife.

Throughout the day, as she tended Eagle Feather, Tache-chana could see her father moving from tepee to tepee, talking to his people. Some did not appear to welcome the news, protesting loudly. Others shrugged as if resigned to be pawns in the hands of the white fathers in the East.

Arriving at Eagle Feather's tepee, Great Bear asked, "Has my daughter told you that we will be going back to the Pine Ridge Agency on the reservation?"

"But I cannot go back!" he objected.

"You will travel by travois. Tachechana will help strike your tepee, and she and Plainsfeather will care for you on the trip."

"I cannot go back!" the brave insisted. "If I register with a bullet hole in me, they will know I have fought the white soldiers, and they will hang me."

"We will hide you until you are well, then you will register and live at peace on the reservation."

"What if I choose to join Crazy Horse and fight?"

Great Bear slanted a dark look at the warrior. "You have made my words a lie once. If you try to do it again, you will not have to worry about an army rope around your neck. I will kill you myself and hang your scalp beneath the tail of my horse."

Tachechana had never heard her father speak so harshly. Even Eagle Feather was intimidated by the outburst, and his eyes sought the floor of his lodge. Were it not for her father's stern countenance, she would have giggled.

Four days later, June 28 by Tachechana's reckoning, the village was alive with activity. On the next day, the tepees would be taken down at sunrise and the long trek to the reservation would begin. Normally everyone would be in high spirits, anticipating new hunting and fishing grounds. But this time they were filled with uncertainty and apprehension, dreading the arrival at their destination.

Several of the younger braves left the village to seek out Crazy Horse and Sitting Bull. While the chief permitted them to go in peace, he reminded them that they must never return to his village again. It was indeed a day of many sorrows.

Even the unexpected guest who arrived near mid-morning did nothing to cheer them, though he brought good news. Little Bear, who might have been his brother's twin, rode directly to the chief's tepee.

"Is my brother well?" he called from his horse.

Great Bear sprang through the doorway, "He is well. Is my brother well?"

"He is well." Little Bear slid from his horse's back. "Call your people near," he said, "and let them hear news from the camp of Sitting Bull."

Scarcely were the words out of his mouth than he was surrounded by all the adult males of the village. Even Eagle Feather hobbled over to hear what was going on.

"There has been a great battle at the villages of Sitting Bull, Crazy Horse, Gall, Two Moons, and Lame White Man. A great victory has been won by your brothers and the Cheyenne," he began, his voice strong and confident.

Assured that he had the undivided attention of all, he took up the narrative in detail. "Three days ago we were preparing for a dance at the Little Big Horn River. It was the largest village anyone had ever seen—six large villages coming together to make one that extended six miles down the valley. It was a happy village—good hunting, good fishing, much greasy grass for our horses.

"Our scouts told us soldiers rode up Rosebud Creek, but we thought they traveled to the camp of General Crook. With over two thousand armed warriors, they dared not attack, and we continued with our feasting and dancing.

"About noon a hunting party galloped in from the

southeast, saying more soldiers were coming. Some of the warriors began to paint themselves for battle. When we saw the soldiers on their horses, we grabbed our weapons and ran out to meet them. They charged and we began shooting them off their horses.

"When the chief, the one called Major Reno, saw how strong we were, he told his men to get off their horses and fight from behind logs and tufts of grass. We shot them down as if they were prairie dogs. Then those who were still alive ran to the trees along the river and continued the fight from that protected place.

"Finally the soldiers caught their horses and scrambled to the top of the hill east of the river. There, they dug into the hill like badgers, and it was very hard to shoot them except when they came down to get water.

"A warrior brought us news that more soldiers were attacking at Middle Ford, so many of us left to fight there. When we came to a deep ravine, we left our horses behind, and I crossed the river with Lame White Man and Gall. Halfway up the ravine, we were cut off by soldiers shooting at us with big rifles from the top of the hill.

"Lame White Man and his warriors decided to charge. Many braves were killed, including Lame White Man, but all the white soldiers with their chief fell, too.

"Now the soldiers were few. Their chief sent some men down the hill a way to keep us out of the deep ravine, but we hid in the grass and sagebrush, and we would pop up, shoot at them, and hide again until they used up their bullets.

"Then those soldiers did a curious thing. One by one they shot themselves in the head." A murmur of disbelief rippled through the audience. "It is true. Rather than fight us, they killed themselves." Little Bear was silent for a moment, as his listeners tried to understand why brave soldiers would take their own lives. It seemed the act of cowards.

"With those dead, we drew very close to the soldiers on the north end of the ridge. Though they had no chance, they formed a circle with their horses and shot them. From behind the bodies of their dead horses, they aimed at us, but there was little fire from their guns. We began shooting our arrows into the air, letting them fall into the circle. When our brothers Crazy Horse and Gall charged, they found all white soldiers dead."

Tachechana cringed. How must God feel about the deeds of her people this day? The white soldiers had been their helpless victims.

Little Bear continued. "Two Cheyenne women who were with Black Kettle on the Washita came to the circle to collect the boots of the white men. When they saw the white chief, they began to sing and dance. They said he was the long yellow hair, General Custer. 'You did not hear our cries for mercy!' they shouted. 'Now maybe you will hear our song of victory!'

"By the next day, more soldiers rode in from the south, but it was Sitting Bull who finally said, 'Let them go. There has been enough killing in this place.'" Little Bear paused in his long monologue, his head held high in pride.

"You have won a great victory," Great Bear congratulated his younger brother.

"Yes," Little Bear replied, "but it may be the last. Never again will there be so many of our brothers gathered together in one place. Many horses require much grass, and there must be much game to feed all the hungry mouths. We have proved to the white man that we are warriors. Still, we cannot continue to fight them. Their railroad brings them food and supplies, even grain for their horses. Though we kill many, more always come to take their place." His voice dropped, and his arrogant stance gave way to one of dejection.

"We have only three choices. We must do as the whites tell us and return to the reservation, go north to the land of the Great Queen, or fight until we are no more."

"What will Sitting Bull and Crazy Horse do?" Great Bear asked.

"Crazy Horse will fight. Sitting Bull is moving his people north to Canada."

"And you, little brother?"

Meeting Great Bear's level gaze, he replied sadly, "It will be soon enough to decide . . . when the white man finds my village. Now I must return to my people. They wait for me where the white man pans for gold in the rivers."

The brothers embraced, and Little Bear rode off toward the south.

The people of the village clustered around their chief, waiting for his counsel. Great Bear looked into each face, and Tachechana knew his heart was heavy. One thing was clear. They could no longer remain here. The soldiers would seek to avenge the death of their chiefs—especially the one called Yellow Hair. And this time there would be no polite talk.

Great Bear spoke at last. "My people, at first light we will move out . . . back to the reservation."

chapter

11

MOVING DAY DAWNED HOT, DRY, AND WINDLESS. As the searing sun slanted its first rays from the horizon, the people of Great Bear's village were packed and waiting at the river for their chief's word to begin the march to their new home and uncertain future.

For the next seven days or so, they would be a group of traveling nomads. Their circle of life had collapsed when they struck their lodges, and with that collapse came the knowledge that their life would never be the same in the square houses provided by the great White Chief in Washington.

People and animals alike filled their bellies with water. It would be a long hot ride before they reached the Belle Fourche River, where they would camp for the night. With more and more white goldminers coming into the territory every day, they wondered if there would be space enough for a camp on the river.

"Tachechana," Great Bear called, "should we carry the flag Captain Baker gave us?"

"I don't know, Father. If the whites see it they may think you took it from the soldiers at the battle. If our brothers from other tribes see it, they might see us as traitors."

"Do you think Captain Baker's men will attack us if we do not fly their banner?"

She shook her head. "He knows we are on our way to the reservation. I don't think he wants to fight any Indians."

"But he is no coward."

"No, but he would like to be a friend to the Sioux. To him, we are all brothers and should not fight and kill one another."

When Great Bear glanced up, his people were looking to him. The time had come.

He told them to wade their horses well into the stream before turning north, downstream, and not to touch or leave anything along the riverbank that would indicate the direction of their travel. Once they left the river, it would be easy to follow the tracks of their unshod horses and the drag marks of the travois.

He sent four braves ahead to scout the trail, leaving two warriors behind as a rear guard. Then, like a monstrous brown snake, the people slithered through the serpentine wanderings of the river for almost two miles.

A small broken twig on the east side of the river alerted Great Bear that his scouts had left the river and now rode out on the open prairie. With a wave of his hand, Great Bear signaled the spot where the travelers were to leave the river. The water was now muddied by the sloshing feet of the animals and those who chose to walk. Slowly, the procession filed out of the river and onto the sun-drenched prairie.

Except for an occasional dust devil, which Great Bear viewed as a bad omen, the air was still. While this made it harder on the people who had to breathe the dust kicked up in front of them, Great Bear rejoiced. At least the dust was falling quickly back to the dry earth rather than blowing in long plumes, announcing their passage to everyone in the area.

The sun steamed the water from the deerskin clothing before an hour elapsed. By the end of the second hour, everyone suffered from the heat, but they sought no comfort in complaining. Occasionally, a baby would cry out and an older brother or sister would be commissioned to entertain the child or tend to some other need.

Tachechana's keen ears were especially attuned to the sound of an infant's cry these days, much to the amusement of the older women who remembered her days as a "warrior." Now she offered to comfort the small ones and applied herself to learning the meaning of their gurgles and grunts.

"How long will it be before I hold my own babe in my arms?" she asked Plainsfeather as one of the little ones cried out.

"It will probably come in the month of heavy snow."

"So long?"

Plainsfeather chuckled. "Time crawls like the turtle until the child comes forth. Then, so I am told, the years take the wings of the eagle."

"You are wise, Plainsfeather. Do you think I am carrying a girl-child or a man-child?"

"Only the Great Spirit knows," she replied enigmatically. "But you could have both at the same time."

"How can such a thing be?" Tachechana's eyes widened.

"Once, I have seen it—two babes just alike." Plainsfeather shook her head as if she still could not believe what she had seen.

Tachechana looked down at the swelling mound beneath her deerskin dress. "Then two babes might be growing in my belly?"

Plainsfeather measured her abdomen with her eyes and shook her head. "Too small. You want more children in your tepee, you find new husband."

"Then I shall give all my love to this one, for no other man can take Nathan's place."

The sun had passed its zenith when a large clump of cottonwoods was spotted a little south of their line of travel. Great Bear, who had been following the tracks of his four scouts, saw that two of the ponies veered off in that direction while the other two continued to the east. He led the procession toward the grove of trees.

Just as he had expected, all four of his scouts were resting in the shadowy coolness. The two that continued east had circled to make sure there was no one near enough to make a surprise attack.

By crowding in together, there was shade enough for all, and for almost two hours, they refreshed themselves. Jerky and pemican appeared from deerskin pouches, and those who had jars and pots of water cheerfully shared the precious fluid with those who had none.

Dozing beneath a cottonwood, Tachechana failed to notice the scouts' departure, so the staccato-like commmand issued by her father came as a shock.

"Come! Mount up! We must move on. The Belle Fourche is still a hard ride, and we must arrive before dark to make camp."

"Eagle Feather and some of the small ones are still tired, Father," Tachechana informed him. "Must we travel all the way to the river today?"

"There is no water until we get to the river. It is better the children be tired than the horses without water. They are Sioux . . . they will not grumble. As for Eagle Feather, if he cannot keep up, he can be left behind. He has caused us much trouble already."

The sun seemed even hotter as the Indians flowed out of the shade and onto the prairie once again. The prospect of camping on the banks of the Belle Fourche kept them moving, and even before the line of trees betrayed the presence of the river, the horses smelled the water and nickered at the prospect of a cool drink. Their pace quickened.

The scouts picked out a broad bench well above the high water line on which to camp. Since the weather was hot and dry, there was no need to set up tepees. Tonight they would sleep under the stars.

While the horses drank their fill, some of the women gathered wood for cooking fires, and about the time the last horse was picketed for the night, two scouts rode in with the news that they had killed three deer, enough to feed the entire camp.

The women sang as they followed the scouts out to the kills where they would do the work of preparing the carcasses for transport and incinerating the viscera. Within a short time, the first portions of meat were being served to the hunters, then to the rest of the men, and finally to the women and children. When their hunger was satisfied, there was meat left over—enough for the morning and to be eaten along the trail.

Great Bear insisted all fires be extinquished as soon as the meal was complete, lest strange eyes see their smoke and learn their position. *Like Nathan,* Tachechana thought, *he doesn't like surprises.*

She listened intently as he spoke with his scouts before retiring. Where they were camped the river ran to the northeast, then turned and flowed southeast. If they traveled due east for another day, they would strike the river again and find another good campsite. Though it was a bit out of their way, they could possibly avoid the white goldminers.

When a copper sun rose in an azure sky, Great Bear and his people were well on their way east. Four more scouts were added to those sent out the day before. While the wooded terrain through which they were passing made travel easier and more pleasant, they must be ever watchful of white men lurking behind the trees or under cover of the brush that grew in abundance.

Tachechana knew that Great Bear did not fear the guns of the white man, for he was a warrior of uncommon courage, but he knew the mind of his enemy. Innocent women and children were at risk, perhaps even Tachechana herself and her unborn child, should they encounter a group of vigilantes intent on retaliation.

"With the whites so angry with us, why don't we hide in the mountains instead of going to the reservation?" she asked the chief.

"A small group, a family maybe, could hide for a time, but we are forty or fifty tepees and many horses. It would not take the soldiers long to find us. On the prairie we could flee from them, but we are not mountain people. There would be no escape for us." She watched the muscles of his jaw tensing. "We are few, they are many, yet the white man was defeated in a great battle. Now he fears us as he fears the snake, and he must step on us and grind our faces into the dust. It seems the white man must kill everything he fears or cannot understand."

On they rode, until Tachechana remembered she had not checked on Eagle Feather since the night before. She was surprised to find him riding with the braves rather than on the travois she had prepared for him. She questioned Plainsfeather about it.

The woman shrugged her shoulders. "He would not eat my food this morning, and he would not get on the travois. Who am I to tell him what to do?"

Tachechana galloped back to Eagle Feather's side. "Why do you refuse the food of a kind old woman and value your life so little that you ride a horse when your wound is yet unhealed?"

"Why do you pretend to care about the value of my life?" His reply was surly.

"What do you mean?" she demanded.

"I have not seen you since we ate last night. You did not find me a good place to sleep. You prepared no food for me this morning. *You* do not care. Why should I?"

"My father required my help. I told Plainsfeather to care for you, and you rejected her. Even the little ones do not behave as you do!" Tachechana said in disgust.

Angry and frustrated, she flicked her reins sharply and rode off in a storm of dust. Gaining her father's side, she asked, "Why are men so difficult? Just because I refused to be Eagle Feather's squaw, he thinks I care nothing for him. Now he will start bleeding again."

The chief merely grunted.

At that moment one of the north flank scouts came galloping back to the chief, ending the conversation. Excitedly he told Great Bear of a group of white settlers camping at a spring just north of their intended route.

Sensing the chief's concern that the forward scouts might be seen, Tachechana said, "Fox is the fastest horse among us. I'll ride ahead and warn them."

Before her father could present an argument, she was off at a full run, her hair flying out behind her. A short distance down the trail, she met one of the lead scouts returning with the news. Turning to ride back to her father with the information, she met Eagle Feather, who had pursued her on his own horse.

"The daughter of Great Bear must not gallop her horse so hard," he warned.

"But my father needs to know that the scouts saw the

smoke of the settlers' campfires and have turned south. The others will head east," she explained.

She rode ahead with the report.

"We will turn south here," the chief said, and the word passed quickly through the ranks. Soon the entire procession again slithered into motion, but their carefree attitude had changed to one of sullen watchfulness.

"Tachechana must not gallop her horse so hard," Eagle Feather repeated, catching up to her.

"I have been a Sioux warrior," she retorted. "Besides, it is still a long time before Fox will foal."

"I was not speaking of your horse," he returned. "The ride might injure your child, perhaps kill him before he is born. You must be more careful."

Terror shot through Tachechana. How could she have failed to give thought to her baby's welfare?

She nudged her horse off to the side of the procession and reined in so everyone would pass her. She pulled in beside Plainsfeather and rode in silence for a few moments, wondering how to approach the topic heavy on her mind.

Plainsfeather took the initiative saying, "What is troubling the daughter of my chief?"

"I have been galloping my horse," she said with tears in her eyes.

"You have always galloped your horse."

"But now I carry a child within me. Nathan's child. Eagle Feather says I might injure him." The tears were flowing freely now. "Perhaps I have already done so."

"What do men know about babies?" Plainsfeather snorted. "When your belly sticks out like this, you must not ride at all," she said, extending her hands well in front of her. "Still, better to walk horse."

The turmoil in Tachechana's mind eased somewhat, but the

thought of losing Nathan's baby continued to plague her throughout the day. The activity of setting up their camp at the river and preparing the evening meal turned her thoughts from the child growing within her, but at the evening's end, the fear returned, like a flood after the spring thaw.

Wandering away from the others, she found a place where she could be alone to pray. "Father God, I didn't mean to hurt Nathan's baby. If you take him from me, I do not want to live. He is all I have left to love."

Eagle Feather appeared in the eye of her mind. *Why did he bother to warn me of my foolish ways?* she wondered. *Why should he care if I lost Nathan's child? He hated Nathan because my white hunter took me from him forever. It is a great mystery.*

But she could not dismiss the tender look of concern in Eagle Feather's eyes.

chapter

12

EACH MORNING DAWNED LIKE THE ONE BEFORE. By now it was understood that all must be ready to move at first light. The scouts' keen eyes were trained on both flanks as well as those bringing up the rear.

As always, water determined the direction and distance traveled. The Sioux could do without a lot of things, but not water, especially in the extreme heat of 1876. Obstacles such as white camps and settlements had to be avoided, but that seemed a small inconvenience compared to a running fight.

The third day, the first of July by Tachechana's accounting, dawned hot, but the Indians' east-southeasterly course held them close to the river, the only detour around a settlement that had recently sprung up. Likewise, the route for day four followed a similar pattern, the monotony of the journey broken only by the sighting of a small family of buffalo.

The braves, acting as one person, gave chase and cut the big bull from the rest. The chief himself rode up beside the ponderous beast and drove an arrow into its heart, all within sight of the cheering travelers.

"The people are tired," Tachechana told her father. "This is a good place to camp for the night. Must we move on?"

"If we rest here tonight, we will have to camp without

water tomorrow night. There is enough daylight left to move on. Tomorrow, we cross south to the Elk River."

Since time was the determining factor, even the men, who normally would think it below their dignity, helped with the care of the buffalo. Meat, hide, horns, sinew, stomach, and certain bones were loaded onto a travois, and soon the entourage was snaking its way down the Belle Fourche. It was almost dark when they were met by one of the advance scouts who was doubling back, looking for them. A mile and a half ahead the other scouts had cooking fires ready for them.

To Tachechana's surprise the next day her father continued to lead the people southeast along the river until about noon, when he got off his horse and motioned for them to stop for water. The horses were loosed to graze on the tall grasses and to drink their fill at the river's edge. Thus fortified against the heat, Great Bear motioned them forward, across an extremely arid section of land.

There was not a breath of air stirring, and Eagle Feather, still weak from his injury, soon felt the effects of the unrelenting sun beating down upon them. When Tachechana checked on him late in the afternoon, he appeared in such poor condition that she instructed Plainsfeather to rig a blanket on sticks to form shade for him.

Tachechana, not yet fully recovered from her fever and now suffering from her advancing pregnancy, began to wilt.

"Is it much farther to the Elk River?" she asked her father.

"If your eyes were the eyes of an antelope, you could see the line of trees on the horizon," he answered.

Try as she might, the only thing she could see was a shimmering haze, like the ripples in the river as seen from a great distance. "My head . . ." and a blessed covering of darkness shut out the blazing ball in the sky.

She awakened to find herself lying on the bouncing travois,

Plainsfeather walking on one side and Eagle Feather stumbling along on the other.

"Stop!" she cried. "What will our people think of the daughter of Great Bear. She acts like a weak one who cannot carry her share of the burden."

The chief, riding by, overheard her complaint. "Your secret is no more. It has gladdened the hearts of our people to learn that you carry Gray Wolf's pup."

Indeed, the happy news rippled through the procession like the wind through the cottonwoods. Thus buoyed for the next few days, they made their way through the rest of the desert region, again reaching well-watered country with many trees.

Lightning flashed and thunder grumbled around the campground that night, but no one seemed the least disturbed. This time of year brought little rain to the parched prairie, and the few drops that fell were welcomed by all as relief from the dusty heat.

Enough water flowed in the Elk River to quench the thirst of both man and beast, but not enough to bathe even a small portion of the people. In another week or so the stream might be completely dry to the untrained eye. But the Indians knew they could get water to drink by digging beneath the undercut banks on the outside of a curve in the river.

The storm did have a cooling effect on the area, and true to Great Bear's prediction, the next morning dawned much cooler than any day of the trip thus far. Not only that, the forest all around them reminded Tachechana of some of the country Nathan and she had trapped the year before. Huge ponderosa pines shaded the needle-carpeted floor of the forest, gold shafts of light giving it a mystical, almost sacred aura.

"When we leave the Cheyenne River tomorrow, you will not see anything like it again. Only the hot bad land with its milky colored streams," Great Bear told her.

"I remember the reservation well, Father. But we must try to believe Captain Baker's words. Perhaps soon we will be allowed to return to the Black Hills and to the prairie, where our horses will thrive and the buffalo supply our needs."

"No, daughter. The time has come for us to realize we have lost all except what we can bargain for with the white man. Our people will survive, but our day has ended. It is good that white blood runs in the veins of my grandchild."

While the campsite for the next night boasted clear streams, good green grass, and food in abundance, the idyllic charm of the place had little effect on Great Bear's people. They could see Sheep Mountain Table to the east and knew the next day they would pass south of it and across the barren Bad Lands of the reservation to the White River and their home on the Pine Ridge Agency.

They clustered in tightly knit groups, knowing that within thirty miles, they would be wards of the United States Government. They, who were born and bred to the vastness of the Great Plains, were to be confined and cared for. To be told they were farmers. To be made to live in square houses with floors.

"What does the White Chief in Washington know of the ways of the Sioux?" they murmured among themselves. "Why does he tell us, the sons of Mother Earth, how to live, what to eat? And why does our chief listen to him? Doesn't Great Bear know all white men are liars?"

Sleep refused to come easy that night, and daylight brought no relief from the nagging questions Tachechana overheard. Questions to which she had no answers. Questions she dared not voice to her father lest he change his mind and die on the warpath. She needed him now almost as a substitute for Nathan, not as a husband, but as a rock on which she could stand. She thought he needed her, too. Needed her to help him understand the ways of the white man and to be sure the interpreters at the Agency did not change his words.

Slowly the procession started out across the barrenness of the Bad Lands, the overcast sky relieving them from the heat of the mid-summer sun, but doing nothing to improve their state of mind. Even the horses seemed to understand that this day would be the first of many unpleasant ones. The choking dust settled on horse and rider and mingled with their perspiration until it ran in muddy rivulets down their faces and bodies.

Tachechana was more worried now that the trip would have an adverse effect on her baby. Yet she knew that haste in reaching the White River would harm not only her but also the old, the very young, and the infirm, so she held Fox in check, staying even with her father, who was setting the pace.

"It will be mid-afternoon when we reach the river," the chief told her.

"Will we camp early then?"

"You must remember that the waters of the White River are too thick with mud to drink. We must travel on to where Medicine Creek joins the White. It is not like the good water of the north, but we can drink it. No later than tomorrow, we will be a village once more."

Encouraged by the prospect of resting a few days, Tachechana pulled out of the line and waited for Plainsfeather and Eagle Feather, who had returned to the travois.

Judging from his complaints, Eagle Feather appeared to be improving. He complained about everything—the heat, the food, the flies. He even complained when Tachechana periodically inspected his wound, which had finally closed itself. The bruise surrounding the bullet hole had dwindled to a dull brown smear, only a little darker than the warrior's skin.

"In a few days you will be able to ride again," she said, attempting to be cheerful.

But Eagle Feather even took exception to her optimism. "In a few days there will be no place to go, and we will soon be forced to eat our horses," he grunted.

The thought of eating horses always shocked Tachechana. To her, horses were always more than animals to be used or eaten. They were creatures to be loved, symbols of the freedom she always felt as she galloped across the prairie, the wind stinging her face. Only Nathan meant more to her than horses, and now she began to feel that love ripening in her body.

It was past mid-afternoon when the first of the procession waded into the milky waters of the river. While the water was too thick for the people to drink, almost everyone splashed its coolness on their bodies and completely soaked their clothing before starting the last leg of the journey to their new home. Just a few more miles downstream, and the clearer waters of Medicine Creek would satisfy their thirst.

About two hours before sunset, Great Bear and his people caught up with the advance scouts. They told him that there was a very small village, only six tepees, set up at their old site.

"Are they Sioux?" the chief asked.

"Yes, all old people."

"Are they well?"

"They appear well, but we didn't want to get too close in case."

"I will go," the chief said. He thundered away in a cloud of dust.

Tachechana remembered the sickness on the reservation, how many people had died with measles and smallpox. Now she was beginning to question her own advice to her father, urging him to return rather than fight. Surely death in battle would be preferred to the plagues of reservation life.

In less than a half hour he was back. "They are all well, and they welcome us."

Light-hearted now, the people pushed forward and found only eleven old ones who had been left behind almost a year earlier when the rest of their clan had attached themselves to Sitting Bull. The six men and five women nearly danced for joy when they saw the size of Great Bear's contingent. Now there would be warriors to help them find food, and young women to fetch firewood and water.

Great Bear gladly added the old people to his village. The old men would be able to give counsel, and the squaws' to help with chores.

The six tepees formed a tight cluster at the point of the vee where the two streams joined. A community fire circle was positioned in approximately the center of the tepees, and across the Medicine and south of the White several ponies were grazing. There appeared to be plenty of grass, and Tachechana noticed that several of the boys were already herding the spare horses across the stream.

Soon life will return to normal, Tachechana mused, *Or will it ever be the same again?*

That night, after they had consumed their meal and were enjoying the cooling evening breeze and the cheering blaze of the fire, Tachechana and Great Bear were surprised by a visit from Eagle Feather.

He stood in ceremonial stance, arms folded across his chest which barely concealed the purplish bruise of his wound. His proud head erect, Tachechana thought she had never seen him looking so well. He had obviously spent much time preparing for this encounter, for his jet braids gleamed with bear grease, and he was wearing new deerskin breeches fringed at the sides.

For some time he stood without speaking. At last, his words broke the silence. "The things done by Eagle Feather were not right," he said in the detached manner of a Sioux apology.

"They have happened, and it is done," replied Great Bear, accepting his tacit confession.

A rare smile tugged at the corners of the chief's mouth. "Sit with us and share our fire. The night breezes blow chill."

Eagle Feather sat, placing a discreet distance between himself and Tachechana, then fell silent while the conversation flowed around him.

"Daughter, tomorrow we will hunt and make our village. The next day you come with me to the Pine Ridge Agency to register our people. Then we will be given beef and flour. The old ones say the flour has no sawdust in it now, and some beef is not filled with worms."

"Maybe what Captain Baker said is happening," the young woman responded.

Unable to restrain himself longer, Eagle Feather interjected, "Does Tachechana have to make the long trip?"

Great Bear frowned. A visitor at a Sioux campfire never spoke unless he was first addressed. "She knows the white man's words, and she will speak my words to him so he cannot twist them."

Sensing the importance of this day, Tachechana felt her blood pulsing through her body. Never before had she been permitted to go to the Agency. In fact, she had always hidden from the agent and his men when they visited the village. Many of the prettier Indian maidens often disappeared after such visits and were never seen again.

But, as Nathan's widow and obviously pregnant, she would be safe. *Ah, Nathan,* she thought, *even from the grave, you protect me.*

chapter
13

ON THE DAY SHE WAS TO ACCOMPANY HER FATHER to the Indian Agency, Tachechana awakened, her blood singing with the old spirit of adventure that had marked all the days of her girlhood. She was eager to see white people again, to speak their language. Perhaps it was because of her deep bond with Nathan, she mused, or perhaps it was just that the warrior in her simply would not die and would ever seek new challenges.

They rode at a leisurely pace, stopping often for Tachechana to refresh herself. She longed to be able to burn a hole in the wind, her horse flying across the prairie. But those days, at least for now, were behind her. Despite their circumstances, the easy companionship with Great Bear was comforting.

"It is good to be riding with you again, Father," Tachechana said.

"Hmmm. Only if our ride is successful," the chief answered.

"Do you have any doubts about our success? I thought all we had to do was register the number of people in our village."

"By now, the whites have heard of the defeat of their army at the Little Big Horn. They may be hostile toward all Indians."

"But we had nothing to do with it."

"Will the white agent believe us?" The question hung, unanswered, between them.

Anxiety shadowed her earlier exhilaration as they neared the Agency. That she was nervous, Tachechana could not deny, but it puzzled her to feel as she did. A year ago, as a Sioux warrior, she would have dared to challenge anyone she met. Now she was aware of the name she bore—Mrs. Nathan Cooper—as well as the precious burden beneath her heart.

"What is the Agency like?" Tachechana asked.

"First, you will see a few scattered tepees," her father described. "The Agency itself is a square building with several rooms. You'll soon see for yourself."

Topping a small rise, they were unprepared for the scene that met their eyes. The "few scattered tepees" now numbered a few hundred, spreading out in all directions. Many small tribes and families had moved onto the reservation, their peaked lodges etched against a barren sky like a miniature range of mountains. The small building housing the office of the Agency had become five buildings, and the sleepy atmosphere was now a maelstrom of activity, with hundreds of people, both red and white, milling about.

They entered the building and stood uncertainly at the door. After what seemed an unnecessary wait, a man glanced up from a pile of papers at his desk and brusquely acknowledged their presence. "Yes? What is it you want?"

Although he didn't rise to greet them, Tachechana could see that he was a tall man, his shoulders and back straight for a man of his years. She figured him to be even older than Nathan, judging from the sparse gray hair on his head and the crinkles around his eyes. Those eyes now shifted from one to the other as Great Bear began to speak, and Tachechana interpreted.

"We have come to register our village."

"Where did you learn to speak English?" the agent demanded, his eyes roaming Tachechana's figure.

"My husband taught me."

"Where is your husband now?"

"He is dead."

A smile flickered on the agent's lips. "Do you have a list of names of everyone in your village?"

"There is no such list. We were not told we needed one."

"Well, you do. That is unless . . . you have no objections to doing some eh . . . favors for us here."

Suspecting the man's intentions, Tachechana kept these words to herself and asked, "What kind of . . . favors?"

He eyed her knowingly. "I'm sure a pretty girl like yourself, who has been married, can think of something." He gave a short, ugly laugh.

Enraged, Tachechana looked the man directly in the eye and hurled a challenge. "If I were to translate to my father, the chief, what you have just suggested, your scalp, poor as it is, would decorate his tepee tonight!"

"It was just a thought . . ." He shuffled some papers and proceeded with the business at hand. "Now, where is your settlement?"

"Where Medicine Creek and the White River meet."

"How many men?"

"I don't know."

"Then how can I be expected to register them?" he snarled. "If I am to supply blankets and food, I'll need to know how many men, women, and children in your village."

Suddenly another man, younger and more powerfully built, entered the room. "Is there a problem here?" he asked, smiling at Tachechana and Great Bear.

"We are trying to register our village as we were told to do

133

by Captain Baker of the Second Cavalry," Tachechana explained.

"Then you must be Great Bear." The man addressed the chief.

"How do you know my father?" Tachechana asked.

"Captain Baker sent a message with the courier from Fort Fetterman. He said to be on the lookout for you. If this is Great Bear, you must be Mrs. Cooper. I'm Reverend Baxter. How can I help you?"

"Reverend? Then you are a Christian?" Tachechana blurted, relieved to find a kindred spirit in this alien place.

"Yes, a missionary here to help the Indians and teach them God's ways."

"I'm a Christian too! My husband—"

"I know," Baxter interrupted with a smile. "Captain Baker told me all about you."

Turning to the agent, he frowned. "Is there any reason why these people can't be registered—promptly?"

"No, Reverend. I just need an accurate nose count. I can't send numbers to Washington without verification."

"It seems to me you never had trouble keeping your count high enough before. Give me the census sheet, and I'll go list them for you."

Thinking the missionary was surprisingly severe with one of his own kind, she offered, "If a paper must be filled out, I can take care of it."

Almost in unison, the two white men asked, "You can read and write?"

Their reactions to the news were noticeably different. The preacher seemed delighted, while the agent registered disgust and uneasiness.

Handing the missionary a handful of papers, he said, "Here! Just so's these get filled out, I don't care how it gets done!"

Smiling, Tachechana tried to explain to her father what had been going on as the big missionary led them out of the building and across a yard to a chapel. The chief seemed unsure of himself when she told him they were entering God's house. She remembered the first time she heard Nathan pray, how she looked around, trying to see the God to whom he was speaking. She understood her father's dilemma.

"Where are your people?" Baxter asked.

Tachechana explained. He knew the place well.

"Tomorrow I'll go with you to the village, and we can list the names. You'll be needing your allotment of supplies from the government. Do you have a place to spend the night?"

"We can camp along the river. By traveling up the White Clay, then down the White, we will have shade most of the way. It is easier for me."

"If you can spare the time, I'll take you in my wagon tomorrow. I'll rig up a cover to give you all the shade you need. In the meantime, you're welcome to use my quarters for the night."

After relaying the offer to the chief and hearing his reply, she said, "My father has friends living here at the Agency. We will spend the night with them and be back at sunrise."

They mounted their horses and rode out through the cluster of tepees the same way they had ridden in.

"I didn't know you recognized anyone."

Her father's face was grim. "You are too quick to trust. We will camp . . . there." He pointed toward a heavy grove of cottonwoods and willows. "If someone comes looking for us or our horses, we will not make it easy for them."

"But surely you trust the missionary. Reverend Baxter is a man of God!"

"I trust only those who have earned my trust."

Great Bear carefully picketed the horses that night very close to where he and Tachechana slept.

135

As the sun split the eastern horizon, Tachechana and Great Bear rode up to the missionary's clapboard house, more than mildly surprised to see him attempting to roll a large barrel up two heavy planks and onto his wagon where four other barrels already stood. One barrel remained on the ground behind the wagon, along with ten large sacks.

Seeing the man's struggle, Great Bear slid from his horse to help. Tachechana could not help comparing them as they worked. The missionary was a bit taller and much heavier than her father, his muscles more pronounced than Great Bear's, but her father was lithe and quick. Their physical attributes reminded her of the differences in her father's war pony and the great work horses she had seen at Fort Fetterman.

Together, the men loaded all the barrels and sacks on the wagon, along with some tools, picks, and shovels, and a small keg of fresh water.

The horse hitched to the customized wagon looked much like Rowdy in size and color, but it was evident that this animal was no match for Nathan's great stallion. The missionary's horse was narrow in the chest and too extreme in his taper. Even her pack mare was a better horse.

Gently the reverend helped Tachechana to the springy seat. "There is room for your father if he would like to change his mind."

"He thinks wagons are for women, children, and old men," she laughed.

For the next several hours Reverend Baxter plied Tachechana with all sorts of questions about her past, the people of the village, her father, and Nathan. When it became apparent that the discussion was depressing her, he changed to a more pleasant topic.

After a lull in the conversation, she ventured a question of her own. "Do you have a wife?"

The preacher's brows knit in a frown. "No. The young lady I planned to wed said she couldn't bear this wilderness, away from family and friends."

"Then why did you come?"

"I knew God wanted me here, helping Indians learn about God's Son. Teaching your people is the most important thing in the world to me, even if it costs me Jane or even my own life."

She ached to see the pained expression in his eyes. "You love her much."

"Yes . . . but I must leave that in God's hands."

"When my husband was dying," Tachechana began, looking off into the distance, "he told me that God gives and God takes away. But when he takes, he always gives back something better."

For a long time they rode in silence, each contemplating the other's words. Tachechana felt a strange affinity for this big jovial man as they plodded across the plains.

She broke the long silence, "What do you have in the barrels and sacks we are carrying?"

"The first allotment of food for your village—cornmeal, beef, and flour," Baxter explained. "The tools are for digging a well so you can have fresh, cool water whenever you want it."

"Why do you take this trouble to help us? Is this not the job of the agent to deliver food and supplies to our people?"

"If that scoundrel had his way"—the big man scowled—"the Indians wouldn't get anything. He'd rather sell it to the fort sutlers and put the money in his own pocket, then each family would have to come to the Agency and pick up their goods. That's why so many of the Indians live right there. They have too few horses to do what is necessary."

"What happened to their horses?"

"The poorer ones were used for food, and the better ones stolen. I suspect the thieves are the agent and his men. They then sell them to settlers or trading posts. Good ones, like the one you were riding, might even be sold to the army."

Tachechana's heart sank. "But without their horses, my people cannot hunt for their food. They will become more and more dependent on the man who steals from them."

"That's why I'm here." The missionary's expression grew even more sober. "Changes have to be made in both your society and mine. The only answer to these problems is that both the Indian and the white man learn to practice God's love, and his way."

"But that is not possible unless they first ask Jesus to live in their hearts."

"Exactly," he said, turning to smile at her. "That's the message I'm trying to bring to both races, but we must first gain their trust."

A straggly line of trees betrayed a watercourse to the northeast, the direction in which they were traveling. "Is that Medicine Creek?" Tachechana asked.

"Yes. We'll water and rest the horses there. Then it's only about two more hours to your village." There was another few moments of thoughtful silence. "Tell me, are there many wounded at your village?"

"Why do you ask such a question?" She evaded the issue.

"Surely you heard of the great battle at the Little Big Horn two weeks ago. I have to report any wounded men to the Agency. Those who killed Custer and mauled the Seventh Cavalry will be punished. If I don't see any wounded, I won't have to report any."

There was a moment's hesitation before Tachechana confided. "We have only one wounded man, Eagle Feather, and his wound is older than that battle. It is almost healed."

"It would probably be best if he weren't in the village tomorrow when I take the census. Is he well enough to ride?"

"Yes."

"Perhaps he could be persuaded to go hunting tomorrow—early." He smiled.

"Perhaps." Her lips curved in an answering smile, perfect understanding between them.

chapter

14

THE NOVELTY OF SEEING A WAGON AT CLOSE RANGE had not worn off the next morning as the people of Great Bear's village gathered round. The old ones, remembering the barrels of beef and sacks of flour from their last stay on the reservation, wanted to be on hand for the distribution of goods, but none wanted to appear anxious about it. The last hunt had not been as successful as they had hoped, and though proud, they realized they needed more than this poor land could provide.

Great Bear waited until Eagle Feather rode away before calling a council. At the missionary's suggestion, he told his people to sit on the ground in family groups in order to speed the registration. Afterwards, the Reverend Baxter would go to each lodge to check on any sick or wounded. But before he began to write down their names, he insisted that they listen to his words as Tachechana translated.

He began by teaching them to say his name, "Mr. Baxter." Some of the Indians laughed as he insisted they pronounce it just right. Briefly he told them why it was important that their own names be listed correctly on the census.

"But there is one name you should remember above all others—Jesus. I am your friend and will do all in my power to help you. But Jesus is your Best Friend, and his power is greater than any man who walks on the earth. Someday I will tell you what he has already done for you."

Tachechana watched their faces for any sign of understanding. They listened politely to their guest, but their minds were on the provisions in his wagon.

His short sermon at an end, Reverend Baxter turned to practical matters. "The water of these streams is not good for you to drink. I have brought shovels and picks so you may dig a well," he told them. He seemed encouraged when so many of them smiled at his statement, but Tachechana explained they thought his words were foolish. They had drunk river water all their lives.

"But many of your babies die needlessly. A well will mean that more of your children will live to be strong and grow old."

If it was important for Indian babies, Tachechana thought, it would be more important for white babies—like hers.

To add emphasis to the missionary's words, she told the people the Agency would not give them more food until the well was dug.

Family by family, the village was registered, the lodges examined, and the wagonload of goods deposited in the new tepee. The missionary suggested the beef be opened one barrel at a time, and each family come as they had need. In that way, the flies would be denied the whole lot at one time, and the meat would last until the next shipment.

Great Bear, who by now was less suspicious of the missionary, declared that there would be a dance in his honor and dismissed the people to their tasks.

The women spent the day preparing the food and foraging for other things needed. The musicians got out their drums and eagle bone whistles, and a renewed feeling of hope permeated the village.

142

As the bloody sun touched the purple gray mountains on the western horizon, a smiling group of Indians gathered at the large council circle in the center of their village to consume great amounts of food. At the end of the meal, the drums began their throbbing, and the men got up to whirl and soar through motions depicting the hunt, the battle, and the victories of their lives. Tachechana loved to see the men of the village displaying their acts of courage and daring. The rhythm of the drums and whistles sent her pulses reeling until she was not watching a dance, but reliving the exploits of the warriors.

Tiring at last of the frenetic activity, the men sat down one by one, and the beat of the drums slowed. Then the younger women rose and began to flow around the inside of the circle, feet shuffling, backs straight, eyes fastened on the ground in front of them. At every fourth beat of the drums, they bent their knees ever so slightly in a small curtsey, their arms stiff at their sides.

"What is the significance of this dance?" asked Reverend Baxter, who was sitting next to Tachechana.

"Some of the women are dancing for their husbands; others," she said with a smile, "to please the men they wish to win for their husbands. They remain stiff and straight to show their strength and beauty, then bend their knees to show how they will obey their men. It makes the braves very proud."

"Why don't you join the dancers? Any man would be proud to claim you," he said, giving her a look of frank admiration.

"I am married—to a man who . . . is not here," Tachechana replied, a wave of despondency displacing her joy in the approaching birth of her child.

"Surely, as young as you are, you'll marry again."

"But I have no desire to marry again," she said simply.

"It is still too soon after your husband's death to make that kind of decision," he counseled. "As time goes by, you'll change your mind."

She shook her head firmly. "When we were married, I promised to love Nathan forever. How could I forget my vow to him and deny my promise to God?"

"Your promise to God was only 'till death do us part.' You will undoubtedly love Nathan always, but there is room in your heart for someone else. You're a fine woman, Tachechana, a good Christian. Life is just beginning for you."

She was grateful when the tempo of the drums increased, making further conversation impossible. The villagers swarmed like bees to the circle—men, women, and children prancing and strutting in a wild display of joy. Only the elders, Great Bear, Tachechana, and Reverend Baxter sat watching, absorbing the beat of the drums and the wild gyrations of the dancers.

How wonderful this moment would be, she thought, *if only Nathan were here to enjoy it with me.*

When the sun was mid-way on its path through the sky, the men of the village gathered at the site the missionary had suggested as a good place for their well. There were grunts of dissatisfaction at having to rise so early to satisfy the white man after a night of feasting. But Great Bear had spoken, and their chief's decisions were always right.

Reverend Baxter, who had remained overnight to begin the project, threw himself into the task with great vigor. Quickly, Great Bear followed suit, taking the shovel from him and plunging it deep into the earth. One by one, the reluctant onlookers picked up their implements and began a halfhearted attempt at digging. Others were instructed to carry the dirt to the front of the tepee used to store the supplies.

Certain at last that everything was well underway, the

missionary took Tachechana by the arm and led her to where his horse and wagon waited. "I must go back to the Agency now, but I'll return in about a week. Your people don't trust me yet—don't believe this well can save lives. Try to make your father understand. They'll listen to him."

"I will try."

"And don't forget what I told you at the dance last night. . . . Someday, when your heart has healed, you will learn to love again."

She looked at him, confused and embarrassed, watching long after his wagon had rumbled down the dusty trail.

Soon after Great Bear retired to his tepee, work on the well slowed, finally coming to a complete stop. Concerned, Tachechana went to her father and reported the malingering among the men.

"The work will get done." He shrugged. "But few of our people will pull water up from the ground with a rope when they can scoop it so easily from the river."

"But we will have no provisions next month if the work is not done," she argued. "Our people will go hungry."

He waved her away like a pesky fly. "It is a hot day and the men are tired. They will do the work, but they will do it in their own way and in their own time. They do not like to take orders from the white man."

Her father was right. It was useless for a small fawn to try to move the great bear, so she turned her energies to something more productive. Leaving Great Bear's lodge, she walked to Plainsfeather's tepee.

There, she found the old woman hard at work, weaving something soft on a small frame. She had cut rabbit skins into narrow strips, sewed them together to produce long ropes of fur, and was now intertwining them through the loom.

"What are you making, Plainsfeather?" she asked.

"Rabbit skin blanket, very warm," she said.

"But it's too small for a blanket."

"*Baby* blanket." The old woman chuckled.

Tachechana didn't know what to say. She rubbed the soft fur on her cheek and was surprised when it came away salty wet.

Plainsfeather smiled her one-toothed smile and held Tachechana's smooth hand in her gnarled one. Tachechana looked at those beloved hands and brought them to her lips in a tender gesture of gratitude.

"It is time I began collecting things for my small one," she said. "I must make some clothes . . . but . . . I never learned how to sew." She dropped her eyes in embarrassment. "Will you teach me?"

The old woman regarded her fondly. "The daughter of the chief learn fast . . . how to ride horse . . . shoot arrow. Now she learn the ways of Sioux woman. I teach."

Fascinated by the nimble fingers of her old friend, Tachechana took up some strips of the fur and, instructed by Plainsfeather, began an awkward attempt at sewing them together. The work was difficult, and she pierced her finger more than once with the sharp bone needle.

Through the open doorway, she saw Eagle Feather leaning against a cottonwood near the river. "Did Eagle Feather eat for you this morning?" she asked.

"Humph! I stop taking him food. He too grumpy. He take care of self."

"Then I'd better see how he's feeling," Tachechana said, grateful for this diversion.

"I tell you how he feel. He feel better when he see you," Plainsfeather crowed, cackling with delight.

Tachechana glared. "You know we're only friends. Nothing more."

"We shall see."

Eagle Feather stood a little straighter at Tachechana's approach. *I don't know why no one believes I will honor Nathan's memory as my father has honored the memory of Green Eyes,* she thought. *I'm not a crazy woman, chasing after men.*

"Why did you send Plainsfeather away again without eating the food she prepared for you?" she demanded, ignoring the proper Sioux greeting. "Don't you want to grow well and strong?"

"I am well enough . . . and strong enough." He stared at the braves who were reluctantly chipping in the dirt. "Why are those braves digging in the ground? What are they looking for?"

"They are digging down where the water runs clean and pure. It is called a well. Reverend Baxter says it will keep our children healthy."

"Ha!" he snorted in derision. "The white man! What does he know? The Great Spirit told the Sioux where to find water long before the white man came!" He cocked his head in her direction, and she could feel his penetrating black eyes probing hers. "You were with the white missionary much. Why?"

"He doesn't know our language. I was telling his words to our people."

"And did you dance for him, too?" Eagle Feather's voice was laced with sarcasm.

Tachechana felt a surge of hot anger. "And what concern is that of yours? When will you stop pursuing me like the hunter pursues the deer? I can never be your squaw!"

Eagle Feather snatched up his rifle and stalked off in the direction of his tepee.

Watching him go, she felt the heat in her cheeks cool, then she sought her father's counsel once again.

Finding him in his lodge, she asked, "Did all the maidens of the tribe try to take my mother's place after she died?"

Startled by her question, Great Bear looked at his daughter for a long time before answering. When he did, he spoke with deliberation. "There were those who let it be known they would be happy to live in the tepee of the chief. Why do you ask such a question?"

"Eagle Feather! That's why! He expects me to be his squaw. It isn't in my heart to be anyone's squaw. I am Nathan's wife. Why can't he understand that?"

"It is hard to fight a dead man . . . a memory. If Nathan were alive, Eagle Feather could fight him with the hope of winning you. Since Nathan is dead, he cannot understand why you won't marry him."

"It is a simple thing. I don't love him."

"What about the soldier with the red hair?"

Tachechana thought of the merry-faced O'Connel and suppressed a warm chuckle. "We too are friends—though he would kill our people if ordered by his superiors, I suppose."

"And the missionary?"

"I have much respect for his work. In time, he will probably become a friend like O'Connel and Eagle Feather."

Great Bear eyed her thoughtfully. "If my daughter wishes to remain as she is, she will not nurture the tender hearts of young men. She may know the difference between friendship and love—but they do not."

Walking along the riverbank a little later, Tachechana considered her father's words. They were wise words. He had known the great sadness of losing one he loved and had chosen to remain one with her even after her death, somehow making it clear to the young maidens that he was no longer eligible for their attentions.

She thought again of Eagle Feather and O'Connel. It was

clear that they found her pleasing, but why had her father mentioned Reverend Baxter? Surely he was not interested in her, except as one who could aid his work with the Indians.

She tried to bring his image to the canvas of her mind. Tall, powerfully built, kind, and gentle—he would make a good husband. But Jane still filled his heart.

Deep down, as she thought of these men, she felt the primitive stirrings in her body. She must bury them forever, as Nathan had been buried. When the child arrived, there would be no room for silly daydreams. She would keep to herself, she decided. She must forget her warrior days when all men were her friends and companions.

As she lay on her buffalo robe that night, she was surprised to find Reverend Baxter appearing in her thoughts once more.

How foolish to think of him. Such a man would never look at an Indian woman, except through the eyes of God. She yawned sleepily. *Besides, there is Jane.*

And she fell asleep, wondering if Baxter had meant he would return in a full week of seven days . . . or if he might come sooner.

chapter
15

WORK ON THE WELL PROGRESSED LITTLE during the first three days after the missionary left Great Bear's village. It was hot, and the men of the village had no heart for the work. At Great Bear's suggestion, several would throw a few scoops of dirt out of the hole, then remembering something of great importance that must be done elsewhere, they would scramble out and stride away. For Tachechana, the most disturbing thing was her father's apparent indifference.

She sought him out. "Reverend Baxter will return any day now, and the well is no deeper than when he left. Does my father, the chief, intend to let his people go hungry because the men of his village are too lazy to dig?"

His chest swelled in indignation. "You call our warriors lazy? In battle and in the hunt, none can compare with the Sioux for strength and valor!"

"Then why do they shirk a duty that will make our children strong and healthy?" she pressed.

"Do you think I care not for my own grandson?" He slanted her a fierce look.

"*Grandson?* " she echoed coyly. "So you think I will give you a small warrior?"

Tachechana struck a pose that never failed to divert her

father's line of thought. Lower lip extended, she exhaled a little puff of air, this action producing the desired effect.

Against his will, the chief's lips trembled in an ill-concealed smile. "When you play such games, Great Bear cannot hold anger. Do not worry, my daughter. You and your missionary will have your well if I have to dig it myself. Now . . . go from my sight. I have weightier matters to ponder than whether this one will be a small warrior or a little princess as spoiled as her mother!"

Later, as Tachechana sat with Plainsfeather, learning to sew with a bone needle and sinew from a deer's leg, she could see her father walking from tepee to tepee, talking with his warriors. In the wake of these visits, she could detect a new spirit of expectancy.

When she questioned him at the evening meal, his answer was even more obscure. "I have declared a day of games to test the skill and endurance of my braves."

Tachechana could not understand her father's reasoning. Why would he want his braves to play games when the well needed digging?

The summer sun blazed down through an azure sky, flocked with great banks of puffy white clouds. The young warriors had gathered early, eager to display their prowess.

The first event was a foot race. The men, lined up near the well, were told to run west up the White River to the place where Great Bear had driven his lance into the ground, cross the river, and return at the point where Medicine Creek joined those waters. The first to reach the opposite bank would receive a prize.

Tachechana cast a worried look in Eagle Feather's direction, sensing his frustration. Fleet of foot, the brave would have been a strong contender if his injury had not kept him from the day's competition. Sadly she watched him stand to one side as Great Bear raised his rifle and fired the starting shot. It was Swimming Otter, strongly challenged by two other braves, who emerged the victor some time later.

After a short period of rest, Great Bear called the warriors together again to explain the rules for the next contest.

"This is a test of strength and skill," he said. "Each man, one at a time, will fill ten buckets with dirt from the well, then shoot an arrow at each of four targets." He pointed first to the south where a jack rabbit skin, stuffed with grass, had been placed about twenty-five yards from the shooting line. Ten yards farther, to the west, was a coyote skin, similarly stuffed. The target to the north was a deer-sized flour sack hanging from a tree on the opposite side of the river. To the east, suspended from a wooden frame, was a worn-out buffalo skin painted to resemble a buffalo.

"The warrior who scores the most killing hits will win the eagle feather. If there is a tie, the distance to the buffalo target will be increased until all the shooters but one have missed. Who will be first?"

Every man was eager to demonstrate his strength and skill, whether it was with the white man's pick and shovel, or his own bow and arrows. The last of them had not finished digging before water began seeping into the hole. It was soon evident that this water was as milky as the river itself, but the warriors quickly left that task to tackle the final contest of the day.

Two days later, the missionary's wagon rolled into the village.

Tachechana was reluctant to pass on the disappointing news about the well. "We struck water," she said, "but I'm afraid it is no different from the water in the river."

153

"Did you wait for it to settle before you tried it?" asked Reverend Baxter.

"No. It was so cloudy that everyone decided to draw their water from the river."

Carefully lowering a new bucket into the well with a long rope, and just as carefully retrieving it, Reverend Baxter showed Tachechana and Great Bear its crystal contents. One sip convinced the chief that his people would no longer be satisfied with river water, and Tachechana beamed, knowing that her small one's health was assured.

The reverend had all the help he needed getting the lumber off his wagon to build the well house. It was said that the water tasted as good as any in the streams flowing through the sacred Black Hills. Tachechana saw the pride in the preacher's eyes and suspected it was not for his own triumph in persuading them to build the well, but because the Indians had bettered their lot by their own efforts.

That night, as he took supper with Tachechana and her father, he made a startling proposition.

"I've been thinking, Mrs. Cooper . . . I'm needing someone to interpret for me in some of the outlying villages . . . tell the people my words about Jesus. You'd be the ideal choice, if you've a mind to try it."

Tachechana's initial enthusiasm for the adventure quickly turned to doubt. "I couldn't do that," she objected. "What would people think if they saw a married woman heavy with child traveling with a man? What would Jane think?"

"As for Jane, it's finished between us," he admitted sadly. "In every letter, she says I must forget my insane mission and move back East before she will marry me. But, of course, you're right. It wouldn't be proper. And there's the child to consider, too." He drummed his fingers on the mat on which he was sitting. "However, I think there is a way you could help me right here . . . if you'd be willing to teach me to speak your language. You could write out the Sioux words as they sound. Then when I come for my visits to your village, you could correct my mistakes. In turn, I'll teach you to understand what the Bible says. Then, perhaps later, we can teach the Sioux some English words so they can read the Bible for themselves."

The prospect was fascinating, but a small finger of doubt still rippled down her spine. Remembering her father's advice, she realized that these lessons would throw the two of them together more often than was seemly. If a way could be devised. . . . Suddenly, it came to her.

"If you will tell me the words you wish to learn, I'll try to write out the Sioux words as they sound."

The grin on the preacher's face told her the idea was pleasing.

Early the next morning, Tachechana found Reverend Baxter standing behind his wagon, scratching on a tablet. Gazing off into space, he stared in contemplation, then wrote some more.

Curious, she approached, eager to see what he was doing.

"Do these words look familiar to you?" he asked, holding out the tablet for her perusal.

She studied the marks, sounding them out, "Man, woman, lost, Jesus, God's Son, love . . ."

"Yes, these are words Nathan taught me."

"Good, then they should make a good start. I'll leave these pages with you, and when I return in a few days, I'll bring more writing supplies and another list of words . . . that is, if you're up to it," he amended hastily.

Looking down at the growing mound beneath her shapeless smock, she laughed. "I'm not helpless yet. I would be pleased to make words for you."

155

His countenance brightened. "Then it's a bargain. And next time, we'll have our first Bible study. Before I go, I'd like to speak to your people once more."

Together, they walked over to greet a group of families resting in the shade of a tepee. Tachechana explained that the missionary wanted to talk more with them about their friend, Jesus, and she nodded for him to begin.

His message was a simple one about God's love. "God, the Great Father, sent his Son, Jesus, to die for you." There was murmuring among them at these words. "You . . . all of us . . . are lost in this world, wandering about with no real home. But God knows and cares and wants to save us from our evil ways, our killing and our stealing. His son Jesus gave his life so that, one day, you would be able to live with him forever in a place where you will never be hungry or thirsty again."

Tachechana walked to the buckboard as the missionary prepared to leave.

"Thank you for helping me today," he said kindly. "Do you think they understood what I was saying?"

She shrugged. "If they had not seen Nathan step in front of the bullet intended for Eagle Feather, they would not understand. But they saw a white man die for one of our people, so there is hope. They heard your words, but I do not think they believed them."

"Why is that?"

"They have always been taught that to kill an enemy will bring great rewards in the spirit world. To kill an enemy is the same as saving a friend."

"But what about God's Word? He tells us to love our enemies."

"Most of my people don't know about love. I myself learned from Nathan, and now I am trying to teach the others. But the Sioux believe they are good people, the

156

noblest of all the nations of the red man, so why should they need someone to die for them? Are they not brave warriors, ready to face death with courage and honor?"

Reverend Baxter's furrowed brow told Tachechana he had much to ponder on the ride back to the Agency.

Soon after his wagon pulled away, she sought a shady spot by the river. Leafing through the sheaf of papers he had given her, she was surprised when three folded pages fluttered to the ground. Opening them, she found a letter written in fine script.

"Dear Donald," it began. "I have received your most recent letter asking again that I come west to be your bride and help in your mission to save the poor lost Indians. Again I must answer by saying that, although I love you deeply, I cannot leave the happiness and security of St. Louis to live in the dust and squalor of that savage land. It grieves me that you care so little for my health and safety to expect such a thing of me."

For two more pages the harangue continued, pleading at last that the young man give up and return to her. ". . . If God intends for those savages to be saved," she said in conclusion, "he can do it without your help."

Perhaps, Tachechana considered thoughtfully, *there are white people, too, who do not understand the true meaning of love.*

She replaced the pages and tried to put the thought from her mind, but the work of translation was not so difficult as to erase the sadness of Jane's words. *If only I could do something to make her understand how badly we need him here,* she thought. *Or maybe Jane is right. . . . Maybe he needs someone who knows the Sioux, someone like . . .* She blushed at the impudent thought and applied herself diligently to her translation.

Whatever she was doing, however, Tachechana could not forget Jane's letter. In the next few days, prompted by Jane's words and the missionary's message, she gave much thought to the idea of love.

As a child she had often dropped stones in the river just to watch the ripples grow in ever-widening circles. Love seemed to be much like that. With Jesus living in her heart, she felt it opening to embrace everyone she met—her father and Plainsfeather, of course, and in a special way, Eagle Feather and Trooper O'Connel, Doc and Captain Baker, and yes, even Reverend Baxter and Jane. But there was still no one like Nathan, who had held her close those precious few nights and whispered words of love against her hair.

Not knowing how to broach the subject of Jane's letter, Tachechana decided not to mention it at all and kept it tucked away in a small deerskin pouch. But the longer she kept it, the more despondent she grew, knowing that the man she loved was lost to her forever, and that Jane was not thinking straight in her head if she let Reverend Baxter slip away from her.

chapter
16

ON A HOT AUGUST NIGHT WHEN TACHECHANA LAY SLEEPLESS
on her pallet in Great Bear's lodge, she felt a feather-light
fluttering in her belly. As quickly as it had come, the feeling
left. She lay very still, thinking she had imagined it. Then it
was upon her again—a movement as slight as the brush of a
butterfly's wing.

Nathan's child! she cried silently so as not to awaken Great
Bear. *Nathan's child moves within me!*

The dark cloud that had settled over Tachechana's spirit
lifted with the stirring of the small one, and she returned to
her tasks with her customary vigor.

Eager now that all should feel the joy she knew, she decided
to share her thoughts with Jane. Taking some of her precious
paper and drawing out a quill pen Reverend Baxter had
brought her, she wrote:

Dear Miss Jane,

This is Tachechana of the Sioux nation. You do not know me,
but I know you because of your man, Reverend Baxter. He talks
of you and carries you in his heart. Most of all, he needs you. I
see it in his eyes. If you love him, come to him soon.

Or he will find someone else, Tachechana thought. *Even I could learn to love such a man.*

To alleviate the woman's fears, she told her something of her daily life on the reservation and how she was once married to a white man and would soon bear his child. She told how Nathan had sacrificed himself trying to make peace between the Indians and the whites. After closing and sealing the letter, she sent it by one of Great Bear's braves to the post office at Wounded Knee.

The winds from the northwest blew colder and colder, and Tachechana marveled at her new figure. "I don't think my stomach can get much bigger without splitting open," she told Plainsfeather one exceptionally cold day in mid-November. "How much longer must I wait?"

"At least two more moons," the old woman said, probing Tachechana's abdomen with practiced fingers.

"If my baby doesn't come soon, both Fox and the big mare will foal first," she said, looking across Medicine Creek toward the corral the missionary had helped to build.

As Tachechana's pregnancy advanced, all the villagers, including the women, showed greater respect and consideration than ever before. She joined in the talk of the women as they stitched small garments. Even Eagle Feather ceased pressing her to be his squaw. It was only when the missionary visited the village that Eagle Feather pouted as before, keeping his distance until Baxter had left.

Another moon passed through its full cycle, and still Tachechana's baby gave no sign of being ready to leave the warm blanket of her body. But Fox dropped a beautiful colt, and Tachechana smiled when the small creature tried his spindly legs for the first time to nuzzle at his mother's soft underside. And when her own child gave a sharp kick, her silvery laughter could be heard throughout the village.

That very week Reverend Baxter stopped by with a load of beef, flour, and cornmeal. Piled high in the rear of his wagon were new blankets for every man, woman, and child.

"But that's not all," he called to Tachechana. "Have the children come to Great Bear's lodge."

Dark eyes wide with wonder, the children and their parents crowded around the lodge and, with Tachechana acting as interpreter, listened to Reverend Baxter tell the sweet story of Jesus' birth—God's great gift to the red man and the white. For the first time, every villager seemed to be listening, really listening.

"And because this is the time of year we celebrate the birth of God's Son, I have some gifts for you," he concluded.

From the boxes in the wagon, he produced red and white peppermint sticks for every child, and apples enough for everyone in the village.

"I will come again later with a special gift for you," he told Tachechana, smiling a mysterious smile as the villagers drifted back to their tepees.

"I have not heard of this custom," she said. "What do you call it?"

"You mean your husband never told you about *Christmas?*" Baxter was incredulous.

"Last year he was unconscious. He could tell me nothing."

The preacher reddened. "I'm so sorry, ma'am. That was thoughtless of me. Captain Baker told me you took care of him all winter."

"Only to lose him, after all." Her voice caught on a small sob. "Sometimes I am still so lonely for the sound of his voice I cannot help crying. But God always sends his Comforter."

Reverend Baxter looked beyond the skin wall of the tepee. "I guess I know something about loneliness." The big man shifted uncomfortably, patting her shoulder with an oversized hand, then reaching for her small one. "My Jane is as lost to me as your Nathan is to you."

"Nathan is dead," she reminded him gently. "Your Jane is still alive. There is hope."

"I'm afraid you're wrong there," he sighed. "I guess God has something else in mind for me." Still holding her hand, he lifted it to his lips.

Tachechana was stunned, first that he would do such a thing, then at her own pleasure. Although she knew she ought to object, she did not. Surely there could be no harm in taking comfort in the touch of a friend.

"If only Jane were more like you," Baxter mused. "I guess she just hasn't learned to trust the Lord enough."

Tachechana tugged her hand away at last. "You . . . you must not give up hope. God can still work in her, giving her the courage she needs."

He released his hold on her hand, but it felt suddenly awkward, as if it no longer belonged to her. She tried putting it to her face, brushing back a strand of hair, rubbing her chin. Finally, to the preacher's amusement, she placed one hand over the other, resting both on her protruding abdomen.

"What's so funny?" she asked, a little frown disturbing the smooth brow.

"Forgive me." But he continued to chuckle. "It's just looks a bit comical to see you that way, with your hands on top of your tummy!"

Her laughter joined his, lightening the mood of the moment.

"How much longer before your baby arrives?" he asked.

"Plainsfeather says it will be another moon, but I don't see how it can be that long. I'm as big as Nathan's mare across the river already." A small giggle erupted.

"Maybe you will be blessed with twins."

"Then my river would run bank full." At his look of puzzlement, she explained. "The river of joy in my heart. Like the river outside, sometimes it runs full, while at other times, it seems to dry up."

"But the river is always there"—he nodded in understanding—"even when it is only a trickle."

"It is there for you, too. Remember that when you are sad or lonely."

He looked at her in frank appreciation. "I thought when I came West, I was coming to teach the Indians. Now I find I am the student."

The sound of galloping horses interrupted their conversation, and Great Bear, who had been hunting, entered the lodge. "We have seen the tracks of many horses with iron on their feet, two miles north."

"Could be a troop of soldiers," Baxter suggested.

"No," replied the chief. "They do not ride, row upon row. They ride more like a pack of wolves."

"Horse thieves!" the missionary exclaimed, jumping to his feet. "Corral your horses, and tell your warriors to get their rifles!"

The chief barked some orders to the men outside his tepee, his shouts bringing the entire village on the run.

"Generally those thieves operate somewhere in the reservation when I'm on the opposite side. Maybe this time I can find out who they are," the preacher told Great Bear and Tachechana. "They generally attack at midnight, so there is time to plan our strategy. I'd like to capture as many of them as we can and send them to the army stockade. If we make an example of them, we might be able to discourage others from that kind of mischief."

After consultation, Baxter and the chief agreed that the thieves would likely attack the herd from the east, keeping the horses and the creek between themselves and the river. The cottonwood trees extending east along the White River would offer cover for some of the Indians, but it would be necessary for most of them to lie on the frozen ground under the scant cover of the sagebrush.

Each warrior carried a buffalo robe, which he spread on the ground, furry side up. On it he laid his rifle, extra ammunition, and coup stick. Finally he prostrated himself on half the robe, pulling the other half over himself. The color blended so well with the earth that the preacher, who had taken a position just inside the east fence of the corral, could see only mounds of dirt as he surveyed the area.

Down by the river, an owl hooted, with an answering call from the sagebrush.

"They are coming," Great Bear whispered, and at his signal there was absolute silence as the braves waited..

A half-hour later, a group of men on horseback could be seen, walking their horses quietly toward the corral, unaware that forty or more guns had been trained on them ever since they rode into sight.

Reverend Baxter waited until one of the thieves threw a rope over one of the fence posts before he shouted, "That's far enough! Drop your guns! You're surrounded!"

One of the outlaws fired in the direction of the preacher's voice, and before the echo died away, Great Bear shot him off his horse. All the Indians scrambled from their hiding places with war whoops that sounded like hell casting out its demons.

"Drop your guns, or I can't be responsible for your lives!" Baxter called.

"Do what he says!" the leader yelled to his men.

With the butts of their rifles, the Indians prodded the thieves off their horses. Once they had dismounted, the captors made sport of them, feinting and dancing wildly around them with shrieks and war whoops. Then, tying the rustlers' hands behind them, the braves motioned the men across the river in single file, forcing them to wade, hip-high, through the icy water.

In the village, a roaring fire had been built in the central-most location.

It was a disturbing sight, even for Tachechana, who was accustomed to Sioux tradition. The prisoners were made to sit in two rows of six, back to back. Their dead companion lay in Baxter's wagon. The drums throbbed as the warriors continued to hurl taunts and jeers at the captives, though, under Great Bear's watchful eye, they did not touch a hair of their heads.

Tachechana stood near him, her heart thudding in rhythm with the drums. "What will you do with them, Father?"

There was a long, almost unbearable pause. "This time," he said gravely, "I will try the white man's way. At sun-up, we will deliver this . . . vermin . . . to the Agency, and the white men can put them in their own cages!"

Fearfully, Tachechana turned to Baxter. "And what will happen to them then?"

"Normally, nothing." His jaw tensed in anger. "The agent would let them off scot-free, claiming too little evidence. But he can't deny my eyewitness report, and God helping me, I intend to see that these scoundrels are brought to justice!"

A dozen braves stood guard over the prisoners throughout the night, and another dozen, including Great Bear, rode out with the missionary in the morning. Great Bear said he wanted to be present when they turned the horse thieves over to the army.

Watching the procession disappear down the wagon trail the next night, Tachechana was vaguely uneasy. She had not slept well. Now, drawing in her breath, she was caught off guard by a sharp pain low in her back, and she bent double.

Eagle Feather, who was never far away these days, bounded to her side. "Tachechana, is it your time?"

"I don't know," she gasped. "Get Plainsfeather."

By the time the old woman returned, a crowd had gathered around Tachechana, murmuring and pointing with concern. Plainsfeather's ample form shunted them aside, and she squatted beside Tachechana.

"You hurt here?" She pointed to the corresponding portion of her own anatomy.

"Yes, though the pain comes and goes away again."

"Your baby wants to be born. Come. You rest."

The old woman and Eagle Feather helped her to her feet. Half-walking, half-carried along, Tachechana managed the distance to Great Bear's tepee, where Plainsfeather gave her a foul-tasting compound to drink. Nearly retching, Tachechana lowered herself to her sleeping pallet and lay still until the nausea passed.

"Is my child well?" she asked with concern.

"All is well. This is the way of women." She instructed Eagle Feather not to leave Tachechana's side until she returned with some articles she would need.

The moment the old woman disappeared through the doorway, Eagle Feather knelt beside Tachechana, brushing the glossy hair from her eyes. As an exceptionally angry contraction seized her, she took his hand and squeezed it. Looking into his face, she saw her pain mirrored there. For a moment she thought of Nathan when she was caught in Running Coyote's snare. He had looked at her with that same tenderness. She smiled to herself, realizing that the warrior's brash air was nothing more than a façade, lest anyone should see him as he really was and mistake his gentleness for weakness.

When Plainsfeather returned, she ordered Eagle Feather out, ignoring the pleading look in his eyes.

"I will be outside the door if you need me," he told the old woman, glancing with concern at the sleeping form of Tachechana.

In her drug-induced state, she saw another woman, a white woman with auburn hair and green eyes, lying on this very pallet. Instead of Eagle Feather, however, it was Great Bear who was watching over her as she gave birth to a girl child. In her dream, she could see that the woman was dying, and the baby was being placed in Great Bear's arms. The woman looked lovingly into her husband's face and said, "Her name shall be . . ."

". . . Tachechana! Tachechana!" Plainsfeather's voice drifted to her through the fog. "Do you have much pain? You moan in sleep."

"I was dreaming about my mother," she said weakly, refusing the thought so close on its heels—that maybe she, too, would die.

At that moment Great Bear entered the tepee, home from his mission to Pine Ridge. "How long has my daughter been like this?" he asked gruffly, attempting to conceal his deep emotion.

"For one full cycle of the sun," Plainsfeather replied. "It is the way of some small ones to wish to remain in warm nest." She shrugged her broad shoulders. "This one is Sioux—no worry."

Tachechana attempted a smile. The blood of her white mother also flowed in her veins—and her mother had died giving birth to her.

chapter

17

FOR THE NEXT FEW DAYS AND NIGHTS Tachechana drifted in and out of a stuporous sleep. When she was conscious, her normally even disposition raged out of control, and those nearest her became the target of her complaints.

On Christmas Day, Reverend Baxter stopped by with a basket of apples and green ribbons for her hair. Tachechana brightened to see him and even tied one of the ribbons in her braids. Her enjoyment was short-lived, however, for the excitement of his visit started a fresh spasm of pain that took her breath.

"It is time. Leave now." Plainsfeather tried to shoo the men out the door, but Reverend Baxter stared her down.

"I have not only come to rejoice with you in the birth of Christ, but to pray that the birth of Tachechana's child will go well."

Kneeling beside the pallet, he took her small hand in his. To her surprise, Eagle Feather knelt, too, taking her other hand. There was such agony in his countenance that she had to look away. No longer could she deny the depth of his love for her.

The missionary's prayer, spoken in reverent terms, gained conviction as he asked God to speed the birth and sustain

Tachechana through the pangs of delivery, concluding with heart-felt gratitude for hearing and answering their prayers. "Praise God and Amen!"

"A-men," came an unexpected echo from Eagle Feather.

Opening her eyes, Tachechana found his head still bowed. While he had understood few of Reverend Baxter's words, he, too, was imploring the Great Spirit in her behalf. The rush of warmth she felt for him at that moment was overpowered by a wrenching pain.

"I eeeeee!"

The men left quickly, allowing Plainsfeather to take over the task at hand.

Tachechana moaned a low-pitched moan that increased with each crescendo of pain. "Plainsfeather!" she cried out. "I am dying . . . just like . . . my mother!"

"You talk crazy talk," the old woman scolded. "This is time of life—not death. You work harder than ever before," she warned, "but when you see small one, you forget pain."

But for all her efforts, there was no sign of the child waiting to be born, and when, at the breaking of the day, Great Bear reappeared with Eagle Feather and Reverend Baxter, Plainsfeather could only shake her head sorrowfully.

All through the long day Tachechana labored, until her father could no longer bear the sound of her screams and fled to the river to pace frantically. Outside the tepee, both Reverend Baxter and Eagle Feather kept their vigil, not daring to leave lest she should call out for one of them.

When the moon rose full in the night sky, Tachechana was spent, and Plainsfeather could only stand by helplessly, tears streaming down her wrinkled cheeks.

"Fa . . . ther . . ." Tachechana attempted to speak. Great Bear was at her side instantly. "I try . . . so hard . . . but I die. . . . So . . . sorry. . . ."

Dry-eyed, Great Bear dropped his head, unwilling to witness that which had happened twenty years earlier, when the life of another green-eyed woman had ebbed away, leaving his heart empty and aching.

The young preacher fell to his knees and prayed as he had never prayed before. Admitting his ignorance of God's ways, he asked that Tachechana's life be spared. "But, Father," he prayed, "thy will be done . . . thy will be done."

Only Eagle Feather, it seemed, would not accept the inevitable. Springing to her side, he took one of the small hands and covered it in both of his. "Tachechana, listen to me," he begged, looking down into the pale face, her brow glistening with beads of sweat, her hair damp and lank. "You cannot die! I love you . . . more than my own life. Your God will not let you die . . . not now. I wish to believe as you believe. . . . Live, Tachechana, live!"

She smiled weakly at her childhood friend. "God . . . wills it. . . ." Then, seized by a blinding pain, she gave a little scream. Barely had she recovered from that onslaught than she was aware of a gush of water soaking her pallet.

Drawing near, Plainsfeather looked up, her face beaming with delight. "*Now* small one come! Go quickly!"

Consumed by the searing pain, Tachechana felt herself rising as if on some giant wave of the ocean she had never seen, then crashing into the depths of a black abyss. Again and again, she rode the swelling tide until at last her body was at peace.

When she opened her eyes, it was to see a tall figure holding a squalling infant in his arms, but to Tachechana's clouded mind, he was wearing buckskins instead of a black suit, and the face above the string tie was Nathan's.

"We have come to be with you, Nathan—your child and I—just as you said we would someday."

171

"It's not Nathan. It's Don Baxter." The man was smiling. "And you'll have to postpone that reunion for a while longer. You have a fine healthy son." He knelt to show her the child, warmly wrapped in the rabbit skin bunting.

"Oh, Nathan, how beautiful he is—like you," she said, looking at the babe through eyes glazed with fatigue. "I love you, Nathan."

Then, while the missionary knelt beside her, his arms filled with the newborn child, she reached for him. Pulling his head down, she lifted her lips to his, then slipped peacefully into deep slumber.

The sun was shining brightly when Tachechana was awakened by a tugging at her deerskin shirt. She opened her eyes to find Plainsfeather cutting a slit down the center of the shirt. Then the old woman turned, lifted a small bundle, and placed it in Tachechana's arms. The bundle stirred, nuzzling her soft breast and quickly finding the source of nourishment.

A thrill coursed through Tachechana. She was alive, and her baby was alive! As the infant gently sucked, she felt her heart being drawn from her chest, her love nourishing him as much as his mother's milk.

"Oh, Plainsfeather, he's beautiful! If only Nathan could see him."

"Perhaps he see, from his heaven. But I know men who walk the earth who love him too."

"Where are they? Father? Reverend Baxter? Eagle Feather? Have they seen him yet?"

"They see. They like." She cackled, her one tooth gleaming. "Mission man go back to Agency. Chief, Eagle Feather outside."

"Then call them in quickly, Plainsfeather." She gave the sleeping infant to the old woman, smoothed her hair, and

172

arranged her shirt modestly. She would not be like her Sioux sisters, she decided, nursing her baby for all to see. She was a lady—like her mother.

Great Bear went immediately to the sleeping child and picked him up. Only rarely had Tachechana seen that look in his eyes when he gazed at her. Pride and gratitude and great joy mingled there.

"The child must be given a name," he said reverently. "It must not be said that the grandson of Great Bear goes unnamed."

Eagle Feather, who had dropped down beside Tachechana upon entering the tepee, now spoke. "Will he bear his father's name?" he asked.

"No," she said slowly, watching Eagle Feather's guarded expression carefully. "There can be only one Nathan. But there is a name my husband loved. Caleb. Nathan's son shall be called Caleb."

"Caleb? ... And what is the meaning of such a name?" Looking up from the tiny bundle in his arms, Great Bear turned an inquiring gaze on his daughter. "It is no Sioux name."

"Caleb is a name in Nathan's Bible. He was a man like Great Bear and Nathan ... and Eagle Feather," she added quickly, "who was a great warrior and always spoke the truth."

"Then Caleb must have been a Sioux," the chief said with a roar of laughter. "I didn't know the white man's Bible spoke of the Sioux."

The minutes sped by like the flight of the bumblebee, and Tachechana felt herself tiring. Under Plainsfeather's scrutiny, she felt both protected and dominated, for soon the old woman was sending them all away so she could gain her strength.

173

"He good man," Plainsfeather mumbled when they had ducked through the doorway of the tepee.

"My father?" Tachechana asked, curious that the old woman should speak so. "I have always known that. Now Caleb will know him, too—his wisdom and strength. . . ."

"I not talk of Great Bear," she said mysteriously. "I talk of Eagle Feather."

"Eagle Feather?" Tachechana cocked her head to one side, eager to hear more.

"Do you remember when you say you dying?"

Tachechana nodded, her green eyes wide.

"Eagle Feather not let you go. . . . He love you much. He pray for you."

Tachechana sighed. *Poor Eagle Feather,* she thought. *First I marry Nathan who takes all my love, and now I have Caleb. Who will love Eagle Feather?*

"He not only one," Plainsfeather said. "Baxter love you, too."

"Oh, Plainsfeather, stop your teasing. Reverend Baxter is engaged to wed another woman. Besides, I'm a mother now."

"You woman first . . . with no father for child." The look in the old woman's eyes was sobering.

Day by day, Tachechana grew stronger, absorbing herself in the care of her child and taking delight in every new discovery. His round eyes were grey as the morning fog, and his complexion, though not as dusky as her own, looked as if it had been kissed by the sun. Unlike other Indian babies, his dark hair curled in downy ringlets.

She happened to be alone in the tepee with Caleb when she heard the sound of Reverend Baxter's wagon rolling into the village at a faster pace than usual.

"Tachechana!" he shouted as the wagon pulled to a stop in front of the tepee. "Tachechana!"

174

"What is it?" she said as he stepped through the door. "What is wrong?"

He scooped her up in his powerful arms and swung her around. Then, realizing what he was doing, he deposited her gently on the earthen floor.

"What a marvelous woman you are!" he exclaimed. "You've brought about a miracle—an undisputed miracle!"

She shook her head in wonder. "It is not I who brought the miracle," she said, eying him curiously. "Caleb is a miracle, but God heard your prayers, and Eagle Feather's, and saved us from—"

"No, no!" He beamed. "Little Caleb is, indeed, a miracle, and we all love the little tyke and thank the Good Lord for sparing him . . . but I refer to a letter you wrote to Jane some time ago."

Tachechana gasped. The letter! She had forgotten all about it. Perhaps Jane had released him from his proposal of marriage, and now he was here to claim Tachechana herself. His prayers had great power. She was much in his debt. If not for Reverend Baxter, she and Caleb might not be alive today. But did she love him enough to—

". . . so she is making plans now to travel west so we can be married," Baxter interrupted her tangled thoughts. "And I owe it all to you!"

"Oh," she said in a small voice.

"Is that all you have to say? I would have thought that, of all people, you would be rejoicing most. If I recall rightly, you delivered some pretty powerful sermons about trusting God and—"

"Oh, Reverend Baxter, I am most happy for you . . . and for your Jane!" she hurried on. But there was a strange sense of loss that dimmed the joy she felt for him, like the sun suddenly covered with a thin veil of clouds. Once Jane arrived, things between them could never be quite the same.

Tachechana did not fail to note Eagle Feather's reaction to the news. The rest of the day he walked around the village with a smile that reminded her of the expression on the face of a coyote with a jack rabbit in his mouth. No matter how hard he tried, he could not conceal a broad grin each time he chanced to see her.

The grin changed to a grimace of distaste when, that very afternoon, Captain Baker's Second Cavalry rode into the village. It was easy to find Tachechana after the soldiers arrived. All Eagle Feather had to do was look for a patch of red hair. It was certain to be in the vicinity of Tachechana. And when he saw Trooper O'Connel sitting on the ledge of the well with her, he stalked off in a huff.

"Ah, Miz Cooper, 'tis a fine lookin' lad ye have there," the young trooper said, admiring the baby on his cradle board.

"Thank you. I think he looks like his father, don't you?"

"Aye, that he does, and he's a boy any man would be proud to claim as his own. . . . Meanin' no offense, ma'am, but a lad such as he deserves a father."

She laughed. "Caleb has many fathers. Every man in the village gives him love and attention. Soon, I fear, he will be greatly spoiled."

"Oh, to be sure he has all the attention he needs . . . at least for the time." Tachechana smiled to herself as the red of his hair seemed to bleed into his cheeks. "Beggin' your pardon for rushin' ye, ma'am, but I would count it a pleasure and an honor to give the boy a proper home if ye could be waitin' for this campaign to be over."

"It is I who am honored, but I'm afraid I must refuse. You see, I don't intend to remarry at all. My child fills the lonely place that Nathan left when he died. Somewhere, though, I know there is a woman, perhaps a fine Irish girl, who could share your home."

176

"I kinda' thought that's what you would be sayin', but I had to speak my mind. I'll not soon be forgettin' ye, Miz Cooper."

"And I'll never forget you." There was genuine regret in her voice.

With that, he turned on his heel and marched back to rejoin the soldiers who were mounting their horses for the ride out.

"Well," Tachechana said to Caleb, who was sleeping nearby, "if only Eagle Feather would believe my words as easily as the other two, I could take up my life again and be happy with you, my small one."

chapter
18

THE WARM APRIL SUN DOMINATED A FLOCK of sheep-like clouds as they wandered across the blue pasture of the sky. Their meanderings cast shadows on the hills and plains below that, at an earlier time, might have been mistaken for herds of buffalo roaming the prairie. In spite of the loveliness of the day, Tachechana's heart was heavy, for only one year ago on a day exactly like this one, she and Nathan had ridden off to Fort Fetterman to be married.

Sitting by the swollen waters of the White River, she looked down at her child. He was staring at her face, and his smile of recognition lighted the dark corners of her heart. The sun shining on his hair made it appear more brown than black. But it was his eyes that were his most arresting feature. Now past the early months of his infancy, his eyes had darkened to a grayish hue, a color that could be as warm as dusk in summer, or as cold as the clouds in winter with a change of his mood. It was agreed by all that Caleb's eyes spoke for him long before he uttered a sound.

She kissed her finger and placed it on his lips. "That is from your father," she crooned.

His chubby little fingers wrapped around her slender one, and he waved it vigorously, kicking his feet up and down with a chortle of joy.

Tachechana could not restrain the giggle which erupted from her own throat, quickly followed by a string of silly sounds she would have been embarrassed to make in the presence of others. Seeing his plump little body filled her with a joy unlike anything she had known, and she murmured a prayer of thanksgiving.

"God has given me the only love I need," she said aloud.

Lifting Caleb into her arms, she followed the path to the village.

The creaking of leather and the squeaking of wheels announced the arrival of Reverend Baxter's wagon almost before he drove into sight. Normally Tachechana would be looking forward to his visit, but this was different. Today he brought his new wife to the village for the first time—his wife from the city of St. Louis.

As soon as the wagon wheels rolled to a stop, the missionary sprang to the ground.

"Tachechana," he called, "can you help us? Jane is not used to traveling long hours by wagon. She's exhausted. Will you take her to your tepee to rest while we unload the supplies?"

"Of course. Come." She handed Caleb, cradle board and all, to Plainsfeather and helped the preacher assist his wife from the wagon. They entered the tepee. Tachechana motioned to her own pallet, and Jane fairly collapsed onto it.

Looking down at her guest, Tachechana could see why Donald had never been able to put her out of his mind. In spite of the fatigue caused by the long journey and the woman's apparent frailty, she was fair to look upon. In fact, Tachechana had never laid eyes on a creature more pleasing to the eyes. For a fleeting moment, she wondered if her own mother might have looked something like Jane Baxter.

She looked on in fascination as her guest untied the strings of her bonnet with elegant, tapered fingers. A cascade of honey-colored hair tumbled over slender shoulders. The woman shook out the tangled curls, and even in the subdued light of the tepee, Tachechana felt as if the sun were shining. The glorious hair framed an oval face and blue eyes that were staring back at Tachechana with equal interest.

"So you are Donald's Sioux princess," the golden one said.

"I am Tachechana, daughter of Great Bear," she replied, drawing herself up to her full height. She must not let the woman know that she was awed by her presence.

"I'm so happy to meet you at last . . . glad for this chance to chat a bit . . . undisturbed." She glanced around, seeing the men still busy about their task of unloading.

"You wish to say things you do not want your husband to hear?"

"I suppose so." The woman's laughter was like the tinkle of a bell. "I want to thank you for writing to me. It was your letter that helped me realize how much I loved Donald and needed to be with him. Your kindness gave me the courage to try."

"He loves you very much."

The lady slanted her a curious sidelong look. "But we were separated for quite a long time. You must have known that he was enchanted with you—that you could have had him all to yourself."

"But I am married—"

"Yes, yes," Jane interrupted. "I know all about your dead husband." Catching sight of Tachechana's stricken face, she put out her hand. "Oh, dear! I shouldn't have said that! It's just that Donald and I have discussed your situation so often. And he thinks you're in love with a memory and are shutting out any other chance for joy and happiness." Seeing Tachechana relax a bit, she went on. "God gives us fond memories so we can heal . . . but there comes a time when we must no longer live in the past, but look for the future he has planned for us."

At that moment Plainsfeather entered the lodge with Caleb in her arms. "The small pup whines for his mother," she said in Sioux, assessing Jane boldly with her eyes.

Tachechana took the child from her. "I see no tears."

"He is with his mother now," Plainsfeather responded, her gaze never leaving the golden-haired guest.

With a smile of understanding, Tachechana translated the old woman's words and explained the curiosity that had prompted her presence in the tepee. When the two younger women burst into laughter, Plainsfeather joined them.

"May I hold the baby?" Jane asked.

Tachechana untied the boy from his cradle board and handed him to Jane, whose eyes took on a lustrous sheen of pleasure. She held his soft cheek to her own and hugged the baby close.

Seeing them together, Tachechana felt a stir of uneasiness. Her baby could pass for white even now . . . and when he grew up. . . . Would he forget his Sioux ways? A lump lodged in her throat. The old ways were passing. Soon they would be no more if the white man continued to rule the prairie.

When Caleb began to whimper, his eyes clouding over with the approaching thunderstorm, Plainsfeather reached for him and took him away to rewrap him in a clean blanket.

Jane stared after the old woman thoughtfully. "She reminds me of my own grandmother, who, I'm afraid, spoiled my sisters and me outrageously." Turning to Tachechana, she bestowed a radiant smile on her. "I have so much to learn about your people. I'm beginning to suspect, though, that there are more similarities than differences. I do hope we can be good friends."

"That is my hope, too," Tachechana admitted, "ever since Reverend Baxter ... your husband ... first spoke of you. I wish to learn how to be more like ... like you."

"Me? Why, whatever for? You're beautiful just as you are. My friends in St. Louis would turn green if they could see your striking coloring. . . ."

Tachechana was horrified. "Turn *green?*"

"Oh, my! I can see how difficult our language must be for you. I only meant that you are a very beautiful young lady."

"Yes, a lady is what I most want to be, but I am just a clumsy Sioux squaw." She dropped her eyes in embarrassment.

"You mustn't belittle yourself that way, Tachechana," Jane scolded gently.

"My mother was white ... a lady ... like you. I want to be like her. Will you teach me?"

Jane studied her face intently. "I think you are already quite a lady. But if it would make you happy, I'll teach you anything you want to know. . . ."

Their conversation halted as Great Bear, Eagle Feather, and Reverend Baxter entered the tepee. Donald introduced his bride to the two Indians, using a mixture of English and the little Sioux he had learned.

"How do," Great Bear said in English, to Tachechana's great surprise, extending his hand in the manner of white men. Jane took it with a ready smile.

Eagle feather grinned widely, showing even white teeth. "Tell her she is welcome. Now I need not worry that the *Wasichus* will win Tachechana from me."

Tachechana was both embarrassed and angry, but a quick survey of the couple's expressions told her she had no cause for believing that either of them had understood.

"What did he say?" Jane asked.

"Just that he is happy to meet you," Tachechana replied in English. Annoyed, she turned to Eagle Feather. "How can anyone win me from you when you don't own me?"

Donald and Jane exchanged knowing looks. Seeing this, Tachechana dashed out the door, saying something about fetching firewood to prepare the evening meal.

Safely outside, she muttered under her breath. "Why can I not live in peace? Why is it that everyone wishes to see me married? If I am ever ready to be wife to a man again, only I will decide!"

By the time she returned with an armload of wood, she had regained her composure.

Great Bear caught six catfish in his fish trap that day and had them all cleaned and skinned when Tachechana brought the smoldering ashes of a fire back to life with some slivers of dry wood. It seemed only minutes until the aromas of broiling fish and fresh bread filled the lodge.

Jane appeared amazed that Tachechana could actually bake bread over an open fire. "It never occurred to me that one could actually wrap dough around a stick and twirl it near the fire until the crust was such a lovely golden-brown."

Later, at the meal, Tachechana noticed that Jane was having difficulty gathering up her skirts to sit cross-legged on the ground, but she managed, licking her fingers like the others to catch every morsel of the food cooked over the glowing coals.

The meal was hardly over when the drums began to throb near the heart of the village. Jane moved closer to her husband, obviously frightened. Reverend Baxter smiled reassuringly and patted her hand.

"The chief has invited us to a dance," he explained.

"Is it right for Christians to be involved in pagan ceremonies?" Jane asked Donald, keeping her voice low.

Tachechana listened carefully to his answer.

"This isn't a pagan ceremony," he said. "It's a chance for us to get better acquainted with these people and show them our interest in their culture. Besides, the dance is being given in our honor."

The dance proved an exciting event for Jane. She was intrigued to see the warriors spin and whirl, depicting various stages of the hunt or battle. And when the women began to dance their own slower steps, gracefully bobbing and bowing before their husbands or special friends, she clasped her hands together, blue eyes wide.

But even Tachechana was surprised when her father rose, took Donald Baxter by the hand, and led him into the circle of dancers. In the very center of the circle, Great Bear helped Donald remove his jacket and placed on him a buckskin shirt, the symbol of the warrior. Then the chief led him around the circle in a slow dance step. By this time all the braves had formed a circle, each with a willow switch in his hand.

As Donald and Great Bear passed by, the braves would reach out to lightly tap Donald with the switch. But each time the chief placed himself between him and the switch and received the stroke on his own back. When each of the braves had taken their turn, the two danced again to the center. Immediately, the drums hushed, and there was complete silence.

Great Bear removed a deerskin thong from around his own neck and tied it around Donald's. "With this thong you are bound to Great Bear and to his village. You are forever Lakota!"

Bewildered, Jane turned wide eyes on Tachechana. "What does this mean?"

"It means your husband has been accepted into our tribe," she explained with a smile. "It means he is Sioux now, and will always be honored and welcome among us."

185

chapter
19

THROUGHOUT THE LONG HOT SUMMER OF 1877, the river of joy in Tachechana's heart ebbed and flowed in turn. Nothing gave her greater joy than watching Caleb's growth as he said his first lisping words, took his first halting steps. She doted on her firstborn. But, at times, he seemed more to her than a child, and she even found herself calling him by Nathan's name.

She thrilled to see the antics of her father when he played with the boy. Never had she seen the chief so animated. His usually solemn countenance came to life each time he glimpsed the child.

Eagle Feather, too, was always at hand to keep a close watch over the boy and to delight in his progress. But Tachechana wondered if he would have been so attentive had she not been Caleb's mother. Still, it was comforting to know that her son would not lack for the love of good men.

Because of Plainsfeather's devotion and the hovering presence of the men, Tachechana was free to pursue her own tasks. The words she wrote phonetically and defined for the big preacher were beginning to develop into a large dictionary.

When Reverend Baxter began to speak to the Indians in

their language, they listened with new interest. Sadly, though, they could not comprehend his message of God's love, nor could they understand how a white man's death on a cross so many years ago could affect them. As prisoners on the white man's reservation, they would listen politely, but they were singleminded in their desire to return to their sacred Black Hills and live as they had always lived.

Meanwhile there was constant fear accompanied by times of great sorrow. News often drifted into Great Bear's village of bands of Sioux who were attacked by soldiers and dragged back to the reservation. Others fought rather than give up their freedom, and their blood painted the prairie red just as Captain Baker had predicted. In the Bad Lands to the north, patrols of blue-coated soldiers hunted up small groups of Indians like so many cattle and either marched them onto the reservation, or shot them down in cold blood.

Some chiefs voluntarily brought their bands to the reservation when they ran out of ammunition or food for their people. Some came, like Great Bear, with the hope that soon they would be back in their homes on the land they loved.

Word came that the Rose Bud Agency was stricken with a plague of smallpox. Panic clamped its iron hand around every heart. Many would not believe Reverend Baxter when he tried to quell the rumor, explaining that this was chicken-pox—a less dangerous affliction. As time passed and most of the people recovered, the fears subsided, but the dread epidemic still lived in their memory. Another like it, and the white man would never again have to worry about the Sioux menace. What rifles and cannon could not do, sickness would.

When Reverend Baxter's wagon arrived with the Indians' August supplies, Tachechana noticed it was not nearly as full as it had been on previous trips.

"Something happened to part of the shipment on the way to the Agency," he said with a frown when Tachechana inquired. "They say everything will be back to normal next month."

"But is there enough to last until you return?" she asked.

"Probably not," he admitted with a frown. "You may have to supplement your rations with fish."

She shook her head. "August is not a good time to catch fish."

"I know. That's why I brought this." He handed her a small, heavy sack. "Don't open it now," he cautioned, looking around. "It's ammunition for the braves. They may need to do some hunting. I could get in trouble for giving it to you, but I trust you to keep it from any who might turn hostile."

Feeling a burden of guilt, she took the sack to her father's lodge and put it under her sleeping pad. She would tell him about it after the missionary left. *It is good to have bullets for our rifles,* she thought, *but will we find game?*

"What was in the sack the missionary gave you?" Eagle Feather asked after Reverend Baxter left.

"It was something for my father," she replied evasively.

"Why didn't he give it to your father then?"

"He wanted me to give it to him." She did not meet his gaze.

"He gave you a gift, didn't he?"

"No . . ."

"Why do you accept gifts from him and not from me? He is a married man. Are you going to be his second wife?" He stomped off before she could reply.

Great Bear, who had been observing from afar, walked up. "Why is Eagle Feather angry?"

"He thought I accepted a gift from Donald . . . Reverend Baxter, but it was some ammunition for our rifles so we could hunt for food."

"So, it begins again," said the chief. "What good are bullets when the buffalo have all been killed? And why does he think we could not hunt with our old weapons? Does the preacher think we have become white men who need guns to hunt?" He glowered. "The missionary wants us to worship like he worships, speak like he speaks, hunt like he hunts." He spat. "We are not white! We are Sioux!"

Tachechana felt his frustration. "Father, becoming a Christian is not the same as becoming a white man. God is the Great Spirit of both Indians and whites, and Jesus is his Son."

"The Great Spirit is Indian!" he insisted. "He created the Ancient Ones, the Hopi, from whom we have all sprung."

She knew her father's anger, but dared to press him. "You know the Hopi legend well. You know it teaches the Great Spirit also created a White Brother for the Hopi and that he would come to this land to be reunited with his Indian Brothers."

"But the White Brother left the way of the Hopi. He lives *koyaanisqatzi*—the crazy life."

"You are a wise chief, my father, and I am your daughter. I will not argue with you. But I must ask one more question. Do the Sioux live the same life as the Hopi?"

Tachechana knew she had struck the target. Many things had changed in the days since the Hopi were the only Indians, farming the land and living in square houses. Could it be that the Sioux themselves were living *koyaanisqatzi*—a life out of tune with the song of Mother Earth? Since Tachechana had asked herself this question, she knew the struggle of her father by the cloud that seemed to drift between them.

"Where are the white man's bullets?" he asked abruptly.

She knew the subject was closed for now, but her father would remember her words. "Under my bed in the tepee," she answered.

That night Tachechana was surprised to find the sack where she had placed it earlier. *I wonder why he didn't take the bullets,* she thought. *Is he upset that Donald Baxter thought he needed them to feed our people?*

Her prayers that night were for her father—that he would accept the Jesus Way. If peace could not come to the prairie, at least it could come to their hearts.

At dawn's breaking, the village was astir. Great Bear had announced there would be a hunt, and all the braves were mounted on their ponies, ready to ride out to look for buffalo. The chief, however, had made provision for the protection of the women and children and the herd of horses they would leave behind.

It was decided that the warriors would be divided into three groups. One armed group, with Eagle Feather in charge, was to remain at the village in case of a raid. A second band was dispatched to the highest places, the mud stone pinnacles, to watch for army patrols. When they were satisfied that no white soldiers marched in their area, they were to build a small fire of dry wood so the trail of white smoke would tell the hunters it was safe. If a patrol should be sighted, they would add green wood or greasy grass to the fire to cause ballooning clouds of black smoke to alert their brothers to danger.

Great Bear led the third group on the hunt, but only after each of the spies sent up their white columns of smoke.

Throughout the day all eyes were on the seven white wisps of smoke as the village busied itself with their daily tasks. The women and children, accustomed to seeing hunting parties leave the village, tried to ignore the armed sentries guarding them, yet those wraiths of smoke were reminders to all that their homeland had become a land hostile to them.

A fire was kept burning in the village with a large supply of greasy grass stacked nearby. If something should happen at the village, the black smoke could easily be seen by those on the pinnacles and relayed to the hunters. Black smoke would bring all the braves into the village at a gallop.

But there was no black smoke. Just before dark Great Bear and his hunters rode into the village from the east, splashing across the river. There was no talk. Tachechana knew it was a bad sign. Then she saw two deer tied on horses behind two of the hunters and was puzzled by the mood. While two deer would only last a day or two, it meant there was still game in the vicinity. They would not starve.

Then she saw the body of one of the hunters slung across the back of his horse, and heard the death chant begin its mournful wail.

"What happened, Father? Who was hurt?" she cried, running to greet Great Bear.

"It is the young brave, Black Dog. He was bitten by a rattlesnake."

"How could that happen?"

"Living on the white man's food made him forget the ways of the Indian. He was climbing up a rocky pinnacle to see if there was game for the hunters. He put his hand higher than his eyes, and the snake bit him here and here." Great Bear indicated two places bearing fang marks on his right arm. "He died quickly."

The work of caring for the meat and hides progressed with the usual Sioux thoroughness, but none of the lightheartedness that helped to ease the work. There was no retelling of the hunt, no laughter. The wail of the death chant and the flickering light of the fire, with its bloody reflections on the walls of the tepees, kept all the villagers in a somber mood.

"What will we do about Black Dog's funeral?" Tachechana asked her father as they ate their venison supper.

"It is not safe to try to take his body back to the burial grounds in the Black Hills, and we are not permitted to bury our dead in the way of the Sioux on the reservation. We will put him in the ground as the white men do."

"Will you send someone to ask Reverend Baxter to pray for him at the burying?" she asked.

"No. We are not whites, and Black Dog was not a Christian. He would not have died if the white men had left us alone to live as we always have. We will put him in the ground without the white man's prayers."

"Does my father forget that his wife, my mother, was white and a Christian, and my husband Nathan?"

"They were only white on the outside. In their hearts, they were Lakota."

"You also called Reverend Baxter your brother." Tachechana knew the chief was touched by her argument, but saw the resolve in his eyes. Black Dog would be buried without the benefit of the missionary's prayers.

"Is my father thinking of leaving this place?"

"No," the chief answered after a long silence. "As much as I want to see my horses standing in grass up to their bellies, I know the dangers you and my grandson would face if we left. I grieve to think that the young Gray Wolf will never see the way of the Sioux as it once was. We must tell him and the other children of past glories. They must never forget what a great people we were."

"We are the same people we always were, Father. Once there is peace on the prairie, things will get better."

"Even if the white man and the Indians live in peace, we will be forever caught up in their *koyaanisqatzi*, the life of turmoil. Nothing changes that."

"May I speak hard words to my father?"

"Speak."

"My father, I have found an answer to the life of turmoil. When I took up the Christian way, God gave me a new life. That new life takes the turmoil out of living—even in the strange world of the white man. It helped me when my husband died, and God's Book says the new life I have will live on after my body dies and I enter the Spirit World."

"But I am Lakota of the Sioux." His head rose in pride and defiance.

"And I am your daughter."

"There is much of your mother in you."

"Do you deny me my Sioux birthright?"

"No. You are my daughter."

"Then the Jesus Way is for you as it is for me . . . for all people."

"We will talk more of this later," the chief said as he got up and walked to where his horse was grazing. Calling back over his shoulder, he said, "You shall decide where Black Dog will be buried."

Will he ever really listen to me? Tachechana asked herself as she watched him leave.

Early the next morning Tachechana visited Black Dog's mother. "My father, the chief, says Black Dog is to be buried in the ground because we cannot go to the Black Hills for a tree burial."

The grief-stricken mother nodded in mute agreement. Her son would be buried in the white man's way. Everything was done in the white man's way. The way of the Sioux was passing.

She went with Tachechana to find a suitable place for the grave. They walked together south of the village, up Medicine Creek. On a grass-covered knoll, they stopped to look around. To the south, they could trace the course of the creek by the trees that lined its banks. To the north, they looked down on all the lodges of the village. Black Dog would rest here.

But Tachechana felt a shock of alarm. Remembering how carefully Nathan had situated his cabin at the box canyon so that no one could fire down upon it from the surrounding hills, she realized suddenly how vulnerable her father's village was. If held by white soldiers or renegades, this hill could be the rallying place for a massacre. She would talk to her father about it. They would never be safe as long as this hill remained unprotected.

At Tachechana's request, several villagers dug a grave for the youth. She helped the mother prepare Black Dog's body and selected the weapons that would be buried with him. Then, on a travois pulled by the horse he had ridden just the day before, the young brave was escorted to his eternal resting place.

Six armed braves were left behind to guard the horses while the rest of the village walked slowly along behind the body, wailing the traditional death chant. Tachechana and Black Dog's mother walked directly behind the body. All the way up the hill, she looked at the lifeless form of the young Indian, wondering if any of Reverend Baxter's words had touched his heart.

At the grave Great Bear made the decree that Black Dog's horse was not to be killed and buried with him. Though the braves were visibly disturbed, none would challenge the chief's decision. Tachechana knew their thoughts. They did not want to send a brave off to the Spirit World with no horse on which to ride. Yet, they knew the hunt had not been successful. Black Dog's horse would provide enough meat to feed the village for a week.

The rest of the day was spent in quiet mourning. Most conversations eventually reverted to talk of the old days, when the Sioux were free to roam the prairie and the beautiful Black Hills with their deep lakes and clear running streams. A spirit of restlessness settled on them along with the shadeless heat of late summer. The day droned on, but night slowly crept across the Bad Lands, bringing with the darkness, cooler air and sleep.

The next day dawned oppressively hot. Children were splashing in the milky water of the White River before some of the adults had stirred from their sleeping pads. It was the playful chatter and squeals of delight made by the children that awakened Tachechana. Surprised that her father had already left the tepee, she leaped from her bed to prepare his morning meal.

When she didn't see him in the village, she looked across Medicine Creek. His favorite war horse was not among the others. She rushed back inside the lodge and discovered his rifle missing too.

"I wonder where he has gone," she said aloud, though no one was near enough to hear.

It was well past noon when Great Bear rode into the village from the west. Tied on either side of his horse directly behind him were a pair of flour sacks. Each sack contained about twenty pounds of freshly caught catfish.

"Call the women of the village to the council circle," he told Tachechana. "I want you to talk to them for me." No chief would deign to speak directly to an assembly of women, she knew.

Obediently, Tachechana started for the nearest tepee and called some girls to help her spread the word. Nearly all the men followed at a distance to see what was going on.

"Dump the fish out on the grass," the chief ordered Tachechana.

There were many cries of surprise and pleasure when the women saw the size and number of fish.

"Tell them there are many more where these came from, but they must learn to catch them a new way."

Tachechana relayed the message, and waited for the chief to continue.

"Tell them the fish are in the colder water of the deep holes. They must build their traps downstream, then get in the water and drive the fish into the traps."

Again Tachechana relayed the message, even though the women could hear Great Bear's speech for themselves.

"Tomorrow you must find many deep holes in both streams. Catch all the fish you can. Then dry them as you do venison jerky. You must catch enough fish to feed the village until the aspen leaves begin to fall and it is once again safe to eat jack rabbit."

At the thought of a good supply of fresh fish in late summer, an almost festive mood prevailed throughout the village. They did not relish the corned beef and salt pork provided by the white man's government. And while the prospect of jack rabbit was not much better, at least it was something they could provide for themselves.

"Tell the old ones to help themselves first, then the others," the chief instructed, following the way of the Sioux.

"How did you find the fish?" Tachechana asked her father after selecting two choice ones for their supper.

"It was something your husband taught me the first time we met. He was fishing with a stick and string, trying to land a large trout when I killed a big rattlesnake that would have bitten him. It was then he told me fish like cold water in the summer. He always fished the deep holes."

A lump of sadness twisted itself in Tachechana's throat as she thought of her fishing trips with Nathan. Then sadness mellowed into pride. Long after his death, Nathan was still a part of the life of the village just as he lived on in her every thought.

chapter

20

ANTICIPATION RIPPLED THROUGH GREAT BEAR'S VILLAGE as the women and children assembled at the council circle the next morning. Since Great Bear talked to the women through Tachechana, everyone assumed she was the leader for the fishing expedition, an honor and responsibility she accepted naturally. She could not help smiling at the thought. Only a little over two years ago, they had denounced her for trying to act like a brave instead of a squaw. Now they looked to her for leadership.

She divided the women into three groups, keeping the same number of tall people in each group. These would be needed to walk through the deep holes to drive the fish into the traps. One group traveled up the White River, while another went downstream. Tachechana led the group bound for Medicine Creek. While the older women cared for the babies and toddlers, everyone else gathered sticks as they proceeded. The sticks were used to form the funnel that guided the fish into the narrow opening of the box-shaped trap, where the boys would spear them and throw them onto the bank and the girls would quickly stuff them into sacks. Even Tachechana was surprised at the catch they made at the first hole.

About three-quarters of a mile up Medicine Creek, the group came upon a low glade, surrounded by an abundance of cottonwood trees. Were it not for the size and color of the creek, it would be just like the place where Tachechana used to swim when she lived at the box canyon cabin. The deep hole was longer and deeper than any of the previous three. Even the tallest women found the water to be over their heads when they tried to drive the fish to the trap. The catch was disappointing.

Still, it was such a peaceful place Tachechana decided to allow the group to rest for a while. She sat with the other women and the small ones in the shade, while the older children splashed in the stream. After a few moments of idle chatter, Tachechana rose to scout the area for game to hunt or food to forage. She wandered aimlessly among the trees and back to the high bank that was its west border.

There, in a small clearing, she made a shocking discovery—the ashes from a recent campfire, and footprints . . . the footprints of a white man!

She put her hand into the ashes. "Warm!" she said under her breath. Her eyes were everywhere at once. Her hand went to the knife she always carried in her sash-belt.

Cautiously she began circling the area, her warrior instincts suddenly acutely alive. As leader of this group she felt responsible for its safety. But she could not determine where the tracks led. Even more baffling, there were no horse tracks. How could a white man come to this remote region without a horse and disappear without a sign? She carefully covered her own tracks and made her way back.

"We must return to the village," she called. "The chief will be pleased when he sees how many fish we have caught!"

The children, still splashing happily, objected when their play was cut short but obeyed instantly, and soon the group of fisherfolk were wending their way back down Medicine Creek toward the village. With Plainsfeather in the lead, Tachechana hung back to cover the rear and make sure all her people returned safely. No one noticed the frequent glances she cast over her shoulder all the way home.

"We caught many fish in the first three holes," she reported to her father upon their arrival in the village, "but the fourth was too deep, and we could not make the fish swim into the trap."

"Why didn't you go to the next hole?"

"We had several small ones with us. I didn't want to tire your grandson or the others." She spoke the truth, but it was only a half-truth, for it was better to find out more about the things she had seen than to tell her father and alarm the whole village, she thought as Great Bear walked away.

That evening, after all the fish had been filleted and hung on the drying racks, and the evening meal eaten, Tachechana walked to the edge of Medicine Creek and called to Fox, who was grazing in the corral on the other side. Effortlessly, the horse jumped the fence, splashed across the creek, and pranced to her side. Tenderly she stroked the animal's velvety nose. "Let's ride, Fox," she murmured.

Then, reaching above her own head, Tachechana grabbed a handful of mane, and with a pull and a jump, she was on Fox's back. Riding into the sunset, Tachechana gave the mare her head for a span of almost two miles before reining her in and circling to the south and east.

The last of the sun's afterglow had faded from the sky when horse and rider topped the hill where Black Dog was buried. From this vantage point, halfway between the village and the glade where she had discovered the footprints, she could see a small glow reflecting from the treetops. The intruder was there again tonight.

201

Turning Fox toward the glade at a slow walk, she nervously fingered the knife in her sash belt. Her heart beat faster as she neared the area. While a distance of over a hundred yards from the bank, she dismounted and told Fox to stay. Carefully now, with every sense honed, she proceeded to the high bank and peered over. At first, the small campfire dazzled her eyes, and she could see nothing. Then she made out the form of a man sitting with his back to her.

He appeared to be a big man with wide shoulders, but from the sag of them, Tachechana sensed he posed no threat to her. Still, the figure was vaguely, disturbingly familiar. But how could she learn his identity unless she could see his face?

She picked up a stone the size of a hen's egg and threw it into the brush about twenty yards to the north of where the man sat. To her surprise, instead of investigating the noise, he rolled over backwards and disappeared.

Puzzled, Tachechana waited, her pulse pounding in her neck. Perhaps he was aware of her position and was sneaking up the hill toward her even now. Quietly, on moccasined feet, she sprinted back to Fox and sprang onto her back, nudging her into a full gallop. But when she looked behind her, no one was pursuing her and she could see nothing but the faint glimmer of the campfire illuminating the tops of the trees.

By the time she had corralled Fox and waded the stream to the village, the chill of excitement had dissipated, and her breathing was even when she entered her father's tepee.

He gave her a sharp look. "Where have you been?"

"Giving Fox some exercise," she replied nonchalantly.

"Humph," he grunted. "You should not travel so far from the village by yourself. The night is filled with surprises."

Tachechana recalled her father's admonition from childhood and pursued it. "Is my father aware of anything that might come as a surprise to his people?"

202

"The chief watches over his people always," he replied noncomittally. "It is our way."

Great Bear didn't return to the tepee until long after Tachechana had retired. As she lay on her bed, her mind leaped from one thought to another. Who was the big man in the glade? How and to where did he disappear? How much did her father know of him? Were others hiding nearby? Finally, What would happen to Caleb if trouble arose? A restless sleep ended her questioning.

The sun had risen fully above the horizon when Tachechana was shaken from her sleep by the sounds of the death chant. Her first thought was to look for Caleb, but he was playing with the wooden horse Eagle Feather carved for him.

Without taking time to comb her hair, she rushed out to find one of the old men sitting in front of his tepee, moaning the chant. Without a word, she entered to find her father and several others bending over the old man's wife, who had died in her sleep.

Convinced that her death was caused naturally, the chief backed out of the tepee and sat beside the old man. The others, following his example, joined in the melancholy song while Tachechana and some of the older women prepared the body for burial.

Looking toward the hill where Black Dog lay in his grave, she saw several of the young braves digging once again. *How long,* she wondered, *before that hill is covered with the graves of my people?*

Because of the heat, the chief decided that the burial would take place that afternoon. Every care must be taken to assure the health of the villagers. Still the old man sat, rocking back and forth in his sorrow.

The sun had already passed its zenith when the burial

procession began its mournful journey. The chief, leading one of his own war horses, dragged the travois on which the body of the old woman lay, her husband at the chief's side. The rest of the mourners followed.

At the grave site, Tachechana looked back at the village and was surprised to see several of her father's finest warriors at the corral, watching the horses. Scanning the southern horizon near the location of the glade, she felt Great Bear's eyes on her. *Does he know, or is he trying to read my thoughts?* she wondered.

Throughout the chanting and covering of the body, Tachechana found herself looking into the face of Great Bear, his piercing black gaze exposing the secrets of her heart. She was eager to return to the village, and started the walk back.

In a few strides, her father was beside her. "Is there anything your father, the chief, should know?" he asked.

"I do not understand, Father."

"Let the others pass, and I will show you."

The villagers filed past, and Great Bear led Tachechana to the top of the hill. "Last night," he said, "you rode your horse west out of the village and circled back here at a gallop. Your tracks show you stopped here, then walked your horse to the south. Later, you rode the wind to the village."

"It is true," she admitted reluctantly.

He pointed to footprints that looked as if they had been made by army boots. "A white man without a horse has been here. Who is he and why does he spy on our village?"

Stung by her father's implied accusation, Tachechana did not speak right away. "I cannot answer you. I found these same tracks while we were fishing, but I do not know the man, though it seems I have seen him before."

"My braves and I will find out soon enough." The chief's jaw tensed. "And if he is up to no good, we will make him sorry he found the village of Great Bear."

"No, Father. It may be he is a friend."

"Why would a friend hide like a rabbit in the bushes?"

"Perhaps he is frightened, thinking we are hostile to him. There could be many reasons why he doesn't show himself."

"Very well," the chief said. "Tonight we will learn the answers to our questions." With a quick flip of his leg, he bounded onto his horse's back and rode down the hill at a fast trot.

Tachechana gave the area a parting glance and began a slow walk toward the village. A range of emotions as diverse as the birds chirping overhead swept through her—fear, curiosity, anger, puzzlement. *Where have I seen such wide shoulders?* But the birds made no reply.

Great Bear acted surly all day. As Tachechana served the evening meal, he asked, "Why did my daughter not come to her chief with news of the white man?"

"I was afraid you and your warriors would kill him."

"Do the Sioux kill without reason?" he barked. "Do you not trust your father's honor?"

"But the whites have betrayed our people in the past," she reasoned.

"What about your missionary friends? They come and go in our village as they please."

"They have proven their friendship."

"Then this stranger should do the same."

Try as she might, Tachechana could not convince her father that the stranger might be afraid to expose himself to them. She admitted she couldn't explain what he would be doing there, nor why he had no horse. She wished for the cover of darkness, when they could lay all their questions to rest.

At last it was time. On the way, Great Bear outlined his strategy for Tachechana. He would take her position of the night before while she moved around to the opposite side to get a look at the man's face. If she knew him, she would call out to him. If not, she would shoot an arrow, aimed to miss him by only a few inches and give him time to identify himself. If he became aggressive, Great Bear would rush in to subdue him, killing him if necessary.

Using all the skills her father had taught her, Tachechana crept through the glade to the place where the stranger sat directly between her and her father. Although the brightness of the fire hid her from his eyes, neither could she make out the facial features of the big man.

Once in a secure hiding place, Tachechana hooted like an owl to let her father know she was ready for the confrontation. The chief responded with a coyote howl. She took several deep breaths to steady herself and offered a quick prayer before calling out, "Do not move if you value your life!"

The stranger jumped to his feet as an arrow thudded into the ground beside him.

"That arrow was just a warning!" Tachechana called. "Put your hands over your head and you might live to see the sunrise."

Slowly the stranger raised his hands over his head. "Miz Cooper?" he said, peering into the blackness. "Is that you?"

Tachechana slowly crept from her hiding and into the circle of light from the fire. "Trooper O'Connel!" She issued another signal cry that brought Great Bear into the clearing.

"Aye, ma'am, 'tis I. Am I to be killed and scalped?"

"Not if you have an explanation for what you are doing here." She eyed his curly black locks and gasped. "What happened to your hair?"

The chief touched the trooper's hair and laughed when his fingers came away black and smelling like boot dressing.

"'Tis a long and sad story, ma'am. I'm on the run from the army and some renegade whites."

"What are you doing here?" she asked.

"Well, ma'am, Captain Baker and a small guard, including myself, were in camp while the rest o' the troop were out on patrol, lookin' for hostiles . . . no offense to you, Chief . . . when we were attacked by about a dozen men dressed up like Sioux. They caught us by surprise an' had us outnumbered to boot. Some of us scrambled for the brush, but I'm the only one to be gettin' away with my life. . . ." He dropped his head.

"Men dressed up like Sioux?" Tachechana asked, not comprehending.

"Aye. The devils were white men. I saw them myself. An' after they killed Cap'n Baker an' the others, they scalped them just like the Sioux."

"Why would they do such a thing?"

"To be making the army mad at the Sioux, ma'am. There are people who want all the Indians killed off so they can have the land for themselves."

"Your words are true, but why are you running from your own people?"

"After them renegades gave up lookin' for me, they rode off toward the reservation. When the rest of the troop came back and saw what happened to the Cap'n and the others, they thought I ran away. But the Cap'n, he gave the order for us to make for the brush. 'Tis no coward that I am." He bristled, squaring his broad shoulders. "The sergeant said I left my post and brought me up on charges of desertion under fire, and was going to have me tried and shot."

"Surely someone believed your story."

"Only Doc. He got a horse for me an' helped me escape. 'Tis a mess of trouble I could be gettin' him in for his trouble, too."

"Where is the horse?"

"Ah, the poor creature. In my haste to get away, I rode her to the ground. 'Tis a sorry excuse for a man I am."

Quickly Tachechana interpreted O'Connel's story to her father. The chief, obviously disgusted at the thought of whites posing as Sioux, smashed his tomahawk into the log upon which the trooper had been sitting.

Turning to O'Connel she said, "Why are the men who posed as Indians pursuing you?"

"They're afraid I might recognize them if I be seein' them again. I think the fort sutler is in on it, too. If only I could be provin' it somehow."

"But why did you come here? And why were you spying on our village last night?"

The trooper's gaze fell before her scrutiny. "I didn't know where else to go. My red hair gives me away wherever I go among white folks. That's why I put the boot black on it. I don't think the army will look for me here, an' I'm sure them renegades won't get this close to a Sioux village. But it's lonesome I get. I've been here for the better part o' two weeks now."

His shoulders drooped lower as he sat down on the log. "Meanin' no offense, ma'am . . . but it's no mistakin' how I feel about ye. . . . I was just hopin' to catch a glimpse o' ye when I climbed the hill last night."

Tachechana suppressed a smile, then found herself blushing as she haltingly relayed the trooper's words to her father.

Glad for the darkness, she turned to the trooper. "What will you do now?"

"I don't know." He sighed. "If the army catches up with me, it will be the gallows for me, 'tis no doubt about it. And what can one man do to prove his story, and without a horse at that?"

"We can help you by passing the word from village to

village. Even the Sioux that might be hostile would help find renegade whites. But where can you live while we find out who is bringing dishonor to our name?"

"Right here! Look, there's a cave behind these bushes." He parted the brush behind where he was sitting and revealed a hole between two boulders, just large enough to squeeze through. Lighting a candle, he crawled into the hole headfirst. Then his head popped out. "Come in. There's room for all of us."

"So that's where you went last night when I threw the stone into the bushes," Tachechana said as she slid between the boulders and into a room almost as large as a tepee.

"What you eat?" Great Bear asked in English.

Surprised when the chief spoke to him in his own language, O'Connel said, "I catch fish in the stream, and I have a few snares for jack rabbits."

The chief looked at his daughter. "White man big badger," he said with a grunt.

"And that is what we will call him while we help him capture the renegades." Tachechana laughed. "And we can spare some flour and cornmeal, can't we, Father?"

The chief nodded and reverted to Sioux. "Tell Big Badger to let his fire burn down to coals before it grows dark every night. He is easy to find sitting beside the bright fire. And tell him to wash the war paint from his hair. Tell him he must not shoot his gun unless he wants the whole Sioux nation looking for his scalp. Tomorrow I will send food and buckskin clothes."

Tachechana relayed the message as Great Bear wriggled out of the cave. O'Connel shook her hand as she prepared to leave, holding onto it as if he could not bear to part with her.

"Be sure and thank your father for me, ma'am. And, if it's not too bold that I am, please be comin' back again . . . soon."

chapter

21

GREAT BEAR BOUNDED OUT OF HIS TEPEE just as the sun nudged its way into the hazy, late-summer sky. Tachechana listened as he followed the path toward Medicine Creek and heard him splash across to single out one of his horses. Sticking her head out of the door, she watched him cross White River and gallop north into the most barren of the Bad Lands.

She checked her first impulse to dash after him. If he wanted her to know where he was going and what he was doing he would have told her, or even invited her to ride with him. Whatever his mission, she was sure it concerned Trooper O'Connel.

All day Tachechana schemed how she and her father would help prove O'Connel's innocence, but it was to no purpose. *How can we, who must stay on the reservation, find out who these white men are, and why they killed Captain Baker?* she thought. *We are as helpless children!*

Just as the squaws were building their fires for the evening meal, Tachechana noticed a plume of dust rising in the northwest. She hurried to Eagle Feather and pointed it out to him. A war whoop brought all the braves in the village on the run.

"Get your horses!" shouted Eagle Feather.

From the mad scramble, an orderly line of fully armed warriors formed, and at Eagle Feather's command, they splashed across the White River and dashed toward the approaching riders.

The dust driven up by the Indian ponies obscured the incoming band. Afraid a fight would ensue, Tachechana told all the young maidens to gather the children and go hide in the brush. The older women and boys armed themselves with whatever weapons they could find and positioned themselves defensively. It seemed the dust would never settle.

Finally, through the haze, Tachechana could barely make out the figures of the horsemen. Leading the procession was her father on his favorite brown and white pinto. From their hiding places the villagers rushed down to the water's edge.

Above the excited babble, her father's voice rose, strong and sure. "My people, there will be a council fire tonight. At that time, I will tell you what we have learned."

Tachechana kept her peace, not questioning her father about his ride, though her silence took all her stoic resolve. She found additional tasks to busy her hands though her mind roamed free. *There will be a council fire tonight,* she told herself. *All your questions will be answered then.*

That night Great Bear stood at the council circle, his muscular arms folded in front of him. "Today I rode north and climbed the rim of the Bad Lands. Above the rim there is much grass. The white man fences in the grass to keep our uncle, the buffalo, out and his cows and horses in.

"Other white men, wearing Indian moccasions, came and cut the fences to break them down. They steal their brothers' cows and horses and bring them down into the Bad Lands. There, they take the animals east where they are sold to other white men.

"The men who steal the animals dress in the clothes of the Sioux and the Cheyenne. Soon many white men will band together and come looking for us, thinking we steal their cattle and horses. Those who chased me today now know where to find us. We will not be safe unless we do two things."

There was no sound except for the gurgle of the river and the call of the night creatures. Every ear was tuned to the words Great Bear would speak next.

"First, we must set guards on the hills to the north to warn us if the white man approaches, so we can be prepared to fight to defend our village. And"—his countenance darkened—"we must find where the white men hide the cattle and horses they steal. We must catch those men, but we must not kill them. We must give them to the army to prove we are not thieves. We are Lakota!"

"How will we look for the thieves and still defend our village?" Swimming Otter asked.

"Tomorrow I will send messages to our brothers who live nearest us. They will watch for our smoke signals and send help if we are attacked. They will also send out their scouts to help us in our search for the stolen cattle. When we find the thieves, our brothers will help us capture them and take them to the army."

Eagle Feather rose, pacing. "Why can't we just kill the thieves?"

"If we kill them, then we, too, are men without honor. If we capture them and turn them over to the army, the Great White Father in Washington might reward us by giving us back our land."

"Ptoo!" Eagle Feather spat. "The Great White Chief is not our father! He cares only for his white children!"

"That may be so, Eagle Feather, but they are many, and we

are few. If we fight and die, we are honored, but what will happen to our wives and little ones? Who will teach them the old ways?"

Walking back to the tepee after the council fire, Tachechana asked, "How many men chased you today, Father?"

"Only four, but there was not a fast horse among them. Many of their horses have been stolen. I saw the tracks of horses without riders coming over the rim and into the Bad Lands."

"Do you think you will be able to find them?"

He drew himself up proudly. "The Sioux can track anything all the way to the door of the Spirit World."

"But why can't the white men track so many animals all moving at the same time?"

"North of here the land is very bad. Many canyons and narrow passes. A few men with rifles can drive off many who follow the herd. These men are very smart. They know the Bad Lands and where they can hide so many animals."

"Then how will our braves ever be able to find them?"

"We will track them backwards. We will go first to where they have not yet been."

"You speak in riddles, Father. How can you track them before they make tracks?"

"As the eagle sees, we will see all of the Bad Lands at one time," the chief replied, then quickly moved to another subject. "Have you taken food to Big Badger?"

"No, I was afraid someone might see me. I planned to ride Fox in the river after the village is asleep."

"If you take Fox, you will be followed." He leveled her a warning look. "No one must know of the Big Badger's den — no one! The safety of our people may depend on it. Now, only two of us know. It must remain so. I alone will take him food. No one will question the chief who rides in the night, his eyes open to see that no danger comes to his people."

Recognizing the wisdom of her father's words, Tachechana penned a note of encouragement and some Scripture verses on a page of her tablet and placed it inside the cover of one of the books she had brought with her from the box canyon.

"Please give this to him," she said. "It will help him pass time while he waits for you to catch the men who killed Captain Baker."

It was very late when Tachechana heard Great Bear slip out of his blankets and through the doorway. The last sound she heard was the flap of the tepee, but she closed her eyes in sleep only after her father's safe return.

Early the next day Tachechana watched as her father moved quietly from tepee to tepee, giving orders to his warriors, who sprang to the task without question or argument. Only the day before they had appeared lethargic and unwilling to work. Today, some of the old spirit showed itself.

Her father and a small party of warriors were the last to leave the village. They wore no war paint, but each was armed in some way. Great Bear and several others carried rifles.

When the last of the warriors rode out of sight, Plainsfeather approached Tachechana. "What shall we do with fish when they finish drying?"

"When they are dry, we should put them into the new tepee, along with the food the Agency supplies," she replied. "Then we will always know how much we have and how soon we should get more."

"When we fish again?"

"Not for many days. We must give more fish time to find the deep holes."

"Not much meat in tepee. We build drying racks there."

She nodded in approval. "Get some of the other women to help you, but don't build them too big. Reverend Baxter said we should get our regular amount of food this month."

"The last time we stay on this reservation, we get less and less . . . almost starve," Plainsfeather grumbled before shuffling off to her tasks.

Throughout the day, Tachechana kept busy with her child. Seeing how fast he was growing, her thoughts turned to the cold months when he would be needing warm clothing and moccasin boots. Even thus preoccupied, she found herself looking constantly toward the signal peaks for signs of smoke.

She worried about her father, out trying to locate the renegades . . . about O'Connel, hiding like an animal in a hole in the ground . . . about Caleb and what would happen to him if the village was attacked . . . and even about Eagle Feather, wondering if his violent temper and hatred for whites would yet bring him trouble.

The unexpected rumble of the missionary's wagon broke the somber stillness of the village about mid-afternoon. Tachechana, always glad to see Donald and Jane, was guarded as she greeted them. *What will I say if he asks where the warriors are?* she thought.

The children squealed with delight as the big man greeted each one with a toss in the air, a hug, and a piece of candy. The little ones clung to his breeches when he at last made his way to Tachechana.

"What brings you here two weeks before your time?" she quizzed.

"Two things. First, a small shipment of salt pork came in to make up for the missing corned beef. Second, I have some bad news for you. One of your old friends, Trooper O'Connel has turned bad. He ran out on his captain in a fight, then broke out of the stockade and deserted. Some feel he might have come this way." Reverend Baxter gave her a searching look. "A posse is out looking for him."

"Why do they think he would come here, to the reservation?"

Reverend Baxter shrugged. "He was heading this way. They found his horse, lame and abandoned, about fifty miles west of here. But what seems strange to me," he mused, "is that they couldn't track him down. A big man like that must have left footprints."

"Who tracked him?" she asked, attempting to conceal her concern.

"Some men from Fort Fetterman and a small group of soldiers. Well now," he said, turning to the wagon, "you and Jane visit while I get someone to help me unload these supplies."

Tachechana always enjoyed Jane's visits, but today her thoughts scattered like leaves before the wind. It bothered her that the trackers from the fort hadn't been able to trace O'Connel's whereabouts. He was a big man and rather clumsy. Any one of the children of the village knew how to spot footprints—and to identify what kind of animal or human had made them. *Someone wants to kill him,* she concluded. *But as long as the soldiers are around, they will not make their move.*

Reverend Baxter walked up to ask the question she had been dreading. "Where are your father and all the braves?"

"They are hunting," Tachechana replied, almost too quickly. "Can you see how much Caleb has grown?"

"Where are they hunting?"

"Oh, Father sent them out in many directions." She tickled Caleb, hoping his happy giggles would distract the preacher.

"Are they finding much game?" he pressed. "All I see is fish in the food tepee."

"This is only the second hunt. We ate all they brought before, while it was still fresh."

"Then they found no buffalo?"

"No, only some small deer, and it cost the life of Black Dog. He was bitten by a snake."

217

"I'm sorry to hear that. Where is his lodge? Jane and I will go talk with his mother."

Reluctantly, Tachechana pointed out the tepee, fearing the grieving mother might reveal the true nature of the braves' expedition. She offered to go along to interpret for the Baxters, but he smiled and said he needed to practice his Sioux. All Tachechana could do was to pray.

"Poor woman," Donald said when they returned to find her busily stitching on a buckskin moccasin for Caleb, "every time I asked her about the hunting party, she burst into tears. She is quite distraught over the death of her son."

Tachechana smiled a sympathetic smile, grateful that the woman had given a convincing performance. "Yes," she said. "She will miss him greatly. Black Dog was her youngest."

"Do you think your father would mind if Jane and I stayed here in the village tonight?"

"No, of course not," Tachechana replied. Her mind raced. What would Reverend Baxter think when the braves came in with no game? "The tepee will smell of drying fish, though. How will you sleep?"

Donald smiled. "We have brought our own lodge. Come and see." He and Jane led Tachechana and the ever curious Plainsfeather out to their wagon.

After inserting several steel hoops in sockets along the sides of the wagon, Donald threw a canvas over the frame while Jane unrolled a large bedroll onto the floor. In a moment the old freight wagon had become a rolling lodge.

All the women, Jane among them, were gathering wood for the evening cook fires when the first group of braves returned. To Tachechana's surprise, one of them had a fat buck fastened behind him on his horse. The women sprang to the task of skinning and cutting up the animal, and before they had the job done, a second group came in with another deer. The women began singing as they worked, and even Jane, covering her skirts with an apron, fell to the skinning with enthusiasm, paling only when the animal's brains were scooped from the skull.

A third group of braves rode in just as Tachechana finished describing to Jane the use of animal brains in tanning buckskin. Looking up, she was relieved to see her father's braves riding in with another deer to add to the village stockpile. He seemed annoyed rather than pleased by the missionaries' presence and only grunted when Tachechana told him of their plans to stay overnight.

The village feasted on fresh venison late into the night, then listened while Reverend Baxter told about Jesus, the God-Man. Though his Sioux was improving, he frequently looked to Tachechana for help with a word, and once he used the word *pig* for *cross,* much to the amusement of the tribe. They were pleased that he was learning their tongue, unlike the government men, who demanded the Sioux learn English.

When the Baxters finally retired to their wagon and the villagers to their tepees, Tachechana asked her father what he had learned on his day's ride to the Bad Lands.

"We have not yet found the place where the white men hide the animals they steal. I went far to the east and found only old tracks, much older than the ones I found yesterday. Swimming Otter found fresh tracks east of where the wind blows through a hole in the rocks. The herd was between us. We will find it tomorrow."

"So soon? Then Timothy . . . Trooper O'Connel will be able to go back to the army a free man."

"Humph! First, we must find them. Then, we must capture them. And then the army must be convinced they are the same men O'Connel claims he saw."

"I must go and tell him the good news—that we are getting closer to—"

"No!" the chief interrupted. "You are to stay away from the glade where Big Badger hides. It is not good for you to be there."

"But, Father, I was a warrior once. I can take care of myself." She kept to herself the fact that she longed to spend time with the gentle giant who treated her like the lady she longed to be.

"You are watched all the time. Eagle Feather watches you, and Baxter watches you."

"*Reverend Baxter* watches me?"

"He thinks you know more about Big Badger than you say with your mouth. Your eyes tell all."

Shortly after the village quieted for the night, Great Bear slipped noiselessly from his tepee and disappeared into the darkness. About an hour later he was back, but Tachechana had prayed the entire time he was gone.

Lately, it seemed her prayers were more questions for which there were no answers. Always, she asked why God had taken Nathan from her. But there were more, many more. Why were Indians hunted and killed by the whites? Why didn't all whites become Christians? Why did her father refuse to discuss the Jesus Way? "Why am I even here?" she whispered just before her father's return.

Then she remembered something the preacher at the fort had said when they buried Nathan. "The answers to all our questions are in the Bible. If we want to know God's will, he will show us from his Word." She fell asleep, determined to be more diligent in reading and studying Nathan's Bible.

It was still dark when Tachechana and Great Bear were awakened by a harsh cough outside their tepee. Great Bear slipped through the door, and though Tachechana strained to hear what was said, she could not make out the whispered words.

Great Bear stuck his head through the open flap and said one word as he grabbed his weapons. "Soldiers." He disappeared again, and Tachechana knew he was alerting the rest of the village.

Shortly before sunrise, a bugle call sounded to the south and east of the village. Tachechana scooped up Caleb and hurried out of the tepee to find a skirmish line of soldiers some distance from the village.

At that moment a similar line of warriors sprang from the grass and brush to face the soldiers, but her father was not among them, and only half the braves were present.

The soldiers lowered their banner and another tied a white flag to its staff. Then three of the soldiers, one bearing the flag, advanced to within thirty yards of the braves. Eagle Feather stepped out to meet them.

"Are you the chief of this village?" a soldier asked in very poor Sioux.

"No."

"Where is he?"

A wicked smile curved Eagle Feather's lips. "Right behind you."

The three snapped their heads around. There, forming a third skirmish line, stood a group of mounted Sioux, formidable in war paint. They flanked a magnificent warrior with a trailing war bonnet of eagle feathers. It was Great Bear.

chapter
22

REVEREND BAXTER PUSHED HIS WAY PAST EAGLE FEATHER. "What's going on here, sergeant?" he asked.

"We're here looking for beef-stealin' renegades, Reverend."

"Then you're looking in the wrong place. I can vouch for these people. There's not a scrap of beef in the village except for the wormy stuff the government sends."

"If they're so innocent, then how come they were waitin' for us and surrounded us like this?"

"How would you act if you were treated as they were?"

"You're soundin' more and more like an Injun-lover all the time. That's not healthy for a white man 'round these parts."

"Are you threatening me?"

"Just statin' a fact." He shrugged casually. "But we intend to search this village. I've got my orders."

"You go back and tell your captain I said there was no fresh beef in this village and that the Indians will not permit a search of the village without a fight. And, I might add, you are at a distinct disadvantage should it come to a fight."

The three envoys wheeled their horses around and galloped back to the main body of troops. After a moment's conversation, the captain barked a short command. Forming a column of twos, the contingent of soldiers reversed their position and stood ready to make their departure. As the column approached the line of Indians, it parted, Great Bear and his braves neatly backing their horses to allow the soldiers to ride through the gap, then closing their ranks as the last of the soldiers passed by. Riding to the southwest, they were followed for a distance by four of Chief Great Bear's braves mounted on the swiftest horses in the village.

The chief rode back into the village with a stormy look on his face. "What they want?" he asked.

"To search the village for stolen beef," Reverend Baxter replied. "They claim they were after the renegades, but I didn't like that fellow's attitude." He stared after the departing troops.

"Why they leave?"

"I told them they'd be in for a fight if they tried it."

"You told them good words," the chief said shortly. "Now we eat."

But before the food could be placed before the warriors, one of the scouts sent by Great Bear to escort the soldiers raced into the village. "The soldiers are headed for Tut-we's village up on the White River," he reported.

Great Bear walked over to two piles of wood. With a brand taken from one of the cooking fires, he set them ablaze and threw a large armful of green grass on the one to the west.

Within seconds a wisp of smoke appeared on a pinnacle to the northwest. Seconds later the wisp turned to a thick billow of heavy black smoke.

"Tut-we will not be surprised by the soldiers now," Great Bear said, and the villagers again settled down to their morning meal.

"Chief, how did you know the soldiers were coming?" Reverend Baxter asked.

"We have learned the white soldiers like to attack as the sun rises. Each morning, well before sunrise my warriors . . ." He checked himself, his eyes hooded.

Tachechana, sitting nearby, took up the slack. "These are troubled times, Reverend Baxter. My father begins to suspect that even the trees have ears. I am sorry," she apologized. "He fears he gives away his secrets."

The missionary sighed. "He's beginning to distrust even me, isn't he?" He pondered his next words. "Then tell your father that, while I may have the same color skin as those soldiers, I do not approve of all their methods. I am here because I want to help the Sioux. God, your Great Spirit, sent me with his love in my heart for you and your people. It's because of his love that I bring you the message of his Son, who wants to give you eternal life in heaven."

Great Bear looked up, probing Reverend Baxter's face with eyes of black granite. Finding no guile there, he spoke through Tachechana. "If all white men were as you, I would become a Christian. But most whites hate us and want to kill us. How could I, a chief of the Lakotas accept the white man's religion when so many of them don't practice what their religion tells them?"

"But, Chief, Christianity is not the white man's religion only. . . ." Baxter broke off, seeing the veil once more covering the chief's eyes.

"It will do no good to tell him now," Tachechana said sadly. "If more of the Indians followed the Jesus Way, it would be easier for my father. He is afraid to be the first for fear he will lead his people down a bad trail."

Baxter watched from a distance as Great Bear and his braves planned the day's hunt. That he wanted desperately to join them was apparent, but no invitation was offered, and it was common knowledge that a white didn't invite himself to a Sioux hunt.

"Will you spend the whole day with us?" Tachechana asked when all the braves had ridden out.

"If you think your father will have no objection. Jane enjoys visiting with you, and I hoped I could tell some Bible stories to the children. They laugh at the way I fracture their language."

About noon, as Tachechana and Jane sat talking in great Bear's tepee, one of the older girls who had been caring for Caleb stuck her head in the door. "Tachechana, come quick!"

As the women exited the tepee the girl pointed to the northwest pinnacle. A steady flow of black smoke drifted upward. The north pinnacle responded in kind, soon to be followed by the northeast lookout.

"Throw grass on all the fires still burning," Tachechana instructed the girl.

"What's going on?" asked Reverend Baxter as he walked up to the two women.

"Trouble," Tachechana replied, and set about ordering the girls to take the children into the brush to hide, and everyone else to get weapons.

"What kind of trouble?" Reverend Baxter asked as Tachechana set the village's defenses.

"I don't know, but we will be ready for it. Do you have a gun?"

"A rifle . . . in the wagon, but . . ."

"You better get it . . . and take Jane there for cover!"

Reverend Baxter took his obviously frightened wife to the wagon and told her to stay there, but she was by his side when he returned.

In a short time, braves from a neighboring village began riding in, and a defense line was formed on the north side of the White River. Reverend Baxter started to join the braves, but Tachechana stopped him. "You stay here to protect your wife if it becomes necessary. The warriors don't want a white man on the first line."

"Do you have any idea who might be attacking?"

"Maybe the army is coming back. Maybe the ranchers whose beef was stolen. Some of them pursued my father two days ago."

Great Bear rode into the village and quickly surveyed the defenses. He sent two of his most trusted scouts off to the south and southwest just as a plume of dust became visible in the north-northwest.

Before the riders were close enough to be seen, the scouts returned with about ten Indians Tachechana had never seen before, but she heard the name Tut-we and realized a sizeable group was forming to meet the opposing force.

When the dust cleared, Tachechana counted fifteen horses standing in a straight line opposite the first line of Indian defense. They were white men, but not soldiers, and they stopped short of the Indians by two hundred yards.

Great Bear splashed across the river to join his warriors. About twenty of them mounted their horses and formed a line with their chief in the middle.

Slowly, the mounted Indians closed the gap between themselves and the white men. Fifty yards shy of them, they stopped. The two groups sat looking at each other, no words passing between them, hearing only the pounding of their hearts and smelling the dust that was settling all around them.

"Do any of you speak English?" called one of the white men.

The chief had learned enough to parley with them, but he called back in Sioux, and the message was relayed that Reverend Baxter should be sent as interpreter. Tachechana quickly mounted a horse and rode with him to the chief's side.

"Ask them what business they have here," The chief said.

"Who are you and what do you want?" Baxter called.

"We're a posse looking for a deserter and horse thief."

"Who deputized you?" Baxter wanted to know before he replied to the chief.

"We sorta deputized ourselves."

"Then you're nothing more than a bunch of bounty hunters."

Tachechana began to interpret what the chief could not understand.

"You might say that, but there's a deserter around here somewhere and we intend to find him an' . . ."

". . . kill him?" Baxter completed the thought.

"We intend to take him in. Course, if he won't come peaceable, we'll do what we have to."

"Since you are not legally deputized lawmen, you are trespassing on Indian territory. I suggest you head out north of here. That's the shortest way off the reservation."

The group mumbled among themselves. "We came in from the west. Our camp is west and a little north of here. We'll go back that way."

"That will take you into the vicinity of Chief Tut-we's village. Several of his braves are here now. They'll be glad to escort you out. I suggest you don't try anything foolish. Tut-we is not nearly as tolerant as Great Bear."

Grudgingly, the posse turned their horses around and began riding north, accompanied by the armed warriors.

"Did you see, Father?" Tachechana could not keep the excitement from her voice. "Four of those men wore Sioux moccasins. And I recognized two of them from Fort Fetterman."

"Is there a chief of the Lokata that is blind? Now be still."

"But . . ."

The chief darted her an angry glance, and she realized she had already said too much in front of Reverend Baxter.

Silently she rode her borrowed horse back across the river. The hoot of an owl erupted from her throat, bringing all the maidens out of the brush along with the children in their care.

"What was that you and your father were talking about out there?" Reverend Baxter asked after the village returned to normal. "I mean, that business about the Sioux moccasins."

She knew this man. He was their friend. If he was to help them, she would have to confide in him. As long as her father rejected Jesus, he could never understand the trust between those who followed the Jesus Way. Firm now in her resolve, she began.

"Two days ago my father was hunting far to the north. He saw where white men, wearing moccasins, had robbed cattle and horses from other white men."

"How did he know they were white men and not Indians?"

"Look at your feet as we stand here."

Baxter looked down.

"Now look at mine."

The missionary seemed perplexed. "So?"

"See how your feet point out to the side as you stand and walk? Indians stand and walk with their toes pointed straight ahead. Any child in this village can tell the difference."

The missionary took four or five steps, stopped, and looked at his tracks. "Walk over here by me," he told Tachechana. She did so. "Well, I'll be! Then what Trooper O'Connel said about the attack on Captain Baker could be true. And if it is, he is in more danger from that posse than he is from the Sioux or the army!"

"What can be done about it?" she asked.

"If we knew where he was, we could help him hide until we could prove his innocence."

Not willing to defy her father's order not to reveal O'Connel's whereabouts, Tachechana asked evasively, "How would you go about that?"

"I don't know how we could find him, but I know we have to catch those thieves in the act and have them all hanged for the murder of Captain Baker and the men who died with him."

"For years they killed the Sioux, and no punishment was given," she mused. "Now they have killed a white man, and they are to be hanged. I may be half white, but I don't understand the thinking of white men."

"Tachechana, the problem is simply that many white men just don't take the time to think. If they did, they would all follow the Christian way."

"What can be done to help O'Connel?"

"I'm not sure. When I go back to the Agency tomorrow, I'll tell the soldiers there about this incident and try to persuade them to go easy on O'Connel if they should find him. And we'll pray that we can get enough evidence on those thieves to hang them all."

Great Bear was strangely subdued at the evening meal and ignored all attempts to draw him into conversation.

When the Baxters retired to their wagon for the night, Great Bear walked out to look at the horses and check on his night sentries, and Tachechana slipped up beside him.

"My father was very quiet at supper tonight."

"Um."

"Do you still distrust the missionary?"

"What he does not hear he cannot repeat."

"He believes O'Connel's story."

"Did you tell him where he can be found?"

"No, Father, I did not." She paused. "Reverend Baxter noticed the moccasins those men were wearing today. He

230

believes they are the same ones who killed Captain Baker and maybe even the ones who steal the cattle and horses."

"They are the same."

"How do you know?"

"The one who did all the talking . . . his horse has a special shoe to protect its split hoof. I saw that track where the fence was cut."

"If we could only find the cattle, we could prove those men are the thieves."

"Be patient, my daughter. Maybe tomorrow, maybe the next day . . . we will find them. Then your Big Badger will be safe."

Tachechana flushed. "He is *not* my Big Badger!" she retorted.

But, lying sleepless on her pallet that night, she kept seeing the boyishly handsome face fringed with carrot-colored hair, and she wondered what life would be like in the white man's world. . . . Although it was a warm night, her bed was cold, and she dreamed of a little cabin in a box canyon far away . . . and of a white man's cottage in a city she had never seen.

Great Bear and his warriors disappeared before Tachechana awoke the next morning. As she tended to Caleb's needs and prepared the morning meal, she noticed the Baxters readying their wagon for travel. She had just finished feeding the ever-hungry child when they walked over to her cooking fire.

"Your father is taking quite a chance, pulling all the braves out to hunt, with those renegades in the area," Donald said, anxiety in the furrowed brow.

"All the braves have not gone on the hunt. Those on night watch are sleeping in their tepees, and there are lookouts on the highest peaks. We will not be taken by surprise."

Reverend Baxter laughed. "I should have learned that

yesterday," he said. "Still, I wish you were in a safer spot. Perhaps you and Caleb should come back to the mission house with us until this mess gets straighted out."

"No. I belong here with my people. I must prove I am as much Sioux as they if I am ever to win them to Christ. You saw yesterday how the women look to me for leadership when the men are gone. Father needs me, too. And . . ." she caught herself just in time. She had almost said, "O'Connel needs me."

"I guess you know best. But be careful. If those men are who we think they are, they'll stop at nothing to get what they want."

"We'll be all right. God guide you safely back to the Agency. You are needed there to work for O'Connel."

The rumble of the wagon wheels and the creaking of the harness leather issued an ominous sound to Tachechana as she watched the Baxters' wagon disappear down the trail. They traveled slowly, stirring up little dust. But the still, hot air caused it to linger long after the wagon had rolled on, its acrid odor adding to the bleakness of the surroundings.

The great ball of the sun was edging the western horizon when the warriors rode into the village. Having ridden out in groups of four or five, they returned in one body, their faces betraying nothing of the day's find.

Quickly food was prepared for the warriors. While Tachechana fed Caleb, Great Bear spoke at last. "We have found the stolen herd. They huddle in a box canyon that stands like a great fort. Even an army could not attack and live."

"Then how will we prove O'Connel innocent?"

The chief sat staring into the fire for a long time before answering. "There is only one way . . . but my warriors will not agree. If we attacked by night, we could take them."

Testing, Tachechana ventured a comment. "Your warriors fear fighting at night because, if they were to die, they would roam the Spirit World forever in darkness."

"Yes." There was a long pause in which Tachechana's heart almost stopped beating. "But your mother said . . . there is no night in the Spirit World."

"Do you believe her words?"

"She spoke always the truth."

"Father . . . do you now believe as she believed? Are you a Christian, too?" Her voice was as soft as the thistledown blooming on the prairie.

"No . . . I am Lakota. . . . but sometimes I wish . . . I were like your mother . . . here." He put his hand over his chest.

"If you become a Christian, Father, you would be like her in your heart. Can't you see the change it has made in me?"

"It is fitting that you be as your mother. I should be as my father, Lakota of the Sioux."

A tear coursed down Tachechana's face. "Am I not the daughter of my father? . . . I am Lakota . . . I am Sioux."

"Um," the chief grunted. "There is no finer woman among all the Sioux. That's why I am troubled in my mind. For the first time, I cannot see clearly which trail I should follow. All the Indian ways are not right, yet all the white man's ways are not right. How am I to know which trail to take?"

"Not all white men follow the Christian trail. Being a Christian is for every person to decide, red or white—"

"We will talk more of this," the chief interrupted. "Now I must think how to capture the white thieves."

It was with emotions as changeable as the seasons that Tachechana watched her father walk to the river's edge and sit down, looking off to the north.

"Father God," she prayed, "You have begun your work in his heart. Please don't let anything happen to him before he learns to trust in your Son."

233

chapter

23

ONLY A FEW BRAVES RODE OUT with Great Bear the next morning to scout the fortifications at the natural corral where the renegades hid the cattle and horses. Tachechana knew the urgency of his mission. So much depended on the capture of the thieves—the vindication of O'Connel and her father's village, the solving of Captain Baker's murder, perhaps even better feelings between the ranchers and her people.

The day dragged on. She prayed, she worried, she prayed some more. About noon she decided to go for a ride. Fox, seeing her wade the creek, waited at the fence, her colt by her side. The colt was growing strong and looked like Rowdy. Tachechana crawled through the rails of the fence. Grabbing a handful of the mare's mane, she sprang lightly to her back. Today she would let the colt run along beside them as they rode.

Holding Fox to a canter, she found herself taking the same route as the night she first saw O'Connel sitting at his campfire. She studied every bush and tree lining the White River, then rode west. After turning south she watched for the tell-tale plume of dust that would betray other riders. Skirting the hill that was becoming the village cemetery, she trotted south of the glade where O'Connel lived in his "badger den."

After being sure she had not crossed any new incoming tracks, she guided Fox and the colt into the shade of the trees and headed downstream toward the young soldier's hideout.

About one hundred yards from the cave, Fox stopped, nostrils flared, ears erect. Tachechana slid from her back and led the two horses into the camp on foot.

When she came to the dead campfire, Tachechana called out, and the burly young soldier scooted out of his den so fast both horses shied, and Fox stepped between her mistress and the threatening stranger. Only at a rebuke from Tachechana did the mare back off to nibble on the lush grasses nearby.

"Ah, Miz Cooper, 'tis right glad I am that ye've come."

For the first time Tachechana felt a little awkward in his presence. "You can call me by my first name if you like."

"If you'll call me Tim. . . . Tach-e-cha-na . . . 'Tis so musical it almost sounds like an Irish name."

For a few strained moments silence gripped them. Finally O'Connel blurted out, "Your father doesn't think you should be visiting me. Is that why you haven't come before?"

"Yes," she replied honestly, "but I wished to be the one to bring you some good news. Father and his braves have found the stolen horses and cattle and are trying to find a way to capture the thieves."

"But will the Army believe they're the same ones as killed the captain?"

"The missionary at the Agency thinks they are the ones." She paused. "Couldn't the soldiers who are after you have seen the shoe tracks where Captain Baker died? Indians never shoe their horses."

"Aye, an' I tried to point that out at my first hearin', but they said the savages . . . no offense, ma'am . . . used stolen horses—maybe even stolen army horses, since they found the track of a corrective shoe, for a horse with a split hoof."

236

She nodded. "My father found such a track up on the rim of the Bad Lands, where the horses and cattle were stolen from other white men."

"Ah, Miz Chana, I don't know what it is that gets into people to do such awful things."

"Oh, I do," she said. "At least, since Nathan explained it to me. You see, all people do evil things because their hearts are wicked. The cost for this evil is death, just as you would be facing the gallows if you had been found guilty of killing Captain Baker. But this is the good part! Jesus paid the cost when he took our sins on himself and died in our place." She recalled the Sioux ritual in which her father had taken the lashes of the braves' willow switches on his own back, paying the price for the missionary's acceptance as one of the tribe.

So lost was O'Connel in his own thoughts that he didn't seem to notice her silence. "Yes . . . I've done much thinkin' since the evenin' we talked about it on the Little Powder River. It shames me everytime. It's wishin' there was somethin' I could do about it, that I am."

"There *is* something you can do . . . Tim. Have you read the Bible I sent to you?"

"Aye."

"Then you must do as it says and accept what Jesus did for you."

"But I don't know how, ma'am."

She cocked her head, studying the fringed buckskin shirt he was wearing. "What did you do to get that buckskin shirt?"

"Nothin'. Your father gave it to me. I only took it—and right glad I was to be gettin' it, too."

"It's the same way with God. He gave his Son to die for you. He wishes you to take his gift, Jesus, just as you took the shirt from my father."

There, in the cool green shade, Timothy O'Connel knelt in

the grass and asked God to forgive his sins and let Jesus take control of his life. Both he and Tachechana were surprised to find themselves kneeling with both her hands in his at the final "Amen." In a burst of enthusiasm the big soldier reached out his arms and nearly crushed the air from her lungs.

"Timothy!"

"Oh, Miz Chana. 'Tis sorry I am for takin' such liberty. So fair to burstin' with happiness was I that I didn't realize what I was doin'!"

There was an awkward silence.

"Now that I'm a real Christian, could ye be tellin' me what I should do next?"

"Study the Bible and talk with God every day. And if there is anyone you have wronged, you should try to make it right."

Dark clouds rolled into the young man's eyes. He looked at the ground and scuffed at a clump of grass with his big foot.

"What's wrong, Timothy?"

"There is somethin' I should set straight, but I don't rightly know how. Please don't make me tell you what it is. 'Tis a shameful thing."

"I am your friend, Timothy. I only wish to help."

"Could ye get me some paper, and then mail a letter for me?"

She nodded. "I will bring them late tonight, and Reverend Baxter can mail it from the Agency."

"Does he know I'm here?"

"He does not know, but I don't think he would turn you in if he did. Still, my father says the missionary cannot slip up and say something about you if he doesn't know."

"'Tis a smart man—your father."

"I must go back before I am missed in the village."

Again, O'Connel took her hands in his. "I'm forever in your debt, ma'am."

Withdrawing her hands quickly, she said, "I'll bring the paper, or send it with Father tonight," and bounded onto Fox's back, cantering out of the glade the way she had come in.

Entering the village, Tachechana noticed that the place had changed. No longer did it seem the drab, drear cluster of tepees it had been before she left. *Perhaps,* she thought, *Timothy's decision to follow the Jesus Way has brightened the whole world today.*

She was eager for Great Bear to return with the news of the renegades' capture and the return of the cattle and horses. In this light-hearted mood, she met Plainsfeather with a radiant smile.

"Hmm," the old woman said, hands on hips, regarding her with a puzzled look. "What happen? You ride off somewhere and leave storms behind. Now all is sunshine."

Tachechana hugged her secret to herself, leaving her old friend to stare after her with no answer to her question.

The rest of the afternoon she devoted to Caleb, and as the shadows lengthened, she collected some wood for the evening fire.

The sun disappeared behind the western hills, and still her father had not returned from the Bad Lands. *What trouble had come upon him?* she wondered.

At the sound of the horses nickering from the corral across the river, Tachechana left the three fresh catfish roasting over the fire and ran to greet Great Bear, dusty from his ride. She did not question him, but waited while he consumed his meal with relish and sat, licking his fingers.

At last he spoke. "Tonight I call my warriors together for a war council. We must make plans to capture the white thieves."

Before she could respond, he was out the door, moving from tepee to tepee. And, when the warriors gathered at the council fire, Tachechana left Caleb in Plainsfeather's care and drew as near as possible to hear their talk.

"To take the thieving whites by surprise, we must attack under cover of darkness," he began. There were murmurs of dissent, but Great Bear quelled their complaints. "I want only the bravest warriors to ride into battle. Who will stand with me?"

To a man, the braves lifted their voices in a cry that chilled Tachechana's blood, rallying behind their chief.

"Then sleep well. For, tomorrow, when the night shades fall, we go to restore honor to the Sioux."

Leaving her place on the fringes of the circle, Tachechana fell into step beside her father. "Will there be much danger?" she asked, concerned for his safety.

"There is always danger. But if the Great Spirit covers the moon with his clouds, we will be victorious. Tomorrow, with two braves, you must ride to the Agency and tell Reverend Baxter to bring soldiers to the village. We will hand over the renegades and show them where the stolen cattle are hidden."

The next morning, Tachechana was surprised to see Swimming Otter and Eagle Feather waiting outside her tepee when she rose to prepare the morning meal.

"Why are you here?" she asked.

"Your father wishes us to ride with you to the Agency," Eagle Feather was quick to reply.

"But tonight you ride into battle."

Eagle Feather grinned. "If you are not too old to ride as you did when you were a warrior, we can be back in time to change horses and still ride with Great Bear."

"Then don't lag too far behind"—she cast him a coy look—"for I will be riding Fox."

240

Her pulses singing with the challenge, Tachechana ran to the corral, lifted herself onto the mare's back, and raced with the wind, slowing only when the Agency came into view.

She found the Baxters in a small garden behind their house and delivered the message.

Donald Baxter left immediately for the army post. "Wait for me here," he called back over his shoulder. "Jane and I will return with you in case we are needed."

Dismissing the braves, Tachechana watched as they wheeled their horses around and galloped out of the compound in a cloud of pungent, nose-plugging dust. At the first turn in the trail, Eagle Feather reined up, turned, and waved.

What a loyal friend you are, Eagle Feather, she thought, returning his salute. *May God ride with you tonight—and bring you safely home.*

As the sun reached its zenith the following morning, there was no sign of either soldiers or Indians. There was only the vast, vacant prairie stretching out before them.

Drawing out his pocket watch, Donald Baxter read its face for the dozenth time. "At first, the captain wouldn't believe me when I told him the thieves were white," he related to Tachechana as he had already done many times before. "I certainly hope your father can deliver them as he said he would."

"My father always does as he says," Tachechana replied briskly, with just a trace of annoyance in her voice. "If he can't bring them in himself, he will leave a trail the army can follow."

Shading his eyes with one hand, Baxter squinted toward the south. "Here comes the army!" he declared, his powerful voice alerting the entire village.

There was no skirmish line this time, and no bugle. The

column rode directly into the village, the captain halting only when he spotted Reverend Baxter.

"Well, where are your savages and their alleged captives?" he demanded.

Reverend Baxter threw back his shoulders, and said, "Let's get some things straight, Captain. These people are not the savages you make them out to be. They are men of honor who carry out their promises."

"Have you seen any evidence of them?"

"Not yet, but—"

"Rider coming in from the north, Cap'n!" the sergeant yelled.

All eyes followed the lone rider galloping toward the village. Tachechana recognized Eagle Feather before he reached the river. He splashed across and slid smoothly from the back of his horse, standing tall before Reverend Baxter and the captain.

"Within the hour, Great Bear will be bringing in fifteen prisoners," Tachechana translated. "One of them is hurt, but alive. The horses and cattle are still in a box canyon with an opening so small only one cow at a time can squeeze through. Great Bear himself will show you where it may be found."

The captain nodded. "Our horses are tired. We'll wait for him here. Sergeant!" he bawled. "Give the order to fall out and dismount. The horses need water."

"I'm sure your men, too, need water," Tachechana offered. "They are welcome to fill their canteens at our well."

Noticing her for the first time, the captain gave Tachechana an appraising look that brought a blush to her cheeks. "So this is the squaw who speaks our language and can even read and write."

"Not *squaw*," Eagle Feather corrected in English. "*Lady*."

Tachechana's mouth fell open. Eagle Feather had never

242

spoken the white man's language, and now he was using it to defend her. "How did you know the difference between squaw and lady?" she asked in Sioux.

"You taught me by your actions," was his simple reply.

A dust plume rising in the distance drew all eyes to the northeast. Great Bear crossed the river first, rode directly up to the captain, and drove his war lance into the ground a scant twelve inches from the soldier's foot.

"Now you will see that the Lakota do not steal the white man's cattle!"

Fourteen whites, dressed as Sioux, were tied to their saddles. Each had a rope noose around his neck. At the other end of each rope, a Sioux brave was ready to yank the prisoner off his horse and break his neck if he tried to escape. One white man was slung over the saddle, unconscious.

"Doc! We've got an injured man here!" the captain called.

At the familiar name, Tachechana craned her neck in every direction looking for Doc, but a different medic came to care for the injured man. Disappointed when she did not see her old friend, she followed the soldier to see how he treated a blow on the head, this time a crack from her father's coup stick.

The medic did nothing more than pour cool water over the massive bump, but when the unconscious man's face came into view, she gasped. *The sutler from Fort Fetterman!*

She flew back to the captain and was opening her mouth to tell him when she realized that he was already discussing the matter with Reverend Baxter.

". . . and it was not just the sutler. I just talked to the blacksmith. They were all in it together, but he told me the sutler was the one who killed Captain Baker and his men."

"Then what O'Connel said at the hearing was true."

"Looks that way."

"What will happen to Trooper O'Connel now?" Tachechana could not resist asking.

"Well, if we find him, he will be exonerated of the desertion-under-fire charge. But I'm afraid he will still have to be tried as a runaway from the stockade."

"With what possible consequences?" Reverend Baxter quizzed.

"I'd say he'll probably have to spend as many days in the stockade as he's been away, that time to be added to his enlistment. Of course, the longer it takes us to find him, the worse things will go for him."

"What if he should happen to hear about the capture of the renegades and turn himself in?" Tachechana's eyes flashed.

The captain gave her a measured look. "The sooner he turns himself in, the better." Turning to Baxter, he said, "With the chief's permission, we'll camp a half mile or so up the White River and head back with our prisoners in the morning."

Great Bear agreed, provided he keep the prisoners until morning. He would then send an armed guard of braves to escort them to the post the next day. Meanwhile, the night would have eyes, and every movement of the captain's contingent would be watched.

The last man had not yet disappeared around the bend of the river when Great Bear spoke to Tachechana. "Go get Big Badger. Tonight, he will be one of us. Tomorrow, he will be a soldier again."

Tachechana called Fox to cross the creek, then cut her mare out of the rest of the herd. *I hope O'Connel can ride the bare back of a horse,* she thought as she led the mare at a slow gallop.

Once inside the shady glade, she slid off Fox's back and dropped her lead rope on the ground. She left the horses to graze, hoping to surprise O'Connel.

Moving noiselessly through the dense underbrush, she heard his voice even before she caught sight of him. He was praying aloud. Still too far away to make out all the words of his prayer, she could hear enough to know that he was asking God to deliver him from his trouble and to help him mend his sinful ways. Not wishing to interrupt such a private moment, she was, nevertheless, eager to tell the big trooper that God had already answered at least one of his prayers.

Quietly, she walked back to the horses and led them into the clearing. It was empty.

"Timothy!" she called. "It is only me, Tachechana! You can come out now.'"

"Ah, Miz Chana, 'tis a risk you're takin' comin' here in the broad daylight," he said, squirming out of his cave.

"No more!" She beamed at him. "Father and his warriors have captured the renegades, and the army knows you were telling the truth! Soon you will be a free man!"

In the excitement of the moment he took her in his beefy arms and spun her around, her feet barely touching the ground. "Thanks to you and the Good Lord, I'm free!" he sang. Then, realizing what he was doing, he set her back down with a sheepish look on his face. "How can I ever be thankin' you properly?"

"By accepting my father's invitation to eat with us in our village tonight." Her dusky face was still rose-tinted from the brief moment in Trooper O'Connel's arms. "In the morning, you may leave with the other soldiers."

"An' I'm goin' back a free man," he said again, amazement in his voice. "I never thought it possible."

"God lives in you now, and his power is greater than any on this earth." Her heart turned in her at the expression on the big man's face. "Quickly! Gather your things and let's be going."

245

Moments later, O'Connel reappeared with all his belongings rolled up in a blanket. As he threw the bedroll over the mare's back, Tachechana could see his mind working. How was he to mount up, with no saddlehorn to grasp and no stirrups for his feet?

Turning to her, his countenance was grim. "Before we go back to the village, Miz Chana . . . I have somethin' to tell ye," he began haltingly. "Do ye recall my askin' for paper and pen so I could write a letter?"

She nodded.

"Well, 'tis done. Ye see, I joined the army to run away from my past. Back home . . . in Ireland . . . I was leadin' a rough life—drinkin' an' gamblin' an' . . . carryin' on.

"One night as I played cards, I caught the dealer cheatin' so I up an' called him a thievin' crook. We commenced fightin' an' it's beatin' him that I am, when, all of a sudden, he pulls a tiny gun from his pocket. Well, I grabbed his hand and we rolled aroun' on the floor until the gun went off. I thought for sure I was a goner, but 'twas the other fellow that was shot.

"I could see that he was adyin' so I high-tailed it out of there as fast as my two legs would carry me. I came to America and joined the army for a place to hide. Now I can see that it's back to Ireland I must go, an' face up to my sins."

"Oh, Timothy! I don't know what to say!"

"There's nothin' for ye to say, Miz Tachechana. If God can get me out of the trouble I was in with the army, he'll see me through this. I'll not be worryin' 'bout what anyone can do to me now!"

chapter

24

ALL EYES WERE ON TACHECHANA and Trooper O'Connel as they trotted into the village. Some recognized him at first sight. Others wondered about the big bedraggled white man who rode side by side with the daughter of their chief.

She led him directly to Great Bear's tepee, surprised to find Eagle Feather consulting with him.

Eagle Feather's mouth dropped open. "What is he doing here?" he asked in Sioux.

"He is my guest," Great Bear replied firmly and turned to Tachechana. "Tell him I welcome him to my village."

"But, Father," she objected, "it would mean much to him to hear your welcome in English from your own lips."

"Everyone who can hear must know what is done here today."

Obediently, she relayed the message to the soldier, while Eagle Feather sulked off in the direction of his tepee. Watching him go, she shook her head in frustration.

"How did you capture those villains?" O'Connel was asking her father when her attention was drawn to him again.

"At the victory dance held in your honor," she interpreted, "you will hear from our warriors the account of the stalk. In the meantime, my daughter will show you where you may wash and rest while the feast is prepared."

Leaving the trooper to shave and ready himself for the evening, Tachechana wandered out to the fire circle, where the prisoners were tied, back to back. The fort sutler, now conscious, was moaning and complaining of the pain in his head. She offered him some water, but he struck the earthen bowl from her hands and sent it spinning to the ground.

"Don't you remember me?" she asked.

His glassy eyes stared into her face. "Why should I remember an Injun girl?"

"I was at Fort Fetterman with my husband about a year and a half ago. We were married there." When he made no reply, she continued, "Why did you kill Captain Baker?"

"He was a no-good Injun-lover, not fit to live . . . anymore than you are." His look of utter contempt chilled her blood.

"Why do you hate us so?"

"Because you're redskins . . . and redskins killed my family."

"Only because you stole from us our land . . . our buffalo and our way of life."

"Animals don't own land! You're nothin' but a bunch of animals."

"You call us animals . . . after what you did to your own kind . . . to Captain Baker?"

He glowered, hunching down into his bony shoulders.

"I will pray for you," she said, compassion softening her voice, "that God will forgive you for what you have done."

"Ma'am?"

She glanced down the row, in the direction of the thin, reedy voice. He looked to be a lad of about sixteen summers.

"Ma'am, I heard what you said . . . 'bout prayin'. Would you pray for me?"

"Shut up, boy!" snapped one of the older men.

"No. I won't shut up. I've listened to you too long. Ma'am, I didn't want to do those things . . . killin' and stealin'. My

248

paw made me do it. I'm goin' to die soon, and I don't want to go to hell. I'm skeered ... skeered bad."

She knelt and looked into the watery blue eyes. "There is a white missionary here. I will send him to you. It is not too late for you ... even now."

When next she saw Donald and Jane Baxter, their eyes were shining.

"Hallelujah!" Baxter shouted. "Another soul has come to the kingdom this day! The young boy asked God's mercy and forgiveness and accepted Jesus as his Savior. Now he can go to his death with peace in his heart." The glad expression changed to one of regret. "If only we could find O'Connel, what a day of rejoicing this would be."

So they hadn't seen her ride into camp with the trooper! Tachechana's smile broke like the dawn. "Look behind you."

Two mouths dropped open in unison as the soldier, now clean-shaven and in full uniform, stepped out of a tepee and, with military elegance, offered his arm to Tachechana.

The meal was a happy one, with much laughter and talk. Only one sat at his cooking fire alone, watching the festivities in sullen silence. Eagle Feather.

Seeing him there, Tachechana sensed his gloom and waved for him to join them. Reluctantly, he left his lonely place and made his way to the circle of friends surrounding Great Bear's fire. To Tachechana's surprise it was O'Connel, seated at her right, who made room for the brave.

"Eagle Feather is one of my most trusted warriors," Great Bear said by way of introduction. "He took the most dangerous part in the capture of the renegades."

"Then 'tis this man who gets my most sincere thanks!" O'Connel, his round face merry with relief and good cheer, extended his right hand. Tentatively, Eagle Feather took it, risking a weak smile.

"And, while I'm about it, I have somethin' to say to all," O'Connel went on. "You've all been so good to me that I don't have words aright. But most of all, it's God I'm thankin'. Miz Chana here showed me what a vile creature I was, and how I could be forgiven. Now I'm a Christian, and I'm not ashamed to admit it!"

There was another round of handshaking and claps on the back among the white people, while Chief Great Bear and Eagle Feather looked on in puzzlement.

"Why does O'Connel's decision to follow the Jesus Trail make your hearts so happy?" the chief asked.

Reverend Baxter answered for all of them. "How many horses do you own, Chief?"

"Five."

"What would you do if one of them wandered away and was lost?"

"A Sioux warrior would not stop seeking his horse until it was again safe in his corral," he declared proudly.

"And after that . . . how would you feel?"

"I would feel . . . great happiness . . . here." He placed his hand over his heart, pacing his words with the dawning recognition of their meaning.

"That's how we feel about O'Connel. He wandered away from God. Now he has come back, and we are happy." Encompassing Great Bear and Eagle Feather in his look of loving concern, Reverend Baxter added, "And our joy will come full circle when the two of you come to our Father, the Great Spirit who lives in heaven and in the hearts of his children on earth."

Silence fell over the group, the Christians praying silently while the chief and Eagle Feather sat looking into the fire.

Great Bear rose slowly and spoke with finality. "I am Lakota. Now, it is time for the village to dance to our victory."

Close on his heels was Eagle Feather, but Tachechana noticed as he passed that his eyes were moist, and that he did not turn his face to meet her gaze.

All the braves appeared at the council circle in a hideous array of war paint. While Great Bear had promised the captain that none of the prisoners would be tortured during the ritual dance, neither had he implied that they would emerge unscathed from the experience. The spears, coup sticks, and guns that had aided in the capture were brought to the circle, and fourteen pairs of eyes widened at the sight.

When the chief stood, utter silence fell upon all. Coup stick in hand, he walked to the center of the circle where the prisoners sat in two rows, tied back to back.

Approaching one who still bore a purplish bruise on his forehead, Great Bear grabbed a handful of his hair. "This man is the leader of the white men who thought they could become Sioux."

An ominous murmur hummed through the group of onlooking Indians. One outcry led to another. "He is a murderer, a thief, and a liar!" "He deserves no mercy!" "Kill him!"

Unsheathing his knife, the chief held it to the man's throat. "He will die, but his filthy blood will not stain the weapons or the honor of the Sioux." Releasing the man with a rough shove, Great Bear's eyes roamed the double row of prisoners, pinning them, one by one, with his penetrating black gaze. "They will all die . . . with a white man's rope around their necks."

At his signal, the drummers began the primal beat that was quickly joined by other musicians blowing on whistles made of eagle bone. Crouching over, the chief moved his feet in the curious toe-heel step of the dance. Soon he was joined by the other braves who had been part of the raid.

251

Each of the warriors took up the posturing and, in dance, reenacted the capture of the renegades. Feet moving in rhythm to the thudding drums, they stalked the white men, hiding behind imaginary brush. Then, at the chief's signal, they pounced upon the unsuspecting thieves. The chief delivered a mock blow to the head of the leader, and the drums intensified their savage beat as all the braves of the village now joined in—whirling, jumping, brandishing weapons. Even the squaws left their places in the circle to throw small clods of dirt on the prisoners.

Long before the celebration ended, Jane Baxter had had enough and asked permission to be excused.

"Oh, the poor things!" she exclaimed to Tachechana as they left together, accompanied by Donald Baxter. "I know they are wicked, wicked men and deserve to suffer for their misdeeds, but I just couldn't bear seeing them humiliated that way. Will the prisoners be hurt?" she asked.

"No harm will be done to them. They will be turned over to the soldiers as they came to us. We will pray that, in the time remaining to them, they will repent just as the young one did today."

When the soldiers rode into camp about mid-morning of the following day, their surprise at finding O'Connel guarding the prisoners was evident. After a snappy salute, the captain offered his hand to O'Connel, showing even white teeth in his tanned face.

"It's good to see you alive and well. But of course you realize I must put you under arrest, don't you, trooper?"

"Yes, sir," O'Connel replied happily. "But I'm not worryin' that the army will be too severe on me now that I can prove I was tellin' the truth all along."

When the time came for the departure of the soldiers,

Tachechana slipped away quietly and returned leading her mare from the corral, complete with saddle.

Responding to O'Connel's look of bewilderment, she said, "You have no mount. Take my mare . . . and Nathan's saddle. It would have pleased him."

"Oh, but Miz Chana, you've been doin' too much already! How can I ever repay you?"

"By helping someone else to walk the Jesus Way. Just remember that God has protected you for a purpose. Don't rest until you have found it."

There, in front of the entire village and the cavalry, Trooper O'Connel took her hand in his, looking deep into her eyes.

"I'll not be forgettin' the finest lady I ever met . . . and I'll find a way to return your horse and saddle. 'Tis only a loan. You've not seen the last of this Irishman."

Eyes moist, he swung easily into the saddle and tipped his hat, falling in behind his regiment and not daring to look back.

Tachechana stood watching until all she could see was the thin plume of dust in their wake, rising from the floor of the prairie. Turning at last, she felt Jane Baxter's eyes upon her. Tears pooled in their blue depths.

"Why do you weep? Was Timothy O'Connel your friend, too?"

"Ah, Tachechana," she cried, "I am weeping for you."

"But my river of joy runs deep and wide," she said in surprise, looking about her at her home, the villagers now returning to their tasks, and at her child, happily playing nearby.

"You have so much love to give," Jane said solemnly. "And anyone with eyes can see that Timothy O'Connel loves you dearly and needs someone to take care of him."

Since there were no more words, Tachechana kept silent.

253

But Jane was not finished. "And so does Eagle Feather," she added.

Winter swept across the prairie without warning while the leaves trembled golden on the branches of the aspen trees in the higher elevations. While the storms raged outside, the villagers kept to their tepees, except to check their snares and traps for fur and food. An occasional hunt brought game to supplement the monthly food allotments.

Caleb was taking more and more steps, walking into the hearts of all. And, with every day that passed, he was becoming more and more the center and the circumference of Tachechana's life. Whenever Great Bear or Eagle Feather could entice him from his mother's side, the boy was with one of them, playing some childish game or learning the skills of the warrior. No matter what his behavior, they laughed indulgently and passed off his misdeeds without punishment.

As winter loosed its fearful grip on the land, and the spring thaw was beginning, two families from Tut-we's village sought refuge with Great Bear, fearing an outbreak of measles.

The chief, concerned that they might be bringing the disease with them, at first denied their plea, but later relented, instructing them to pitch their tepee at the westernmost edge of the village and remain in seclusion for a period of two weeks.

But within a matter of days, they found some of the dreaded red spots on their bodies, and like an army of red ants, the disease swept the entire village from west to east.

Caleb was the first in Great Bear's tepee to show the symptoms—high fever and then the rash that caused almost unbearable itching. Both Eagle Feather and Plainsfeather, who had survived an earlier epidemic, nursed the sick child and other villagers as they succumbed, one by one. Occasionally, they had to pause to bury some older person who had been unable to withstand the strange malady brought by the white man.

Caleb was regaining his usual high spirits just as Tachechana felt the first flush of the fever. Eagle Feather gave himself exclusively to her care, scarcely leaving her side until the fever had broken and the rash was under control.

In the meantime, Great Bear went from lodge to lodge, comforting his stricken people and helping to bury their dead in the little cemetery on the hill south of the village.

But one morning the chief could not rise from his bed. Still weak from her own illness, Tachechana touched her hand to his forehead. It was burning hot. All day, he tossed about in his delirium, calling for Green Eyes.

"Ah, Green Eyes," he said once when Tachechana bent near to bathe his face with a deerskin cloth dipped in cold water, "you have come to ease my suffering. Never a day passes that your face is not before me." Then his voice trailed off into an incoherent mumble.

Just before the crescent moon began her descent, he cried out in great distress. "Green Eyes, do not leave me! Where you go I cannot follow!"

At dawn, the fever subsided, leaving him weak and listless and covered with the angry red splotches that caused the insufferable itching. But Plainsfeather's remedy of herbs and leaves applied as a poultice gave him great relief, and he no longer spoke to his green-eyed bride. Still, as the days passed, he grew no stronger and was content to lie silent, staring up through the smoke hole into the spring sky.

The first day he stepped out of the tepee, the villagers spread the word. From a respectful distance, they watched him shield his eyes from the sun and look toward the cemetery on the hill.

"How many?" he asked Eagle Feather with a frown.

Eagle Feather counted the new graves. "Twenty-three," he said.

"Um," replied the chief. "Warriors?"

"Only two."

"Um."

The Chief wandered from tepee to tepee, inquiring if his people were well and expressing his sorrow to those who had lost family members.

"Tonight there will be a council fire," he told each villager as he left.

As was his custom, Great Bear was the last to appear at the fire circle, but there was a subdued gasp of surprise when the villagers noticed he appeared without his feathered headdress. Something was wrong.

Looking past the circle of participants as if they were not present, the chief began the ritual with the lighting of the peace pipe, then passed it to the elders.

"Never have I seen my father's spirit so troubled," whispered Tachechana to Plainsfeather.

"It is the sickness," Plainsfeather said, nodding sagely.

When at last the pipe was returned, Great Bear drove the hatchet side of it into the ground and looked around blankly into the faces of his people. Silence filled the village like a black cloud.

The chief cleared his throat. "I have led you for many snows as our Navajo brothers lead their sheep," he said. "Most of the time I led you down the right trail. I thought it right to lead you here, that we might live in peace. Instead, many have died of the white man's disease. This wrong has caused you all much sorrow. I am no longer fit to be your chief."

A murmur rippled through the group. "No!" One voice rose above the others. "If we had not come here, the soldiers would have killed us."

"Would it not be better to die like warriors in battle rather than in our beds?" Great Bear asked.

"It is not the chief's fault the sickness came!" another voice rang out.

Great Bear raised both his hands to signal silence. Pointing to a brave halfway around the circle, he said, "You. Stand, but do not speak."

The brave obeyed.

"Many times I have been told I had the eyes of a hawk or an antelope. Tonight, at this short distance, I cannot tell who this brave is. The white man's sickness has stolen my eyes. I cannot see enough to be chief of the squaws."

chapter
25

A SHOCK WAVE OF DISBELIEF RIPPLED THROUGH THE TRIBE like a pebble thrown into a small pond, the outer waves bouncing in from the shore before the last of the new waves has filtered to the flatness of silence. The chief—nearly blind—how could it be? What would happen next? Who would lead them?

Tachechana, forgetting the protocol of the council circle, left Plainsfeather's side and went to her father. Kneeling in front of him, she took his hand and kissed it, her tears glistening on his bronze skin.

"Would the daughter of the chief embarrass him by weeping for him before his entire village?" Tenderly he placed his other hand on her head.

"I do not weep for my chief, but for my father whom I love."

"Perhaps it is too soon for weeping. Your father has a daughter and a grandson who can be his eyes." He helped her to her feet and, with a gentle shove, sent her back to the squaws' circle.

Addressing his people, he said, "It is time to select a new chief. There are warriors among you who are brave enough and wise enough to lead you in good paths. I will join the circle of elders, and together we will ask the Great Spirit to guide our decision. Eagle Feather will take my coup stick until you have chosen."

Eagle Feather rose, uneasily accepting the coup stick, the village symbol of authority, though the chief would retain possession of the great peace pipe, which would be relinquished only when the new chief was named.

The council was over before the fire had reached its apex. A moody quiet hushed the village. Most of the villagers avoided the sightless stare of their chief. They understood his infirmity, and his pride. They would not embarrass him by showing pity, but he understood the sounds of silence as he retired to his tepee.

The next morning Great Bear and the elders met at the fire circle, but no fire was lit and no pipe was passed. They sat in a ring around the remains of the old fire. No one spoke, and the villagers knew the old ones had had no food or water since the previous night. Throughout the day they sat without eating, without drinking, without speaking, silently imploring the Great Spirit to give them wisdom. As darkness fell they retired to their tepees, but all of them were again in their places when the sun rose.

Throughout the second and third days they sat, neither eating nor drinking. Shortly after noon on the fourth day, one of the elders lost consciousness and had to be carried to his lodge. Before the day was over, two more had followed him. These did not rejoin the circle on the fifth day when four more passed out, leaving only Great Bear and six others to face the sixth and seventh days. Surprisingly, no one else fell.

As the sun touched the western mountains, the elders who had left the circle earlier began returning, one by one, with a small bundle of wood. A fire was built and Great Bear lighted the pipe, which had remained beside him during the ordeal. The pipe was passed to each of the elders and again driven into the ground.

All the villagers began gathering to hear the results of the elders' meditations. No one spoke. Little Gray Wolf, usually babbling and boisterous, sat quietly on Tachechana's lap, looking inquiringly into his mother's face, then at his grandfather who paid no attention to him.

At last Great Bear broke the silence. "What has the Great Spirit spoken to the elders of the Lakota? Who should be our new chief?" He puffed on the ceremonial pipe and blew the smoke skyward. The elder to his right accepted the pipe, puffed, and blew the smoke skyward. "Eagle Feather." The next elder did the same, and the next. Four times the name Swimming Otter was mentioned, but all the rest spoke the name of Eagle Feather.

"Let Eagle Feather and Swimming Otter step forward," Great Bear said. The two braves stood before him. "Prepare yourselves for the tests of combat. Tomorrow, you will compete to show your worthiness to lead our people. Both of you are honored warriors. Tomorrow night, one of you will be chief of this village."

The two young men turned to gaze long into each other's eyes, measuring the breadth and depth of the competition.

"We have been friends and brothers since childhood," Eagle Feather said. "At the end of the contest, I hope that friendship will remain. . . ."

". . . and that one of us does not have to kill the other before the day is through," Swimming Otter replied gravely.

In the stillness of predawn, both men bathed in the river. After painting themselves and their horses with symbols of courage, strength, and daring, they left the river's edge to walk toward the council circle.

Pausing on the path, Eagle Feather saw Tachechana sitting with Plainsfeather and some of the other women and motioned to her. She left the group and approached him hesitantly.

"Swimming Otter wears some of his wife's hair tied with a thong about his neck. I have no such charm to help me in my quest to be chief. Would you be offended if I asked for . . ."

Smiling, Tachechana did not permit him to finish before turning her back and presenting her glossy black braid to him. Hearing his knife cutting through the thick hair, she was surprised to find he had taken only a small amount, just enough to tie with a deerhide thong and hang around his neck.

"Such beauty should not be plundered," he said. "It is enough that I have your trust."

At the council circle, the two braves stood before their chief, awaiting his words.

"It is good that there are two such as you who are able to lead my people well and wisely, yet a village can have only one leader. To decide which of you will wear the war bonnet, you must win three eagle feathers in contests of skill, strength, and courage. Are you ready?"

The braves' bold stance suggested that they were not only ready, but eager for the games to begin.

"The first contest will be a test of skill with your weapons." The chief explained the rules, which included throwing the knife and the tomahawk, and shooting the bow at a series of deerskin targets, placed at ever greater distances.

Eagle Feather was more accurate at knife-throwing, and Swimming Otter at throwing the tomahawk. It would be the archery contest that would determine the winner of the first feather.

Early in this contest, it appeared the braves were taunting

each other. So great was their skill that Swimming Otter, with his first attempt, scored a direct hit into the heart painted on the grass-filled deerskin, and a cheer went up. But when Eagle Feather's arrow sped through the air and split the first, a reverent hush fell over the crowd.

When they moved over to vie for the second and third targets, it soon became evident that Eagle Feather's arrows, while aimed true, took longer to reach their destination. Observing him carefully, Tachechana noticed him massaging the still tender muscles of his injured shoulder. At about sixty yards, one of his arrows fell short, and Swimming Otter was declared the winner of the first feather.

The second contest was one of pure strength. A large, round stone must be picked up and carried as far as possible, where a lance would be driven into the ground, marking the position.

Swimming Otter was the first to carry. He lifted the stone with little difficulty and began walking toward the west with choppy little steps. When he had covered a distance of some one hundred yards, the stone began slipping from his grasp, and he staggered forward, heaving the stone from him. A brave ran to mark the spot. Gauging the distance he had come, Swimming Otter beamed in satisfaction.

It was a good carry—good enough to cause Tachechana to feel concern for Eagle Feather. The wound in his left shoulder had weakened that arm, she knew. And he must win this and the next two feathers, or he and Swimming Otter would be forced to fight to the death. She was praying as Eagle Feather approached the stone.

He narrowed his eyes, assessing the distance to the lance. Then, bending his knees, he hoisted the large stone to his right shoulder and proceeded to move ahead with a steady, sure-footed stride.

The villagers shouted in approval as Eagle Feather stepped past the lance and called to the chief, "Where does my chief wish me to place this stone?"

With Eagle Feather's win, the score was tied, and the tension mounted.

During the rest period before the third contest, Tachechana kneaded the taut muscles in Eagle Feather's shoulders and back. Bending over him, she murmured, "You must win the next two contests so you won't have to fight Swimming Otter," she urged.

"Perhaps you should tell him to *lose* the next two tests," he suggested with a grim smile.

Ignoring his weak attempt to relieve the tense moment, Tachechana continued. "The next test will be horsemanship. Fox is the fastest horse in the village. Please . . . take her."

"No." Eagle Feather's voice was firm. "If I can't prove myself on my own horse, I have no right to win."

When it was time to mount up for the competition, Swimming Otter chose his paint gelding, a beautiful animal known for his speed and endurance. Eagle Feather was astride the paint that had once belonged to Running Coyote. Both horses pranced nervously, sidestepping and circling with the excitement of the impending race.

As Great Bear explained, the riders were to start at the lance, cross the White River, and ride upstream to Tut-we's village where a lance was driven into the ground at his council circle. They would return by way of the south side of the river, a rougher course because of the dense vegetation. The distance would total twenty-five miles, a real test for both man and horse.

They were off at the blast of Great Bear's rifle and the cheers of the village. Swimming Otter's horse stumbled when it entered the river, giving Eagle Feather an advantage, but before the horses disappeared from view, Swimming Otter had recovered and had gained the lead.

Despite all appearances, Tachechana was not concerned about this event. Both men were equal in ability, but she also knew horses. Barring an accident, Eagle Feather's paint should win with ease.

About noon, two braves from Tut-we's village raced in with the news that Swimming Otter was ahead by a length as the two contestants thundered into the village. Every eye was now trained on the south side of the river. The first horse to come into view was Swimming Otter's gelding, but as they neared the half-mile point, Eagle Feather emitted a vicious war cry and gave his horse his head. Tachechana smiled as the paint, flecked with lather, sprang to life and, in a burst of speed, crossed the finish line well ahead of the other horse.

In her great relief, Tachechana ran to greet the victor, throwing her arms around Eagle Feather's neck as he slid from his horse. He held her close.

"You rode a great race," she said.

"If I knew I would be so rewarded, I would do it all again," he replied, savoring her nearness.

Embarrassed, Tachechana backed away. "It—it's just that I was caught up in the excitement of the race . . . and gladdened that you and Swimming Otter may not have to fight, after all. It is wrong to spill blood, especially the blood of a friend."

Hearing Caleb's cry, she turned to tend her child, leaving Eagle Feather to rest and ponder the next event. Though he now had two feathers to Swimming Otter's one, the greatest challenge yet remained—a foot race, and, in running, his friend had always been the undisputed champion.

At the appointed time, the two warriors returned to the council circle to hear the terms of the race. It would be a long run—almost four miles of rugged terrain, uphill and down, across the river twice and Medicine Creek once. The trial would test fleetness of foot, pace, and endurance.

Eagle Feather did his best, but his bunchy muscles were no match for Swimming Otter's strong flat ones. From the start, it was evident that one worked at running while the other ran. Even in the least difficult parts of the course, Eagle Feather could do no more than hold his own. Swimming Otter had already stopped breathing hard by the time Eagle Feather crossed the finish line.

Each of them now had two feathers. The contest would go on to the fifth and final event, a fight to the death, or until one submitted to the other. Tachechana knew, however, that the Sioux did not submit readily in such a battle and that one of her friends might die this very evening.

As the sun touched the horizon, the combatants faced each other at the council circle. They would wrestle without weapons until the disc of the sun sank into the purple hills. If by then there were no winner, each would be given a knife, and the fight would go on to its only possible conclusion.

At Great Bear's command, the two began circling each other, looking for an opening, diving in, and backing off as they were blocked. Dive, block, parry, grasp, shove. The fight went on.

Tachechana had often watched the boys and men of the village playing at such fighting, and in her own younger days, she had wrestled right along with them. She knew when the fighter saw an opening and how the other would react. She anticipated moves and countermoves, and she prayed that one of them would win before the sun disappeared.

Eagle Feather appeared to be much stronger, but Swimming Otter had the advantage of speed. Once it looked as though Eagle Feather had gained the advantage. He slipped quickly behind Swimming Otter and threw him to the ground, knocking the wind from his body, but Swimming Otter rolled out of the brave's grip until he recovered. All the time the sun sank lower and lower into the distant hills as the crowd cheered.

At length, Great Bear shouted, "Stop!"

Every head turned to the west. The sun was hidden by the hills. The combatants would rest while the fire was built. During this time they would also select the knife they would use for the remainder of the fight.

Tachechana knelt beside Eagle Feather as he sat on the ground, his breathing labored. "Do not continue. Let Swimming Otter become chief," she begged.

"Am I a coward that I should insult my Sioux blood . . . and you . . . by running from danger?"

"How would it be an insult to me?" she asked.

"I wear a lock of your hair tied around my neck. It is for your honor as well as mine that I fight. I will win."

"But that means you must kill your friend."

"Perhaps."

"Have you no feeling for him?"

"For Swimming Otter, I would give my life . . . but not my honor . . . or yours. If your God is as great as you say he is, perhaps he will do something."

Great Bear interrupted, "It is time."

Tenderly Tachechana trailed her fingers along the bronze muscles of Eagle Feather's shoulders as he got to his feet.

"Do not worry, my Skipping Fawn. The battle is not yet over."

He entered the circle with Swimming Otter. "My friend," Eagle Feather said, "I have no hatred in my heart for you."

"Nor I for you," Swimming Otter replied.

"Whatever happens here tonight, I will think of you as a great warrior of the Sioux. If I prevail, I will grieve for you. If you prevail, you have my forgiveness for my fate."

"It is good." Swimming Otter nodded, a smile easing the tension of the moment.

"Begin!" shouted Great Bear.

It was a new kind of fight. No more diving in with the brute force of one man against the other. Now the sharp knives must be considered, flashing blades of death and agony. This was a fight of thrusts and jumps and deft sidesteps, each combatant staring into the eyes of his opponent, trying to predict the other's next move.

Eagle Feather was the first to draw blood. On one of his slashing thrusts, Swimming Otter misjudged Eagle Feather's reaction and received a cut on the outside of his right forearm. Although blood ran down his arm, wetting the handle of his knife, it had no effect on his speed or strength as the fight continued.

Then it was Eagle Feather who bled. In a flashing, slashing jump Swimming Otter managed to get the tip of his blade into the belly flesh of his opponent, about an inch and a half above the belt line, leaving a thin six-inch slice to dribble blood down onto Eagle Feather's breeches. The crowd gasped.

The fight went on. Neither fighter seemed able to get the better of the other. For almost twenty minutes more, they thrust and jabbed at each other to no avail. Each of them became spattered with the blood of the other as they clenched and closed, each holding the other's knife hand with his free one. During one of those hand-to-hand clenches, Eagle Feather managed to get his foot around behind Swimming Otter's knee, and they both crashed to the ground, rolling and grunting in the dust. Sweat, blood, and war paint ran together.

In a slick, strong move, Swimming Otter threw him off and gained his footing. Again the pair circled and thrust and parried. Both had received new cuts, minor nicks, but the strain of the day began to tell in their actions. Again they closed, but instead of pushing Swimming Otter's blade away, Eagle Feather pulled it toward himself and, at the last instant, surprised his opponent by springing him sideways. He leaped up as Swimming Otter began to turn, and scissored his legs around the brave's body.

They crashed to the ground. Eagle Feather's knees were under them both when they landed, and he knew he was finished if he didn't make this instant count. He squeezed hard on Swimming Otter's stomach with his legs, driving the wind from him. Then he noticed that, in the fall, Swimming Otter had dropped his knife.

Taking advantage of his friend's winded condition, Eagle Feather pulled Swimming Otter's head back. "Submit!" he yelled.

"No!" Swimming Otter tried wriggling away, but could not. Eagle Feather put the keen edge of his knife to Swimming Otter's throat.

"Submit!" he shouted, half pleading.

Swimming Otter only closed his eyes, awaiting his fate.

"Enough!" shouted Great Bear.

A hush fell over the village. Eagle Feather, his knife still at Swimming Otter's throat, looked up at his chief.

"Eagle Feather has shown the skill and courage that is necessary to lead the people of this village. Swimming Otter, too, has proven a brave and worthy warrior who does not fear death. For him to die would be a great waste. Let him go."

"It is good," Eagle Feather said as he took his knife and drove it into the ground beside Swimming Otter.

The two braves helped each other up and walked to Great Bear. Two pails of water were brought, and for all the people to see, they bathed each other's wounds.

When this was accomplished, the villagers took their places around the council circle. Sitting at Eagle Feather's right, Great Bear brought out the peace pipe and lighted it, but remained seated as he did so.

"Let all the people of the Sioux hear the voice of their chief," he said. He puffed smoke skyward, then handed the pipe to the elder on his right. So the pipe was passed around the circle of elders, each one repeating the words, "Let the Sioux hear the words of their chief." Finally the pipe came back to Eagle Feather. He rose and said, "Let the people hear the words of their chief." Blowing smoke from the pipe skyward as each of the elders before him had done, he buried the hatchet side into the earth.

"The paths along which you have been led by Great Bear were good paths. He was a wise and mighty chief. He will be honored always because of his deeds of valor and his wisdom. He has led us well.

"Swimming Otter has shown today his great skill and courage. If he had won the fight and become your chief, he would have led you wisely. Swimming Otter will be your leader when I am not near.

"The paths I have chosen for myself have not always been good. I do not yet have the wisdom of Great Bear. I am quick to fight before I think. Now, as your chief, I will listen to the counsel of the elders and of Great Bear. I will do my best to lead you in good paths."

A thrill coursed through Tachechana as she heard Eagle Feather speak, and she could not squelch the feeling of pride that rose within her. Not since the days of her life with Nathan had she felt so.

Into the hours of the night, the villagers celebrated the triumph of Eagle Feather. But afterward, he led Tachechana back to her lodge.

"Did you pray to your God for me today?" he asked, giving her a sidelong glance.

"I prayed that neither of my friends would have to die," she parried, deftly evading the true intent of his question.

As in the battle with Swimming Otter, Tachechana could feel Eagle Feather withdrawing to consider his next move. He spoke at last. "Do you think a chief of the Sioux should have a wife?"

Tachechana paused along the pathway to look full into his face. How could she answer such a question without falling neatly into his trap? "Yes . . ." she began honestly, "but . . ."

Pressing his advantage, he confronted her boldly. "If I were a Christian, would you marry me?"

Now it was Tachechana's turn to take her time, distancing herself from him with her next words. "I would never marry anyone who was *not* a Christian . . . nor would I marry someone who took the Jesus Way to gain my favor."

Thrust. "Would you have me for your husband if I were already a Christian?"

Parry. "Only if your heart were pure in God's eyes."

Thrust. "And if your God spoke to you concerning me, would you obey him?"

There was a moment of indecision. "I . . . ah . . . yes, I suppose so . . ." She was weakening now, feeling the fatigue of defeat. Then, a new burst of insight strengthened her resolve. "But I would have to be sure!"

"Will you ask him if he wants you to marry me?"

How could she refuse? "Yes. I will ask him."

She could almost hear the cry of victory in his voice. "The next time the missionary comes to the village, tell him the new chief wants to talk to him about the Jesus Trail!"

chapter

26

IT WAS SEVERAL DAYS LATER—days in which Chief Eagle Feather learned what was expected of him—when the missionary's wagon rolled to a creaking stop in front of the food tepee. The wagon was full of barrels of flour and corned beef to be unloaded, but it didn't take long for Tachechana to convince Reverend Baxter to visit the new chief before putting the supplies away.

As he ducked into Eagle Feather's tepee, she led Jane up the hill to the little cemetery where Tachechana retreated when she wanted to be alone.

"Eagle Feather has asked for our prayers," she explained to Jane. "This new way is difficult, and he needs wisdom to guide our people." But she did not mention the other request he had made—that Tachechana ask God to reveal whether Eagle Feather was to be her future husband.

In fact, the thought filled her with confusion. Would she not be betraying Nathan? Should she quell the warm feelings that were rising in her heart for Eagle Feather? Surely, God would show her what to do.

Their prayers at an end, they sat and spoke of all that had taken place since their last meeting—the terrible sickness that had filled this place with many new graves and taken Great

Bear's sight; her joy in Caleb's progress; the constant heartache of their people in not being able to return to the life they had known. But there were no words to explain the turmoil that, night after night, stole her sleep.

Looking up, Jane saw her husband and Eagle Feather helping Great Bear up the hill. "Here they come now."

Even from a distance, Reverend Baxter's broad grin signaled good news. "Eagle Feather has something to say, and he wanted Great Bear to witness it," he explained.

Tachechana's eyes flew to the warrior's face. He was gazing down upon the village. "Not many moons ago," he began, "I thought I was strong and brave . . . the mightiest of all the Sioux warriors. No enemy could conquer me. No friend could best me in battle . . . not even Swimming Otter.

"Then, I became chief and I have learned many things about . . . my people. Their lot is my lot. I suffer when they suffer." He paused, his eyes misty with conviction. "No man who walks upon the earth is strong enough or brave enough or wise enough to lead them in good paths . . . without a greater power living in him."

Looking directly at Tachechana, he confessed, "I have decided to follow the Jesus Way. I am a Christian now . . . as you are."

She felt the sting of tears as the river of joy flowed in her heart, but she could not move. Helpless, she could only stand by in wonder as her white friends embraced him, rejoicing in his decision.

Suddenly Great Bear raised his hands, signaling silence. "Wait. I would speak." And, as so many times before, there was instant compliance.

"What Eagle Feather has done this day is braver than any feat of skill or daring," he said. "When I was your chief, I did not have the courage to take the Jesus Trail. Eagle Feather,

274

you are Lakota. You are a chief of the Lakota. If you have such courage to lead these people down the Christian path, you will need much help. I wish to follow Jesus, too."

Quiet tears rolled down Tachechana's cheeks, and she reached out to be enfolded in her father's strong arms. Turning, she found herself standing beside Eagle Feather. He did not reach out for her. It was as if he knew that the stirring in her heart was because he was now her brother in faith—not because she loved him as a woman loves a man.

The dusty days of summer dragged by, with only one incident breaking the monotony of life in the village.

One day, while Tachechana was washing Caleb's garments in the river, she heard the pounding of horses' hoofs. She ran into the village and found a small patrol of soldiers. At the head was Timothy O'Connel, leading not one, but two horses—Tachechana's mare and a little filly looking suspiciously like Rowdy.

"Miz Chana, I told you I'd be back! When we got word about Eagle Feather, the captain dispatched this patrol to bring him our best wishes. I have some business with him, if you'd be so kind as to be tellin' me where I can find him."

Having led him to Eagle Feather's tepee, she returned to her task at the river, but it wasn't long before the big trooper joined her there.

"Do you recall the letter we talked about last time I was here?" he asked.

"Yes."

"Well, I got an answer from my brother in Ireland, and right happy I was to be hearin' from him. He told me that the man who was shot in the fight never died. All I have to do to clear my name is to go back and pay for the damages we did to the saloon!" His smile was as wide as the river.

275

"Oh, Timothy! I am very happy to hear your news. How soon before you will be able to go?"

"Only three more months, and my hitch in the army is up. Then I'll be goin' home."

Tachechana felt a catch in her throat. His leaving would make a big hole in her small circle of friends.

"And there's somethin' else, too, Miz Chana." He scuffed his boots in the dust. "Since I knew I'd never be havin' a chance with the likes of ye, I wrote my old girl back home, Mary. Seems she's willin' to have me back. She said if God could forgive me for runnin' out on her . . . and for all those other things I did"—he dropped his head in embarrassment—"she could forgive me, too."

Tachechana swallowed past the huge lump in her throat. "Then hurry home to her, Timothy," she said through her tears. "And God go with you."

The big trooper nodded, backing away until he had reached his horse. Then he swung easily into the saddle, lifted his hand, and issued a short command. "Company! Move out!"

When the soldiers left, the dust raised by their flying hoofs hung in the still summer air like a brown cloud.

The ninth day of October dawned crisp and clear, the air purged by recent fall rains. The melancholy that marked all Tachechana's days still shrouded her spirit, despite her continued appeals for God's leading. But she could not feel sad today, for Eagle Feather had agreed to host a feast for their good friends, Donald and Jane Baxter, in celebration of the child that was soon to come.

At first, he had objected to her proposal. "How can I entertain them? I have no wife to prepare the food and serve it!" The intensity of his gaze caused her to squirm uncomfortably.

"Plainsfeather and I will share the responsibility," she replied quickly.

"Humpf!" he grumbled. "What I need is a wife!"

Although Tachechana hurried from one task to another, she could not put Eagle Feather's last remark from her thoughts. It was true. He did need a wife, but each time she reviewed the maidens available, she found some flaw in them that would make them unacceptable. For some reason, none measured up to her ideal for her old friend.

When the day for the feast arrived, Tachechana found herself looking often into the distance, hoping to catch the first sight of the Baxters' wagon. At last, she saw it jouncing along the rutted road. Behind it was another, larger wagon with a billowing white canvas stretched over it. It looked for all the world like a cloud rubbing its belly on the ground and sending up puffs of dust as it did so. By the time the two wagons had pulled up, all the villagers had left their daily tasks to investigate the strange new conveyance.

To Tachechana's utter surprise, Timothy O'Connel bounded down from the second wagon and enveloped her in an enormous hug. "Ah, Miz Chana. We thought to be surprisin' ye—my Mary and meself. So we came along with the preacher and his wife here. They've offered to help us homestead, since we won't be goin' back to Ireland again for some time." Seeing Eagle Feather, he stuck out a beefy hand. "And 'tis glad I am to be seein' ye, too, sir . . . chief." He shook the new chief's hand heartily. "And here's me wife, Mary."

With a grand display of care and affection, he helped his bride down from the wagon seat. She was a short woman, only an inch or so taller than Tachechana, and fuller of figure. Her chestnut hair cascaded down her back like a mountain stream finding its way around unseen stones, and its color caught the rays of the afternoon sun, giving it a blinding luster.

"Timothy has been tellin' me so much about ye, Miz Chana," she said. "How can I ever be thankin' ye for helpin' him the way ye did?" Pausing in her speech, she looked from Tachechana to Eagle Feather with frank curiosity. "'Twould be a grand thing indeed if we could be celebratin' another weddin' . . . or have the two of ye already tied the knot?" she smiled impishly, ignoring Timothy's nudge to her ribcage.

"No . . . not yet," Tachechana replied weakly. "That is, we do not plan to . . . Excuse me, there is much to prepare for the feast. . . ." and she scurried out of range before she could be further embarrassed.

Quickly, she mobilized Plainsfeather and two younger women, making sure there would be plenty of food for the extra guests.

By now, the men were engaged in their own conversation, and Jane and Mary sought her out to offer their help.

"Oh, me dear," Mary began, "Timothy tells me I'm talkin' too much," she admitted candidly. "I'm sorry if I put me big foot in me mouth!" Then, chuckling, she explained the strange phrase to her hostess.

"It's all right," Tachechana waved aside her apology. "Your question just took me by surprise."

"Maybe your heart was answering before your head could interfere," suggested Jane, looking prettier than ever in the bloom of impending motherhood.

"I know he loves me," Tachechana mused. "But how can I know if I love him? Or even that God would approve such a thing?"

Jane regarded her fondly. "There is still much of the warrior in you, my dear, and I think you're probably engaged in the biggest battle of your life. . . . I think," she continued without mercy, "that you're fighting the very idea of giving yourself to another man."

Tachechana's eyes filled with tears, and she fondled the little ring Nathan had given her on the night of their marriage. "I never want to stop loving Nathan."

"And ye never will," Mary agreed. "But God can give ye a love for someone else as well—a love that's just as deep and satisfyin' as your love for Nathan. Ye can't ask God to show ye what to do if ye're not willin' to do it, ye know!"

The idea was a new and disturbing one. Her spirit leaped in response. Perhaps that was the reason she had felt that no answers came from God.

"Then if God leads me to love Eagle Feather as I love Nathan, I am ready," she said firmly.

Looking across the compound to the little cluster of men, she was surprised to see a look of concern on Eagle Feather's face.

Throughout the day, whenever she chanced to come upon him, Tachechana looked at her old friend through new eyes. It was true that no handsomer warrior could be found for miles around, no one stronger or braver. And there was a new gentleness, a new humility in his eyes that many of the villagers had noted, thinking it had come with the heavy burdens of his office. But Tachechana knew its source and gave a happy little sigh that this strong man shared her love for Jesus, looking to Jesus as the true leader of their people.

When the time for feasting arrived, the villagers gathered at the fire circle, but with much less formality than at other times. This time they sat in family groups, and there was much laughter and good cheer.

Eagle Feather had insisted that Tachechana and her father sit with him and his guests, using the excuse that he would need her skills as interpreter.

"But Reverend Baxter can interpret for you," she had reminded him.

"I would like to have you at my side tonight." Eagle Feather's tone brooked no dispute.

Answering in kind, her reply reflected the formal Sioux respect for authority. "I would be honored to sit beside my chief."

"I ask you as a friend, not as your chief," he asked, humble now.

"Then, as your friend, I accept gladly."

The events of the evening unfolded without a flaw. The meal was unsurpassed, since a hunting party had brought back three fat bucks for the feast, and the conversation flowed like the river, with shouts of merriment when Timothy relived some comical episode during the days spent in his "badger's den."

As the sky darkened, the drummers took up their beating, and the three braves who had killed the deer danced a pantomime of the hunt. The primitive beauty of this wordless form of storytelling captured the attention of Timothy and Mary, who had never seen anything like it.

When the last deer was killed in the dance and the three hunters presented themselves to the Great Spirit with both arms lifted to the heavens, the rest of the young men sprang into their midst. They jumped and circled, performing nearly impossible acrobatic feats in token of their joy and thanksgiving.

Faster and faster the dancers moved to the pulsing drumbeat. Even the white friends were caught up in the festive mood, their eyes shining with excitement.

Then, one by one, the men and boys left the circle to sit again with their families. The drumbeat slowed, and the young maidens glided to the circle to begin their dance of promise and submission. Straight-backed, they dipped and bobbed, bowing as gracefully as the lilies at the river's edge.

Suddenly, Tachechana was aware of a new maiden in the group. Dancing around the circle, she paused in front of Eagle Feather, her dark lashes fanned across her cheeks, a faint blush heightening their dusky color. Holding herself proudly erect, she kept her back rigid until the moment when, on the fourth beat of the drum, she bent her knees and bowed, then lifted her lovely head, looking directly at him with eyes sparkling with black fire.

Tachechana felt a burst of indignation at this impudent newcomer, then, looking more closely, recognized the young girl who had often helped her tend to Caleb.

Eagle Feather smiled his encouragement. She was hardly more than a *child!* Why, she looked like Tachechana herself when she was but seventeen summers!

In desperation, she looked over at her father, who was sitting at Eagle Feather's left hand. Great Bear's failing eyesight had only increased his wisdom, she thought, for he seemed to see beyond the obvious, looking into all the secret places of her mind.

"Perhaps it is time," the old chief said.

"Yes. It is time," she echoed with determination, and got to her feet.

Weaving through the dancers, Tachechana came to stand beside the beautiful young maiden. Her feet kept the rhythm of the music in her heart, and, dancing in place, she waited until the dance was over. Then, in one adept move, she stepped in front of the girl and bowed before Eagle Feather, her eyes focused on the ground, her heart pounding as wildly as the drums.

Slowly she raised her eyes to look into his face. The smile she had seen earlier was replaced with a look of wonder. Still seated, he extended both hands to her, and she placed her own in his. Gently, he tugged her to a kneeling position close to him.

The drums ceased their beating, but her heart sped on. There was no need for words.

They walked by the river, shining like a silver ribbon under the cold moon.

"You danced for me alone tonight?" he asked.

"For you alone."

Only the night creatures stirred . . . and this rising, nameless emotion within her.

"I have loved you long," Eagle Feather said. "I think before time began, God planned this time," he mused, "and for as long as I draw breath. . . ." His eyes shimmered in the moonlight.

"Hush now," she crooned, drawing him to her. "It has taken me too long to see what has been there all along . . . that there is room in my heart for more than one."

"Nathan was your husband . . . and my friend. He died in my place. God's Book says there is no greater love. . . ."

"Except, perhaps, what I feel for you now. . . ." she said.

Unashamedly he wept, his tears mingling with hers, overflowing the river of joy running, bank full, in her heart.